Mrs. Soul Crusher

By: Jessica Terry

I0629589

MRS. SOUL CRUSHER

First edition. January 5, 2024.

Copyright © 2024 Jessica Terry.

ISBN: 979-8988003670

Written by Jessica Terry.

Super thankful to God for the ability.

To my family, especially my amazing son Langston, for the support.

To my readers for, well, the reading. lol

To my fellow authors, especially my Wordmakers, for the encouragment and the camraderie.

And to everyone else who has shown support for me in *any* way...just, thank you.

Author's Note/Content warning: This book has a main character that's a sex addict. So they do what sex addicts do. If you find sex addict behavior offensive, please check out some of the less risqué books in my catalogue instead. I get it; this isn't for everyone. ☺

Also, depression, brief mentions of STDs and suicide contemplation, and miscarriage.

Chapter 1 – Montrel

My name is Montrel Burns and I'd like to complain about my life.

Many would say I didn't have anything to complain *about*. On the surface, I had it pretty good.

I had my health.

More money than I could spend.

Good friends (for the most part).

I looked damn good.

All of that was plenty to be thankful for. But as great as all that was, I also had a wife that had a knack for crushing my soul, intentionally or not. As my friend Forrest constantly reminded me, though, this was what I got for choosing sex and money over love. As if I hadn't been kicking myself for that every day since I woke up the first morning of my honeymoon to find my new bride Aurora jacking off the gentleman that brought our breakfast. At least she didn't try to say she didn't have enough money for a tip.

I guess it was supposed to make me feel better when she told me I was next. And that I could go ahead and eat; no need to wait for her. She didn't want my omelet to get cold.

How considerate.

And two years later, things weren't much different. Aurora and I lived in the same house, slept in the same bed, but as far as she was apparently concerned, our marriage certificate was the only place we were man and wife. While I can't say we ever shared a love that burned with the fire of a thousand suns, I actually thought that we'd grow to love each other over time. I'd never been accused of being a huge romantic, but that's what I'd hoped for. I mean, since we *were* married and all. Might as well be in love, right?

I don't think Aurora ever got that memo.

Attending funerals sucked. I'd hated them since suffering through my father's when I was ten years old. Ever since then, I tried to avoid them whenever possible, even if it made me look like an insensitive asshole. Many people thought I was one of those, anyway, so I wasn't losing much in the area of public opinion.

But this one was different; I couldn't miss this one, no matter how much I dreaded it. Ms. Debra, my favorite resident at the nursing home where I volunteered, was being laid to rest thanks to a massive stroke. It came out of nowhere; I had just seen her the day before. When I got the call, I literally fell to my knees and cried. Ms. Debra was like another mother to me; I confided in her, doted on her, looked forward to seeing her more than I did my own mother, if I'm honest. Knowing I'd no longer be able to go visit her caused a hole that I knew wouldn't get filled any time soon, if ever.

And how did my wife comfort me? By asking if I wanted some head. (I didn't).

So unfortunately, I was mourning Ms. Debra's passing alone. Aurora was a no-show, and I didn't have the energy to find out why. My mother 'didn't do' funerals, as she so eloquently reminded me when I foolishly requested her support. Forrest would have accompanied me but had an emergency with one of his pediatric patients. His wife Giselle, who I used to be friends with, only gave me obligatory comfort, as she hadn't had much to say to me ever since I 'dogged' her friend and my ex, Claire. A decision I can't say I never regretted; I knew she'd be right there by my side if I'd married her instead of Aurora like everyone (except my mother) constantly reminded me I should have.

But...that was the bed I'd made. And I was stuck in it.

So I sat practically comatose through the memorial service, listening to the preacher and various family members regale the mourners with stories about Ms. Debra and prayers over her soul. Everyone around me was sniffling and sobbing and barely holding it together while I just sat there, dazed. I had no more tears left. Part of me was hoping that it was all some dream I'd wake up from but as I watched Ms. Debra's casket get lowered into the ground, I knew it wasn't.

Honestly, part of me was angry. Everyone there had someone to hold their hand or hug them and comfort them; give them the patented assurances that things would be okay and that Ms. Debra 'was in a better place.' I stood there alone, numb and resentful. And when I periodically checked my phone to see if there was any explanation from my wife as to why she wasn't there with me as promised and found none, my face just got more sourly. At least I could pass it off as grief.

I tossed a long-stemmed tulip, Ms. Debra's favorite, on top of her casket and turned away, unable to look at it anymore. My legs automatically started walking back to my car so I could get out of there. I wasn't going to the repast; I wasn't that familiar with Ms. Debra's family and didn't want to answer a bunch of questions about who I was and how I knew her. Being the lone Black man in a room full of her White family didn't hold a lot of appeal, anyway.

By the time I got back home, the house was empty. Part of me was annoyed; the other part was relieved. I just tossed my keys on the coffee table, not caring when they skidded off to the floor, and plopped down the couch, my head falling back onto the cushions. I don't know how long I was sitting there before I heard the front door open.

"Oh, hey," Aurora greeted, sounding surprised. "I'm didn't expect you to be back so early. I thought I'd have time to come home and change before I met up with you."

"Where were you?" I asked, my eyes still closed.

"I had an appointment that ran long."

"Is that a euphemism?"

"What?"

"Was it an actual appointment or were you riding somebody's dick?"

"There's no need to be crass, Montrel. I understand you're in mourning and all-"

"Aurora, I get that our marriage isn't exactly conventional and funerals aren't the most fun way to spend an afternoon, but this was a tough day for me. If nothing else, we're at least friends, I thought. It would've been nice to have had some support there. You know how much Ms. Debra meant to me."

"I'm sorry." Aurora came over to join me on the couch, placing a hand high on my thigh. I finally opened my eyes, turning my head to look at her. She at least looked contrite.

"I really am. I had every intention of being there but time just got away from me. It wasn't intentional."

"And you couldn't call?"

"I thought I'd have time to at least catch some of it. Or join you at the repast. You didn't want to go to that?"

"No." I didn't have the energy to explain why.

"Can I make it up to you?" Her hand started inching up my thigh. "You've been so sad these last few days; let me help you feel better."

"Aurora," I grabbed her hand before it clamped onto my crotch like the mechanical claw in a game machine, "I love sex as much as the next person but it doesn't fix everything. An orgasm marathon isn't going to hurdle me over my grief."

"Well, I'm not very good in tense situations, Montrel, you know that. We all have our own ways of coping. And you know my love language is physical touch."

"Oh believe me, I know." Rolling my eyes, I eased her hand off me and stood. "You've made that *more* than clear. Now if you'll excuse me, I'm gonna go take some of the pills I pilfered from my mother and hope they knock me out. Maybe the shitshow that is my life right now will be over by the time I wake up."

"Oh Montrel, don't say that," Aurora pleaded, grabbing my hand. Her tawny brown skin almost seemed to clash with my beige coloring in that moment. "I hate to hear you talk like that. Ms. Debra was old; it was just her time to go. But don't waste time being sad; that's not what she would want."

"How would *you* know? You never met her," I reminded bitingly. "Thanks to something always 'coming up' whenever I invited you to visit her with me."

At least she had the courtesy to look sheepish. "I'm sorry."

"No, you're not." Pulling my hand away, I headed towards the staircase in our stupidly-big Cape Cod mansion. We moved into it after we married, since we couldn't decide on which of our respective former homes to move into. And since Aurora was newly wealthy thanks to getting her trust fund after saying 'I do', she insisted on us getting a house way bigger than necessary for just the two of us. I went along with it because, whatever.

I wasn't kidding about those pills. Mother didn't even miss them. After popping two of them and throwing back a cup of water like it was a Patron shot, I toed off my shoes and crawled onto our California king platform bed, lying face down on the duvet. I tried to drown out everything; the cars going by outside, the sound of Aurora moving around downstairs, my thoughts, until the meds kicked in and took over the job.

And I engaged in the daily futile attempt to keep my mind from drifting to my ex. I missed Claire so much and wondered where she was, what she was doing, who she was with now. After I'd announced my engagement to Aurora to her, we hadn't spoken (she'd declined my admittedly insensitive invitation to my wedding) and according to Forrest, she moved away a few months later. I wouldn't be feeling so alone if she was there and I knew it. I could almost feel her warm hand on my back and her voice in my ear. She wouldn't have left my side when I needed her.

But, hey. At least I had on-demand orgasms, right?

Chapter 2 – Montrel

"Man, I told you I don't want to hear it."

"Come on, Forrest. You're supposed to be my boy. If I can't complain about my wife to you, who can I complain to?"

"You're not complaining; you're bitching."

"Semantics."

"And doing all that is pointless, anyway. I told you it was a mistake to marry that woman but you swore you knew what you were doing, so I'm not trying to hear any bellyaching now."

I sighed. I'd gone to my boy Forrest's to get out of the house and try to clear my head of my problems at home, but it somehow morphed into me going into how Aurora stood me up for Ms. Debra's funeral. And Forrest wasted no time letting me know he didn't want to hear it.

"It would be nice to have some support from *somebody*," I grumbled, crossing my arms over my chest with a frown. "You know full well how much I loved Ms. Debra and how gutted I felt when she passed."

"Oh, I'm all the way here for you on *that*," Forrest assured, turning those droopy eyes of his from the television to me. "But you were bitching about Aurora, not your grief. Honestly, I can't tell which one you're more upset about."

"It's neck-and-neck, depending on the day."

"Whatever. Like I said, I don't want to hear about Aurora's bullshit no more. You got what you deserved, marrying somebody just because she turned your ass out.

And she only married you so she could get her money; what did you expect?"

I sighed again. Even though Forrest had a point, I still wanted – needed – some assurance that things weren't always going to be this way, even if it was bullshit. I couldn't see myself living with things as they were indefinitely.

"So I guess I'm on my own, then," I surmised, the realization deflating me. "You won't let me vent to you. Giselle practically hates me for what I did to Claire. You know Mother isn't exactly the comforting type. And anyway, she's been team Aurora from the beginning and probably wouldn't believe me, anyway."

"Giselle doesn't hate you," Forrest replied. "But you did her girl dirty, Montrel. How many times did you dump Claire because things were getting too real, only to go running back when she tried to move on from you?"

My eyes squeezed shut at the reminder. "I'm aware of what I did, Forrest-"

"Then when she got with that other dude, you refused to respect her relationship and seduced her, and the guy ended up dumping her. Now, she was equally as foolish for giving in to you, but she *did* beg you to leave her alone several times and you wouldn't."

"I get it. I should have. But I sincerely loved Claire and seeing her with somebody else...I couldn't handle it."

"Right. That's why you proposed to Aurora instead and then threw it in Claire's face. Actually invited her to your damn wedding. *I* was pissed at you for that shit. Claire didn't deserve that."

He was right. Claire Hutchinson was the only woman I'd ever even thought about sharing my life with, but I was too immature and kept running from it. If I'm honest, there was a tiny part of me that wondered if I could do better, which was now shameful to admit.

But no matter how many times I ended things with Claire, it was only a matter of time before I was missing her again. Yes, part of it was jealousy when she got into a relationship with someone else. I felt she was mine, regardless of my actions. That if she could just be patient, I'd get to the point where I was ready to really lock it in with her and go the distance.

And I thought I'd reached that point. I did a lot of soul searching, because despite what it seemed, I didn't enjoy hurting Claire. And I got excited about the idea of marrying her and having some kids. I'd gone to tell Aurora this, and I succumbed to her seduction for what was supposed to be the last time. But somehow over the course of the night, I let her delude me into believing that marrying her was the better option. I ended up proposing a couple of days later.

My chest burned when I remembered the look on Claire's face when I told her I was marrying Aurora. She was stunned, not to mention hurt. The look in her eyes...it haunted me.

"You're right," I eventually muttered, eyes on the ground. "She absolutely didn't deserve that."

Just then, Giselle came through the front door, laden with bags and her and Forrest's daughter, Jenna. Forrest hopped up to help her, kissing his wife and almost two-year-old daughter as he took the grocery bags from Giselle's hands.

"Hey, baby," he greeted her. "Are there any more bags in the car or is this it?"

"This is it. I only got enough stuff for dinner tonight, plus Jenna was getting cranky. It's almost time for her nap." They shared a loving smile that instantly ignited my jealousy before Giselle noticed me sitting on the black sectional couch. I could see the light go out in her eyes and her smile melted like a snowman in the sun. "Oh...hi, Montrel."

"Hey, Giselle." I stood, starting to go over and give her a hug but thinking better of it. Her expression clearly warned me to stay where I was. "How are you?"

"Fine." She turned her attention back to her husband, striking up a hushed conversation as she turned her back to me. I sank back onto the couch with yet another sigh. I knew when I was dismissed.

I checked my phone as Forrest and Giselle continued into the kitchen, talking amongst themselves and playing with Jenna, momentarily forgetting about me. Feeling compelled, I texted Aurora to see how her day was going. I hadn't had much to say to her since the day of Ms. Debra's funeral, but seeing my boy with his wife and daughter had me wanting to put that grudge behind me and move forward. Maybe we could go out to dinner or something later. But when a couple of minutes passed with no response, the usual wonderings about where she was and who she was with began sprouting in my mind. Just like that, I was frowning again.

"What's wrong with you?"

I blinked. I hadn't even heard Forrest come back into the room.

"Nothing," I grunted, trying to clear my expression. It's not like he'd want to hear the real reason for it, anyway. I sat up and glanced around. "Where's Giselle?"

"Went to put Jenna down for her nap."

"And avoiding me."

"She's not avoiding you, man."

"Come on, Forrest. You know she is. Since I married Aurora, she's barely had anything to say to me. Is she ever going to stop being mad at me for that?"

Sighing, Forrest shook his head. "I've told you, I'm not getting in the middle of that. You two are gonna have to work that out yourselves."

"And I'd love to do that, but it's kinda hard when she runs every time I come around. I get that she's upset about how I handled things with Claire but I didn't think she'd totally throw away our friendship because of it."

"I don't know what to tell you, Montrel. I'd like to say she'll come around eventually; Giselle doesn't usually hold grudges. But you *are* the one that drove one of her closest friends out of town, so..."

I started to respond but stopped myself. What was the point? It wasn't like he was wrong.

After checking my phone and still seeing no reply from Aurora, I suddenly felt the need to be alone.

Standing, I barely looked at Forrest before I started heading for the door.

"Where you going?" he called out.

"My head hurts," I lied over my shoulder, feet still moving. "I'll talk to you later."

"You almost ready?"

I entered our large en suite bathroom where Aurora was running a flat iron through her thick brown hair that hung a couple inches past her shoulders. Everything in there was white; the counters, the large-slate marble tile that ran up the walls in the huge glass-enclosed shower, the fancy toilet, the rug, even the damn flowers on the double vanity. I hated it but it was what Aurora wanted and I didn't care enough to protest.

Her eyes stayed focused on her image in the lighted mirror as I approached. "Ready for what?"

"Aurora, for real? We're supposed to go see my mother. I reminded you this morning."

"Oh..." She slowly finished straightening the lock of hair she'd been focused on before gently setting down the flat iron, taking her time looking up at me. "I'm sorry but I won't be able to go with you."

My face tightened. Here we go again. "And why is that?"

"I told Mecca I'd help her get her books together. Remember when I told you how her accountant turned out to be shady and messed up her finances?"

"Yeah, I recall. And I sympathize but you told me you were going with *me* today. You've already skipped out the last two times. Mecca is your best friend; I'm sure she'll understand that you made a promise to your husband first.

And it's not like we're gonna be at Mother's forever; you can go help Mecca *after* that."

"I can't, Montrel, because she has to go in to work tonight. And this is going to take a while."

"So she's more important than me?"

She sighed, turning to looking at me admonishingly. "Don't do that."

"You know what?" I held my hands up, taking a step back. "Whatever. I don't even know why I'm surprised. You've made it more than clear that my feelings mean nothing to you so my bad for expecting any different. Do your thing, as usual. Hell, spend the night over there, for all I care. It wouldn't be the first time."

"Montrel!" She lunged forward to grab my shirt before I could turn away, her eyes morphing from admonishing to pleading. "I'm sorry; I didn't mean to make it seem like you don't matter. You know that's not true."

"No I don't." My voice was flat as I looked down at her. Her prettiness didn't even register thanks to my annoyance. "And I wish you'd quit lying and acting like you give a damn about me when we both know you don't."

"I do!" She had the nerve to look affronted. Her arms slid around my waist while mine stayed hanging at my sides. "I *do* care about you. I love you."

"You love the money I made it possible for you to get. Let's not act like it's anything more than that. Your actions have proven it and the sooner I stop fooling myself, the better."

"Montrel-"

"Let go of me."

"Montrel!"

"I said take your damn hands off me, Aurora!"

I could tell she was shocked at my anger. It wasn't something I exhibited often. Annoyance, indifference, arrogance, a self-deprecating dry humor...those were my usuals. But anger usually came slowly, so even I was a little surprised at how quickly it hit. This latest brush-off of Aurora's was like gasoline to a low-burning fire and despite knowing what kind of marriage she and I had, I wasn't interested in making myself douse it.

Her arms hesitantly loosened from my waist and I quickly spun on my heel and stalked to our bedroom. To my surprise and annoyance, she followed me, still pleading her case.

"Can we please talk about this?" she pleaded, trailing me into the walk-in closet.

I snatched a tan Boglioli wool and silk sport coat from the hanger, not even looking at her as I brushed past. "Nothing to talk about."

"It's not that I don't get how I treat you sometimes. I don't mean to be cruel. It's just..." Her hands wrung as she tried to find the words. "It's hard to explain..."

"Save yourself the trouble. I don't care."

"Montrel, please..." She reached for me again.

"Will you stop??" I knocked her hands away, both confused and aggravated by her persistence. "You didn't care how I'd feel about it when you agreed to go help your damn friend instead of keeping your word to me. You didn't care about my feelings when you stood me up for Ms. Debra's funeral. I call or text you and you take forever to respond, if you ever do. You didn't even try to hide jacking some random guy off on our honeymoon, or having phone sex when you think I'm asleep. You don't pay me any real attention until you're trying to fuck. So don't insult me by acting like you care now. Now get the fuck out of my way so I can go."

Something shifted in her expression and her chest started to heave. I squared up, ready for whatever she was about to come back with. Aurora and I didn't argue terribly often but I was more than willing to make time today.

She threw me off, though, when she literally jumped on me and started slobbing me down. Her legs clamped around my waist as she jammed her tongue in my mouth, grunting in that way that signaled she was already riled up. It took a moment for this sudden change of events to register, and my arms encircled her almost on their own. My body clearly didn't get the memo that I was pissed at her because arousal began taking over pretty much instantly.

My mouth opened to her, kissing her back with as much intensity as she was kissing me. We fell onto the bed, me rolling on top of her and grinding my hardness against her writhing body. Just like that, I'd forgotten about our argument and what caused it, which I didn't have time to be ashamed about. This felt good, and I deserved to feel good with the shitty few weeks I'd had.

She rolled on top of me, tearing her mouth away as she braced her hands on my shoulders and reared back. Her brown eyes had that look that I was all too familiar with, and I couldn't help but salivate at the sight of her generous breasts straining against her thin camisole, her nipples erect and ready to be sucked. Regardless of everything, Aurora had an amazing body and it often skewed my good sense, as it was doing then.

"Can I make this up to you?" she whispered, slowly and seductively winding her hips on top of mine. Our eyes were locked as she unbuckled my belt with one hand and unbuttoned my shirt with the other. "I need you to know how sorry I am, Montrel. Let me show you how much I love you."

I had no words. My hands just slid up her thighs to her ass, glad that she hadn't yet put on any pants. My fingers tugged at the pale blue thong she was wearing as I sat up so we were chest-to-chest, now as on fire as she was.

My lips captured hers again as she pushed the sport coat from my shoulders, then my shirt. I disposed of her camisole, hungrily going for her breasts. Her head fell back as she released a satisfied groan, her fingers digging into my shoulders.

"You wanna make it up to me?" I whispered, lips back on hers. My fingers pinched and gently pulled at her nipples, which I knew she loved.

"Yes," she immediately gasped, nodding as she sent her tongue out to play with mine, which jutted out to meet hers. They circled and stroked and sensuously battled each other, our bodies now grinding crazily and our over-the-top moans filling the room. She loved doing that, and it admittedly drove me crazy when she did it. It was so erotic, so unlike the ladylike image she portrayed most of the time. "Yes, I want to. Can I?"

"I'm gonna be late."

"Blame it on me. I'm sure your mother will understand you making love to your wife. And I don't plan on this being quick."

I didn't bother responding. I just let her proceed to distract me yet again.

It was almost three hours later when I finally headed to Mother's. Once Aurora finally rolled off me, she went on to get freshened up so she could meet her friend, humming to herself. I got in the shower. We didn't say anything to each other; we just went on about our business as if we hadn't had each other screaming mere minutes before.

I was kicking myself for giving in so easily. Aurora always tried to use sex as a remedy for everything and I thought I'd gotten better about resisting, but the flesh was weak this time. I'd let her have her way with me, despite being pissed at her prior to that. And as good as it felt – hell, as amazing as it felt – I recognized how counterproductive it was now that I was thinking with the right head.

Sighing, I figured there was nothing to be done but resign to do better in the future.

Before I left the house, I took a picture of myself in my outfit, because I looked too good in the tan and royal blue ensemble not to. It was something I did on occasion, when I felt like it. I wasn't a huge user of social media and posting my outfits was the main reason I bothered with it.

Once I finally left, I hoped Mother didn't trip about my being late. She could be rather anal about that kind of thing.

To my surprise, though, she wasn't upset at all. Her characteristic aloofness was replaced with something I'd dare to describe as jubilance, and it threw me off big time. Especially when she threw her arms around me and squeezed like we hadn't seen each other in years. My mother and I didn't usually hug.

"I am so glad to see you, dear!" she exclaimed, still squeezing. "You're looking as handsome as always!"

"Um, thanks."

"I was starting to get a little worried," she pulled back, still grinning. "I'm glad you made it."

"Oh...yeah, my apologies for being late. And for not calling. I was with Aurora and-"

"No need to explain, dear." She grabbed my hand, puzzling me even more. "I understand your wife takes precedence. Are you hungry?"

I eyed her. "Mother, are you all right?"

"Never better. Why do you ask?"

"You're acting differently. With all due respect, are you high?"

She giggled. Actually *giggled*. What the hell was happening?? "Oh, Montrel, you're so silly. If I'm high off of anything, it's euphoria. May I offer you some homemade prosciutto and fontina empanadas? I made them earlier."

"Wait, what?" I legitimately felt like I was being pranked as she led me by the hand into her spacious kitchen, which had almost every amenity you could think of despite Mother only using it to make tea. Her nourishment came at the hands of a private chef; she didn't cook.

Which was why I was floored to see actual pots and pans on the stove and the marble countertops, and various plates and platters of food scattered across the humongous center island. I stopped in my tracks, taking it all in, even more sure that I was in some kind of alternate universe. It was a mess; there were actual spills of some kind of sauce and flour and whatever else on the stove and counters, and she didn't seem fazed in the least by it. Mother usually freaked out when any one thing was out of place, but now, she just looked at me with a proud grin.

"See?" She swept her arms in front of her. "I told you."

"I go back to my earlier question..."

"Montrel, stop that," she scolded, frowning slightly and sounding more like her usual self. "I've just been expanding my abilities. There's no need to act as if I've been taken over by aliens."

I hadn't wanted to say it but that's almost exactly what I thought.

"All right," I finally managed to say. "Well, thanks, but I'm not all that hungry."

"No? You sure you wouldn't like some stuffed potato croquettes or bean tarts?"

"Positive." If she were offering some of her usual catered fare or pastries from her favorite bakery, I'd have partaken. But I was in no mood to get sick off of whatever it was she tried to experiment with in the midst of what had to be some kind of midlife crisis. I'd never even heard of a damn bean tart.

"Very well. I'll send some home with you. Come, we can go into the living room, then."

I trailed her through the house I'd grown up in that had been through numerous changes in the years since my father passed. Mother didn't work; she didn't need to, thanks to Father leaving each of us gargantuan sums of money. She usually busied herself being a wannabe socialite, occasional traveling, and doing unnecessary renovations on the house. And of course, shopping. Mother was the definition of 'buying overly expensive shit just because you can.' Whether she actually needed it or would use it was irrelevant; if it was pricey and popular (and added to her feeling of superiority), she had to have it. Thankfully I made better use of my time and was better with my money than that.

"So where's my daughter-in-law?" Mother asked once we were settled. She carefully crossed her legs, not wanting to wrinkle her wide-leg silk pants. As if she'd wear them again, anyway.

"Aurora had an appointment she couldn't miss. She sends her apologies."

"That's a shame. It would have been nice to see her."

I just nodded. There was no need in telling the real reason for Aurora's absence. That would be too much like confiding. And anyway, Mother thought so highly of Aurora that she likely would have just spun it into something admirable. She'd been the main one advocating for me to choose her over Claire, who she always considered to be beneath me.

"You and Aurora have been married for a while now. When is there going to be a pregnancy announcement?"

Just like that, I was ready to go. And my frustration with Aurora was reignited since I had to endure this line of questioning by myself yet again.

"As I've told you, Mother, we're not ready for that yet," I responded, fighting to keep my voice pleasant. "We're in no hurry to have children."

"I don't see why not. You're both in your mid-thirties. You shouldn't dawdle, especially Aurora. Restoring that figure of hers will only be harder the older she gets."

"She can afford a trainer if she needs or wants one. But it's not a concern right now."

"I wish you'd get her to change her mind. I'd love some grandchildren. But I'll leave it alone for now."

I was glad when she changed the subject. I'd much rather sit through a recounting of the latest gala she attended than have to break the news that grandchildren wouldn't be happening. Aurora made it clear to me not long after we married that she didn't want kids and would be keeping her IUD until menopause took over. I was disappointed to hear that, as I'd always wanted to be a father. And I wished I'd thought to have that discussion before we exchanged vows, but then I had to ask myself just how much of a difference it would have made, given our situation.

Mother claimed to have plans for the evening so she sent me on my way an hour or so later with Tupperware containers jam-packed with her homemade concoctions, that went straight into the trash the minute I got home. Of course, Aurora was still out, and I knew there was no telling when she'd be back. When we were sexing earlier, she'd promised me a romantic evening, claiming she'd wrap things up with her friend Mecca as quickly as possible so she could get back home to me. But I wasn't gonna hold my breath.

Chapter 3 – Aurora

I wasn't proud of myself.

It didn't feel good knowing that I'd disappointed Montrel. Our marriage wasn't a usual one and we both knew that, but it didn't mean I didn't care about him. And constantly upsetting him wasn't what I had in mind when we agreed to marry.

We were supposed to spend the evening together after he got back from visiting his mother, and I finished up with my friend Mecca. I knew getting her financial books in order was going to take a while, but I still had every intention of getting as much as I could done as quickly as possible so I could get back home to Montrel as promised. I gave myself three hours, tops, before I'd wrap things up wherever they were and resume another day, if need be.

But then Mecca started venting about her man and musing about giving him an ultimatum or leaving him, since they'd been together five years and he had yet to propose. When I saw her tears, I couldn't bring myself to leave her like that. And when she brought out the wine, the one glass I agreed to turned into multiple, and Mecca took my car keys. I ended up spending the night.

I knew Montrel would be either furious or apathetic once I got home the next morning. It turned out to be the latter. He acted like I wasn't even there, refusing the breakfast I made for him and sidestepping me any time I tried to touch him. Of course I knew he wouldn't be in the mood for a blow job after that, but I still felt compelled to try. I knew those made him feel good, and that's all I wanted at the time.

This latest rift between us was consuming me, and taking most of my attention as I sat in my office at work. I was supposed to be replying to emails and looking over the pile of reports on my desk, but all of that was ignored as I just sat staring out the window. I barely noticed when my assistant Daria knocked on my door and opened it, poking her head in.

"Aurora?"

I blinked, looking up at her in surprise. "Yes?"

"Did you forget that you're supposed to be in a meeting right now?"

My eyes snapped to my computer monitor, and I remembered the meeting notification that I had snoozed multiple times. Groaning, I briefly pressed my hands to my cheeks but made no move to get up.

"Please let them know I had a conflict and I'll get with Dan to get the rundown of everything later," I told her, scooting my chair closer to my desk and pretending to type something on my keyboard. My eyes were on my screen but I could still see her hovering and hesitating.

"What is it, Daria?" I finally snapped, looking up at her.

Her eyes widened slightly at my tone. "It's just that they're expecting you...*now*. They asked me to come and get you. Apparently someone tried to call from the conference room but couldn't get through."

That was because my phone was on Do Not Disturb and had been since I arrived that morning. I was in no frame of mind to deal with anyone then and I still wasn't.

"I can't step away right now," I insisted. "I have to follow up with a client and I can't delay it for a meeting it's not vital I attend. So again, let Dan know I'll follow up with him later. Close the door behind you, please."

Daria clearly wasn't pleased about having to deliver that news. She pursed her lips and nodded, thankfully not saying anything else and ducking out of my office. As soon as the door was closed, I hurried over and locked it, not wanting any more interruptions.

Work had become a nagging chore in the previous months, and it was getting harder and harder to keep my energy and focus on what I was supposed to be doing while there. Mostly because I didn't want to *be* there, which was crazy considering I was doing what I always wanted to do. Being a portfolio manager had always been my goal, and thanks in part to my late mother who demanded excellence when it came to academics, I'd earned the grades and skills to get a great position as a financial analyst right out of college, working my way up to my current position. And I sincerely did love it, at first.

But it no longer held the same appeal now that I had my trust fund. I'd started to dread going in, resenting having to get dressed and sit in traffic and deal with people about things that had no bearing on my life whatsoever. Constantly hearing my mother's voice in my head was the main reason I hadn't handed in my resignation. That, and I knew Monroe, the man she married when I was seventeen, would be all over my case about it.

I played games on my phone for the next hour until I had to get ready for a client appointment that I wasn't able to reschedule. Since I wasn't interested in coming across as *totally* incompetent, I actually did my due diligence in preparing. By the time he arrived, I'd freshened my makeup, fluffed out my hair, and put on my game face.

"Mrs. Chadwick," Boris Worthy greeted, entering my office with a smile. "Good to see you again."

I moved over to him and placed my hand in his, my own smile in place. "You too, Mr. Worthy. But what is it I have to do to get you to just call me Aurora?"

"Sorry." His bald head dipped graciously. "I keep forgetting. But that means you should also call me Boris."

"Absolutely."

A moment passed before he gently pulled his hand from mine, sliding it into his pants pocket. "Thank you for seeing me today, Aurora. Nice suit you have on there."

"Oh, thank you." I tugged at the lapels of my winter white Alexander McQueen suit jacket. My eyes drifted over Boris's sculpted features, noting that his brown skin was almost the exact same shade as mine. "Would you like anything to drink? Coffee, tea, sparkling water..."

"No, thanks. I'm good."

"Is there anything *else* I could get you?" I heard myself ask. Somehow, I was now closer to his six-two frame than I'd been a moment before. He smelled like sandalwood.

His eyebrows lifted slightly at my question. "No...there's nothing else. Um, shall we get started? I have other meetings today and I'm already running a little behind; it's been a hectic morning."

"Of course." Snapping out of it, I backed away from him and sauntered around my desk, trying to ignore the tingles that were ignited the moment he walked into my office. I motioned towards the chair facing my desk. "Please, have a seat."

We proceeded to discuss the investment strategy I'd devised for his company, and I managed to mostly keep my mind on task, despite the fidgeting that was getting increasingly harder to control. It was a battle to keep still, but at least he couldn't see my legs rubbing together under my desk. Even though I knew our time was limited, I still felt compelled to ask him about his home life, what he liked to do, and if he worked out. It might not have been my business but I felt it was harmless enough; Boris was a relatively new client and I was just trying to get to know him. And thankfully, with the way his phone kept going off, he was just distracted enough not to bother wondering why I was asking all this.

After about an hour, Boris glanced at his watch and stood. "This was helpful, Aurora; I appreciate your time."

"No problem. I'll be sure to have those projections sent over to you by close of business tomorrow."

He started to respond but his buzzing phone snatched his attention. His brow furrowed slightly as he looked down at it, giving me another opportunity to take in his features. Thick eyebrows, broad nose, mustache. He looked to be in great shape underneath that Brioni suit. Part of me hated that he had to rush off; this had been the most interesting part of my work day.

Finally, he lifted those dark eyes back to me, though I could tell he was still slightly distracted.

"Sorry about that," he muttered. "I don't mean to be rude."

"No problem." I rounded my desk, stopping a couple feet shy of him. "As I was saying, I'll have the projections to you tomorrow before close of business. It was a good thing we met today because those acquisitions you proposed make a vast difference. Oh, you said you were going to bring hard copies of the new contracts?"

"Right, yeah." Boris placed his satchel on the chair, absently laying his phone on my desk as he looked for the documents. I eyed his iPhone for a moment before slyly covering it with a folder, then stepping in front of it with my hands behind my back. I smiled when Boris finally whirled around with the paperwork.

"Here you go. I apologize for being so out of it; I have a *lot* going on at once and it can catch up to me at times."

"I totally understand. No problem at all." I laid the documents on top of the folder that was hiding his phone, hoping his jumbled brain had already forgotten he'd laid it there. Smiling sweetly, I stepped forward and placed a gentle hand to his arm as I started guiding him towards the door. "You just be sure to let me know if you think of anything else you need me to do for you."

"I'll be sure to do that." He glanced at his watch again. "I hate to rush off, but I have to get back across town and you know how traffic can be this time of day."

"Ugh, I surely do. No worries. I'll be seeing you again soon enough."

"Thanks, Aurora." With a smile and a brief nod, he exited my office. I bit my lip and strode back over to my desk, uncovering his phone and running the tip of my nail around the sleek trim. I figured it would only be a matter of time before he realized he'd forgotten it.

Sure enough, there was an urgent knock at my door not even five minutes later. Knowing it was him, I grinned and called out, "Yes?"

He hurried in, his eyes darting around worriedly. "I'm so sorry for this, but did I leave my phone in here?"

"Your phone?" I pretended to scan my organized desk, knowing I had already moved the phone to my drawer. "Are you sure you brought it in?"

"Yeah, I just had it a little while ago. At least, I'm pretty sure I did." He groaned, running a frustrated hand over his head. "Damn, I'm out of it today."

"Don't even worry about it. We've all had days like that."

"I need to apologize again, Aurora. I swear I'm usually not this scatterbrained." He started scanning the floor around the chair he was sitting in earlier. "I can only imagine what you're thinking of me right now."

My brow quirked as I eased open the desk drawer where his phone was hidden. "You'd be surprised."

As Boris continued to search and curse himself under his breath, I nudged the drawer closed with my hip before kneeling down to the ground momentarily, then shooting up with the phone in hand and a triumphant grin. "Here it is!"

He shot upright, releasing a relieved sigh. "Thank god...how'd it get over there on the floor?"

"Who knows," I shrugged. "Maybe one of us accidentally knocked it over here and didn't notice."

"Hmm. That's weird. Well, I'm sorry again for the trouble. I'll just take that and get out of your hair..."

"Actually..." I stepped closer to him, his phone behind my back. "There *is* something I'd like to ask of you before you leave."

"Of course, yeah. What can I do for you?"

A teasing smile graced my lips. "Kiss me."

He reared, frowning slightly. "What?"

"I want you to kiss me, Boris."

"Are you...are you serious right now?"

"Extremely."

"I thought you were married." His eyes drifted to my left hand.

"Legally, yes. But my husband and I have an understanding. That's the least of your concerns, believe me."

"Mrs. Chadwick-"

"Oh, we're back to that?" I couldn't help but chuckle. Boldly placing my free hand to his chest, I looked up into his confused eyes. "Look, Boris, let's not make this into a big deal. I'm not asking you to run away with me. It's just a kiss. You already told me earlier that you're unattached. Is your hesitancy because you're not attracted to me?"

He opened his mouth but nothing came out for a moment. I could feel his heartbeat underneath my hand and I could only surmise that I was getting to him, with how fast it was beating. I traced my bottom lip with my tongue and his eyes locked in on the movement.

Glancing towards the door as if he feared someone would come busting in, he finally replied in a low voice, "It's not that."

"What is it, then?"

"This is just...it's not very professional. I'm your client."

"We're both adults. If we both want it..." I stepped closer so my chest was just barely grazing his, "Then there's no issue."

My physical desires had completely taken over by this point. Common sense would usually have spoken up by now and reminded me that this was a place of business and making out with a client wasn't the smartest thing to do. And my door wasn't locked; Daria or anyone could come walking in at any second. Knowing that only increased my desire, though. Every inch of my body was buzzing with anticipation.

"I can't deny you're an attractive woman..." He licked his lips.

"Thank you. Just one little kiss and you can get your phone back and get on with your day."

"Mrs. Chadwick-"

"Aurora."

"Aurora." His eyes darkened and he suddenly reached around and grabbed the wrist of the hand holding his phone behind my back, yanking me closer and drawing a surprised gasp out of me. The sudden aggression sent my arousal into overdrive. "Do you honestly think I couldn't get the phone from you if I really wanted to?"

"Big strong thing like you? I'm sure you could. So the fact that you haven't can only mean one thing, huh?"

His head started lowering towards mine. "I still don't think this is the best idea."

My eyes danced as they zeroed in on his approaching lips. "So?"

Finally, contact. Boris blessed me with what I'd been aching for for the past hour, and my breath hitched as I moaned softly and opened my mouth to him. His phone fell to the floor but he didn't seem to care. If it broke, I'd have gladly bought him a new one.

I know I'd said all I wanted was a kiss, but I couldn't resist easing a hand between us and grabbing a handful of what I'd felt pressing against my stomach for the past several moments. I slowly stroked him through his slacks, and his kisses got increasingly more urgent and aggressive. Both of his hands eased to my ass, and I was *so* glad I'd worn a skirt that day.

I could hear phones ringing and voices and footsteps outside the door, but I couldn't stop. Boris and I continued to make out hungrily, a silent agreement to be quiet outside of our gasps and breaths and occasional hisses hovering over us. He lifted one of my thighs and pressed closer to me, and my hands clutched his shoulders and the back of his neck. I was outside of myself, totally lost in the moment.

Which is why I gleefully complied when he whipped me around and bent me over my desk, biting my lip hard when he entered me moments later. His short pants and grunts littered the air as he started pumping into me, gripping my hips. My gaze fell to my left hand braced on the desk, my wedding ring gleaming especially bright in that moment, and I closed my eyes and refocused on the pleasure I was experiencing. The faint sound of his skin slapping against mine, the feel of his balls hitting me, his fingers digging into my flesh...it was all so heady. So intoxicating, not to mention thrilling, knowing there were people right outside the door who had no clue what was going on in my office.

It felt *so* good, and that was all I cared about; not the fact that my door was still unlocked. Not the fact that Daria's desk was mere feet away. Not how I'd feel once I came down off this high. All that mattered in that moment was getting quietly fucked by Boris and satisfying my urge. I'd deal with the rest later, like I always did.

By the time I was done with work and was meeting up with my friends Mecca and Bron, the whole scene with Boris was being forcibly pushed to the back of my mind. Prickles of regret and shame were already crawling over me for being so reckless. I'd started to go home to Montrel, but figured he was still upset with me, and I didn't want to sit home in separate rooms and let the internal admonishment over what happened with Boris start to take root. I needed a distraction.

Mecca was over the moon, since her man Toronto had just surprised her by proposing that morning, showing up to pop the question not too long after I'd left. I was so happy for her, knowing how long she'd been waiting for this.

"I still can't believe he just showed up like he did right after I'd done all that crying to you last night, Aurora." Mecca extended her thin arm, wiggling her hand and admiring her three-carat diamond ring yet again. "It's almost like it was kismet or one of those things like that. And look at the size of this ring! My eyes almost popped out of my head when he opened that ring box."

"Yeah, girl." I smiled tightly, taking a sip of my champagne. We were hanging out at the Prism Lounge, an upscale place that had glass walls, velvet couches, and pricey drinks. Mecca had been hinting about wanting to go there for a while but could never afford it, so I figured her engagement was as good a reason to treat her to an evening there as any. I felt that was the least I could do, anyway. "Sounds like it was meant to be. I told you that you were worrying for nothing."

"It's wild that he just showed up like that," Bron commented from his spot between me and Mecca at the round cherry wood table. He almost looked like a different man without his customary backwards Braves hat. He had protested going to the Prism Lounge because of the 'no t-shirts or jeans' dress code, but acquiesced because it was Mecca's night. "And you're right; that *is* a big-ass ring. Didn't think he had it like that. Hope he didn't rob the store."

"Hush, Bron."

"I honestly thought my man was never gonna propose. Wonder what made him go ahead and make that move. Did you give him an ultimatum like you said you were gonna do?"

"Nope, I didn't have to go there," Mecca boasted. "He realized it on his own, finally. And it's a good thing because he has no idea how close he was to getting his walking papers. Five years? I've been *more* than patient."

"Have you two talked about all the shit from your pasts yet? Better get it out now so there's not any surprises down the line."

"What? I haven't done anything all that crazy."

"So he knows about the time you and Aurora fooled around?"

I groaned while Mecca's face flushed with embarrassment. Bron liked to bring up that night in college more often than I preferred.

"That was *one* drunken night at a house party," Mecca hissed, glancing around us to make sure no one could hear. "And all we did was kiss for a few minutes."

"You did more than just kiss. I was there. Y'all were in the pantry and when I found you, certain articles of clothing were either pushed up or down-"

"Bron!"

"Am I lying?"

"No, but we wish you'd quit bringing that up," I chimed in, fiddling with the bottom of my champagne flute. "We were both wasted. It meant absolutely nothing. I barely even remember it."

"Well, *I* damn sure remember it," Bron quipped, his dimpled smile widening as he playfully nudged the both of us. "That has provided much shower-time entertainment for years now."

Mecca scoffed. "You're disgusting."

"Whatever."

I waited to see if Bron would spill the beans about the night *he and I* spent together. In truth, it was more than one, the latest being as recently as six months earlier. And we couldn't even blame it on alcohol (the first time, at least)...we were both horny and willing, so we had sex. It was as simple as that and both times, we just went on with our friendship afterwards as if nothing happened. It wasn't something we talked about; it was just something that happened.

But of course, he wasn't broadcasting that. The two of them got to talking about what was going on at Bron's community center and I slid my phone over to check my messages. It actually surprised me to see nothing from Montrel. Usually he'd have at least sent something asking where I was or if I was okay. I felt myself getting frustrated at his lack of concern. Yes, I upset him. But the fact that I was his wife should have counted for something. He couldn't just shut me out because I did something he disagreed with.

I plunked my phone down and signaled for another round of champagne.

"How's Montrel, Aurora?"

Mecca's question slightly threw me off since I'd just been mentally fussing about him. "He's fine."

"Everything good with you two?" Bron asked.

"Oh yeah, everything is great. We're still swimming in the honeymoon phase two years in. Montrel is a wonderful husband."

"Well, I'll ask you like I asked Mecca; does Montrel know about how wild you used to be?"

My face tightened. "I don't know if I'd describe myself as that..."

"Come on, girl," Mecca chimed in, brushing her long sandy brown braids from her shoulder. She gave me a good-natured glare under her heavy false lashes. "You know good and well you were *out* there back in the day. Hell, me and Bron always had trouble keeping up with you."

I didn't respond but I couldn't resist a smile of conviction. If I was honest, I *was* pretty wild once I was finally out of my mother's house and free of her and Monroe's restrictions. My four years in undergrad were some of the most freeing and uninhibited of my life, but while I enjoyed it, I was glad I'd calmed down some since then. As much fun as that time was, it was also draining.

"Okay, I had my fun," I finally conceded when they continued to peer at me. "But that's all behind me. I'm on the straight and narrow now."

Bron chortled. "You might not be wildin' out like you did back in the day but...straight and narrow? You?"

"Yeah, girl, you act like you're a Stepford wife now or something," Mecca added jokingly. "Really, I was surprised when you said you were getting married; didn't think there was a man that could tame you. And are we gonna get some food to go with this champagne?"

My friends didn't know about my trust fund, or that I'd married Montrel to get it. As much as I loved them, I didn't tell them everything. Money made some people treat you differently, and I didn't want something like that to affect our friendship. I didn't want to do anything to risk losing the last two real friends I had.

Well, anything *else*.

After Mecca ordered shrimp toasts, Moroccan stuffed mushrooms, and honey mint lamb skewers, we continued to enjoy the evening. I had finally managed to put the romp with Boris, the rift with Montrel, and the memories of my dalliances with Mecca and Bron out of my mind and just enjoy myself.

That is, until Mecca asked me about Monroe.

"I haven't seen him in a while," she realized, taking a bite of her lamb and giving a brief moan of appreciation. "How's he doing? With his fine self."

My head jerked back a little. "What?"

"Girl, you know I think he's handsome. I've said that ever since I first met him. He has *major* big dick energy."

"If you say so." I shook my head, feeling the frown form on its own like it tended to do when Monroe's name came up. "In answer to your question, he's doing okay, as far as I know. Pretty much all he does is work. He's always off on some business trip somewhere."

"I still don't get why you two aren't closer. I'd think after your mom passed…"

"Monroe and I never established that kind of relationship. I was almost off to college when he came into the picture. And he was gone more than he was home."

As if we talked him up, my phone buzzed with Monroe's call. I hesitated on whether or not to answer it, knowing that if I did, he'd demand I come over there and visit him. My mother had made us promise to stay close after she passed, and he was the main one trying to keep that promise.

Knowing I'd have to hear about it if I ignored him, I hesitantly answered though made sure my voice was unwavering when I declared, "Monroe, now really isn't a good time. I'm busy."

"What are you doing?"

His voice was just as deep and even-keeled as ever. I could remember very few times when I heard him raise his voice or get incensed. He had a quiet dominance that people automatically respected, including myself.

"I'm out with friends, celebrating."

"Celebrating what?"

"Monroe...did you need something?"

"When are you coming by?"

"I don't know. It won't be tonight. Maybe sometime in the next week or so."

"Make sure that happens. We have some things to get caught up on."

"Right. Well, if there's nothing else, can I talk to you later? I'm being rude."

"Certainly. Tell Mecca and Bron I said hello."

"I'll do that."

I ended the call with one hand and drained the rest of my champagne with the other. That was one visit I was not looking forward to; Monroe wasn't the most pleasant host. Not to mention, he could be so critical and pedantic that it made me want to avoid being around him as much as possible.

Anxiety was already spreading and threatening to ruin my evening. I couldn't let that happen. Flashbacks from my earlier romp with Boris were already pinging through my mind, as much as I wished they wouldn't. I so wanted to forget about that whole scene; I couldn't believe I'd been so stupid.

I ducked into the ladies room to call Montrel, but he didn't answer. Huffing an exasperated breath, I scrolled through my contacts looking for someone else to help me relieve this tension, but then I stopped. I'd promised myself I wasn't going to keep doing that.

So I went back to my friends, telling myself that they were plenty.

Chapter 4 – Montrel

Ms. Debra had been out of my life for a few weeks and I still wasn't feeling like myself. There were a couple of times when I'd picked up the phone to call or started to get ready to go visit her, and then I remembered she was no longer there. Then the funk started all over again. I wondered when or if I'd ever get out of it.

I was feeling restless. One thing Ms. Debra had asked me about repeatedly over the course of the time I knew her was what I was going to do with my life long-term. I was fortunate enough to not have to work, and I'd always been fine with that. But now it didn't seem like enough. Especially with so few friends and my up-and-down relationship with Aurora, I needed something steadfast to focus on. Volunteering had been my thing until Ms. Debra passed but I'd refused to step foot inside that nursing home since she was no longer there. And I could only have so many spa days.

I'd finally let go of my frustration with Aurora over standing me up for the funeral. There was no point in holding a grudge for too long, and I was tired of us each pretending like the other wasn't there, though I couldn't imagine what the hell she was upset with *me* for. But she'd come home from hanging with her friends one night with an attitude, and I just let her stew in it. Didn't even bother asking what her problem was because the larger part of me didn't care.

But on this particular night, we were sitting up in bed, her doing something on her tablet and me writing a letter to

Ms. Debra, getting all of my feelings and frustrations out. I'd read somewhere that was a good way to purge after the death of a loved one; getting all the things out that you weren't able – or didn't take time - to say while they were still alive.

"What are you doing?" Aurora asked, peering over at my notebook.

"Just getting some things down." I didn't want to let her know what I was doing; I had a feeling she'd just think it was silly.

"You sure are writing furiously."

"I've got a lot on my mind."

"Anything you want to talk about?"

A few quiet moments passed before I capped my pen and placed it inside my notebook, closing it and setting it aside. "What would you think about me getting a job?"

You'd think I said something about robbing a bank, as startled as she looked. "Why would you want to do that? And what kind of job?"

"I'm not sure yet. I just feel like I'm wasting time, you know?"

She peered at me thoughtfully, putting down her tablet. "Getting bored with your life?"

"I mean, I guess..."

"I suppose I can understand you wanting something else to do. Though I have a feeling you'd be regretting it soon enough. I've actually been thinking about stepping back from *my* job for a little while now."

This was new information. "I didn't know that. Did something happen?"

"No." She shifted and cleared her throat. "Apathy has just started setting in and it doesn't hold the same appeal for me that it used to."

"You mean now that you don't need it for the money."

"Truthfully, yes. It was like I started noticing all the small annoying things that I hadn't noticed before, and I realized I don't *have* to put up with them now. You really don't know how good you have it, Montrel."

"I realize my good fortune. But as far as I'm concerned, it just means I can take my time to figure out what I'm passionate about. You know the saying about how doing what you love isn't like work."

"Hmph. Well, I love what I do but it has surely felt like work lately. Speaking of, I've been summoned to Monroe's Friday night and I've delayed it as much as he'll allow. Would you go with me? You know how he tends to get under my skin and it would be nice to have an ally."

Oh, how I was tempted to be petty. The thought of agreeing and then bailing on her at the last minute like she did me immediately came to mind. It wasn't like I enjoyed visiting Monroe, either. He tended to treat Aurora like she was still under his thumb or something, and I didn't think it was about concern as much as it was about control. He wasn't cruel to her (at least from what I'd seen) but he was still demanding, as if she needed to answer to him. And I don't think I'd ever seen the man smile.

"I don't see why you still bother going over there," I commented. "You clearly don't enjoy it. And you're a grown woman now; what could he do about it?"

"We promised my mother that we'd stay close. Since my father died when I was a toddler and Monroe came along when I was knocking on adulthood, she tried to cram our relationship and get us together as much as possible. I had to call him every week when I was in college, promise to visit every three months, and keep him posted on what was going on with me. Not to mention, reporting my grades and achievements to him like I was a child. He's not as anal about our time together as he used to be but he won't let it stop altogether."

"Are you the only family he has or something?"

"I don't know. I've never met anyone, though I do recall him mentioning his parents are deceased. But Monroe and I have never been close enough to get into all that; our relationship is obligatory. There's only so much we know about each other beyond the superficial."

"And you're satisfied with that? Maybe he could be the father figure you never had if you both put forth the effort."

"Please," Aurora immediately scoffed, shaking her head. "Monroe might not be a bad guy, but the *last* thing I see him as is a father figure. So will you go with me on Friday? I'd really appreciate it. It's better that I don't go alone."

I looked at her. "Why do you say that?"

She shifted, averting her eyes briefly. "I...it just is. *Please*, Montrel?"

I wanted to say no but she was looking so pitiful I couldn't make myself deny her. "Fine, yeah."

"Thank you!" She leaned over and grabbed my face, planting a kiss to my cheek before grabbing her tablet and scurrying out of the room. I looked after her curiously, briefly wondering where she was going, then shrugged. I didn't need to know her every move. I just picked up my notebook and resumed writing my letter.

I knew Aurora appreciated me agreeing to go with her to Monroe's, but I figured that ended with her thanking me. I didn't expect to wake up the next morning with her head between my legs, sliding that warm wet mouth of hers up and down my dick.

"Shit..." I muttered, my hips automatically falling into rhythm.

She looked up at me, clearly pleased at my reaction. Winking at me, she continued with the pleasure, working me over until I was gripping the sheets, screaming her name, and busting in her mouth. I was still convulsing as she continued milking every last drop out of me, refusing to budge when I tried to push her away.

"Good morning, handsome," she finally greeted huskily, giving one last lick to the head before easing herself up.

"Yeah, good morning. You know it wasn't necessary to give me head just because I agreed to go with you to visit your stepfather."

"Since when do I need a reason to pleasure you? I just wanted to give you something nice to wake up to, that's all."

"Can't deny you did that."

"I wish we had time to keep the fun going but-"

"We do." I pulled her to me, her back to my chest, wrapping my arms around her. I kissed the back of her neck but she inched away.

"Montrel, I'd love to lay here with you but I have to get in the shower."

"That can't wait?"

"I wish but, no. I'm behind on some things at work and I'm...kind of on thin ice with Dan as it is."

"Come on, Aurora. Just because we don't have a traditional marriage doesn't mean we can't still be romantic with each other. You keep saying you love me but when I dare try to get closer to you, you switch up."

"Montrel." I heard something shift in her voice, and she turned away further, as if she suddenly didn't want me touching her at all. "I don't have time for this. Some of us *do* have actual jobs, you know."

"What the fuck?" I released her and sat up, my frown in full effect. "You had to go there, huh? Already throwing what I confided in you about just last night in my face?"

She glanced in my direction over her shoulder but her eyes never quite met mine. "I'm not trying to be mean. I'm just telling the truth."

"Yeah, and you were talking like I had it made last night. Now you're implying I'm some kind of bum."

"That's not what I said, Montrel. Can you please stop being so sensitive all the time?"

"What??"

"You're *always* getting in your feelings about something lately. It's been nothing but you moping around here for weeks with your 'woe is me' attitude. You can't deny that."

"Where the hell is all this coming from? Did you wake me up by sucking my dick just to get me to let my guard down so you could throw jabs? 'Cause I'm not sure how we went from that to this in the span of two minutes."

She slid out of bed, the sheets falling from her naked body. All she had on was a hair bonnet. "I don't want to fight with you."

"I can't tell. You're the one who started this bullshit just because I dared to try and cuddle with you. This is clearly stuff you've been holding in the chamber for a while now."

"Montrel..." She held up her hands. "Look, I'm sorry. I'm just...you know I get a little testy when the visits to Monroe roll around. It's like emotional PMS."

"Uh-huh." I got out of bed myself, facing off with her on the opposite side of it. Her eyes traveled down my naked form but snapped off to the side when I crossed my arms over my chest. "You don't bitch like this when you're going through *actual* PMS. And I know you never look forward to visiting Monroe but you've never taken shots at me like you're doing now. So you're gonna have to come with something better than that."

She huffed a frustrated breath and dropped her hands. "As I said, I don't have time for this. I have to get ready for work." And with that, she turned and stalked out of the room.

I didn't know what the hell just happened, but I knew I didn't like it. Aurora was acting like I had *no* reason to be upset recently. One of the most important people in my life died, one of my good friends wanted nothing more to do with me, I'd lost the love of my life, don't even get me *started* on Mother, and I was married to a woman that didn't seem to have much respect for me. Excuse me for not walking on air.

Yanking at the bed sheets, I tried to put that whole scene out of my mind. Whatever was going on with Aurora was her problem, though I had a feeling there was more to it than just her pre-Monroe anxiety. Even with that, though, I never understood why she always got so nervous with him. He wasn't the most pleasant man but he wasn't a tyrant. And she'd insisted that he never did anything out of pocket towards her. So if you asked *me*, she was the one being overly sensitive and getting in her feelings over nothing.

Figuring there was no point in trying to go back to bed even though it was barely seven o'clock, I went to pick out what I'd wear for the day before getting in the shower. I had some errands to run and a doctor's appointment for my regular checkup. And I figured I'd go spend some time at the children's hospital, which was another place I frequently volunteered, reading to the sick kids and holding babies. That was my favorite thing to do there.

I'd just entered our stupid white en suite bathroom when Aurora inched in, looking sheepish. I only glanced at her before proceeding to get the shower going, not planning on acknowledging her.

"Montrel, I'm sorry," she murmured in that soft voice that she turned on when she wanted something. I could barely hear her over the water. "For those things I said."

My brow arched skeptically. "What, you didn't mean them?"

"I shouldn't have said them."

"Wow." I chuckled sarcastically. "Yeah, okay. Whatever."

"Do you forgive me?"

"Does it matter?"

"Montrel..."

"I'm not in the mood for this hot-and-cold thing you have going on right now, Aurora. You have to get ready for work, right? Matter of fact," I stepped back, sweeping my arm towards the shower. "You go first. Since you're the one with the actual *job* and all. I'm going to get me some breakfast."

She grabbed my arm as I tried to walk past her. "Can we go out to dinner together tonight?"

"For what?"

"I thought it would be nice. You said you wanted to get more romantic. And we haven't had a date night in a while."

My eyes narrowed as I looked at her. I could not figure this woman out. Now she was asking me on a date?

"I'm good on that," I replied, pulling away. "I'd rather subject myself to eating ramen and hot dogs than deal with whatever mood swing you're gonna have next."

I didn't care about her hurt expression. She wasn't caring how I felt when she was calling me a whiny jobless bitch.

Tired of looking at her, I left her in the bathroom. For once, I was glad that we had such a big house; it was easier to get lost when I didn't want to deal with her like I didn't right then. While she got ready for work, I holed up in our seldom-used library on the other side of the house. And thankfully, she left me alone and just went ahead and left.

I felt relief when she was gone. This was one of those times when dealing with Aurora exhausted me, as had been the case more and more often as our excuse-for-a-marriage continued. Claire's face flashed through my mind, and as I did probably too often, I wondered what she was doing at that very moment. Was she still a school counselor? Did she still love peanut butter toast and lattes? Was she still a Disney Plus addict? It felt like I hadn't seen her in so long, and the ache from that was making itself known. Again.

Simply put, I missed the hell out of Claire.

And not just because Aurora was far from the ideal wife. I never denied that Claire was the better woman for me. She was loving but she still called me on my shit. She was encouraging and supportive. Funny. Never tried to shame me for the choices I made. And she was incredibly pretty, with her green eyes and pretty legs and smooth brown skin that was always as soft as a newborn's. Sure, she didn't like my mother but if I was honest, I didn't like her half the time my damn self, either.

I wondered if Giselle would give me Claire's contact information if I apologized. Or just begged. Maybe if I admitted how crappy my marriage was, she'd take some pity on me. But I had to dismiss that. She'd probably just tell me I was getting what I deserved.

Maybe I was.

My energy was gone already and I hadn't been up two hours yet. The deflation I felt when I let my rose-colored glasses slip was taking over, and I actually felt heavy as I trudged to the kitchen to get myself something to eat. I admittedly didn't cook, so breakfast was banana coconut overnight oats and an apple. Aurora, who actually *did* use our kitchen for what it was there for, had made a couple of comments in the past about how insufficient I was. I didn't cook. I utilized a cleaning and laundry service. Couldn't do anything with my car but drive it and take it to the mechanic when the littlest thing went wrong. And home maintenance and repairs? Please.

The way *I* looked at it, I was helping to keep all these people in business by using them for whatever I needed. And it wasn't like I hired someone for *everything*; I still ran my own errands. But according to Aurora, I was just spoiled. It certainly wasn't the first time I'd been called that.

I was heading back from the children's hospital later that afternoon when Aurora called. I ignored it, still burning from the things she'd said that morning. But she called right back, and I sighed and cursed under my breath, plunking my head against the headrest.

"What?" I droned, finally answering her damn call.

"Hey, are you busy?"

"Of course not. I don't have a job or anything, so..."

"Montrel, please; I'm trying to call a truce, here. I don't want you to be upset with me."

"Why are you calling me? I thought you were *so* busy today."

"I have some time between appointments. Have you given any more thought to my dinner invitation?"

"The one I already declined? No."

"Can you reconsider? I thought about what you said earlier and you're right; we *could* be more intimate with each other, despite our arrangement. I mean, it couldn't hurt, right?"

"Stop it; I'm swooning."

"Montrel."

"Are you in love with me, Aurora?" I found myself asking, even though I was ninety-nine percent sure of the answer. Guess I liked torturing myself. "You've said you love me several times. But are you *in love* with me? Or am I just someone you feel like you have a debt towards?"

There was a pause, and I felt my hand squeeze the steering wheel tighter. Why the hell did I ask such a question? And why did I care so much about what her answer would be?

"We're best friends, Montrel," Aurora finally responded, her voice softening again.

"Best friends? Us?"

"I care about you...*so* much. You're not just another man to me. Now that I think about it, you're the most important person in my life, especially since my mother passed. I felt like I didn't have anyone after she died."

"What about Mecca and Bron? Or Monroe?"

"You know the deal with Monroe; he and I never had that kind of relationship. And I love Mecca and Bron but they're more for fun; we don't really talk about deep things or anything that serious. I can talk to *you* about anything. The fact that you're so handsome and sexy is a bonus."

My lip automatically quirked at the compliment and I was glad that this conversation was happening over the phone. It was sad that I was so easily charmed.

I forced the frown back to my face.

"Yeah, thanks," I deadpanned. "But basically that was the long way of saying that you're *not* in love with me; I'm just a buddy you're legally bonded to."

"Are you in love with *me*?"

I didn't appreciate her turning the tables on me. She wasn't supposed to ask me that.

"As much as I can be, considering you only let me get so close to you," I truthfully responded. "But you've made it quite clear you're not interested in anything other than what we're doing now."

"No, I told you, I *would* like to change that," Aurora insisted. "Just because our marriage started out unconventionally doesn't mean it has to stay that way. I'd love to get to where we're madly in love with each other; more than you know. Which is why I wish you'd reconsider my dinner invitation. We can get started on that path tonight."

I wanted to say no, but the voice in my head reminded me that this was what I said I wanted; for me and Aurora to be man and wife more than just on paper. I mean, we'd chosen this; might as well make the best of it. And since Aurora didn't want to get a divorce (believe me, I asked), *something* needed to change, because the thought of another fifty years like this made me want to hurl myself against a wall.

"Fine, yeah," I finally conceded. "You're right. We can go out to dinner."

"Great!" I could hear the smile in her voice, and it sent my lips quirking again. "I'm so glad. Thank you, for reconsidering. I'm looking forward to it."

"Me, too."

I felt marginally better after that call. Aurora really seemed to be making an effort, so I figured I should, too.

And it would be better to make it work with the woman I was already married to than to torture myself pining over the woman I drove away. Maybe if things improved between me and Aurora, I wouldn't be compelled to obsess over Claire so much. I could actually appreciate and be content with what I had, which was a big issue in my relationship with Claire.

By the time we were sitting at a cozy back table later that evening at Aurora's favorite spot, the Orange Pearl Bistro, I was actually feeling optimistic.

"You're looking beautiful," I told Aurora, admiring how she looked in her floral cap-sleeved dress that showed an enticing amount of cleavage. I actually had to remind myself that she was my wife and I didn't have to feel guilty for ogling.

She looked up from her menu, grinning. "Thank you. I'm sure you know how good you look already."

"Certainly, but it would still be nice to hear."

"You look very handsome. I love that you have the nerve to wear such a bold color."

Not sure if this was an actual compliment or a backhanded one, I chose to think positively as I looked down at my mustard yellow suit jacket, midnight blue silk shirt, and blue paisley tie and accents. Of course, I'd posted my look on social media before leaving the house. "I've never been one to follow trends."

"I've learned that about you."

"So what else can I learn about *you*?" I put down my menu and folded my arms on top of it, looking at her intently. I wished I felt something other than just primal urges when I looked at her like that but I was sure it would come in time. "Tell me something I don't know already."

"Hmm..." Aurora put down her own menu, looking off to the side thoughtfully. "I've always wanted a sibling; that's something I don't usually admit."

"Do you wish you had a sister or a brother? Or both?"

"I'd love a protective big brother and a sister that I could be best friends with. Honestly, I used to wish I was part of a big family so I could get lost in the mix. I loved my mother dearly but it was hard being the sole focal point of her attention."

"Was she that tough on you?"

"I wouldn't say *tough* but she had high expectations. She was a successful attorney and she just wanted me to be successful, too. Not long before she died, she admitted she was against me getting my trust fund because she wanted me to earn whatever I got on my own. It was my father that insisted on setting it up when I was born. His adding the stipulation that I had to be married to get it was a compromise."

"It was good that you were at least close to your mother, though, despite her expecting so much of you. I can't say the same for my situation."

"Ms. Annie doesn't exactly seem like the mothering type."

"You're being nice about it. She's far from that."

"Do you even *want* a closer relationship with her?"

I had to pause at that question; it was something I honestly hadn't thought about. "I'll admit I'm so used to things as they are that I've never imagined it being any other way. Mother and I have an obligatory bond. I check on her because she's my mother and I feel like I have to. She feigns interest in what's going on with me because I'm her son. She's always cared more about how I make her look than...me."

"Does she know that?"

"I've never bothered telling her. I'd be willing to bet all the money in my accounts that it wouldn't make any difference. She'd probably just tell me I was being silly and dismiss it."

Our server came over and took our orders, and once they were gone, Aurora returned her focus to me. "It's a shame, the main things we have in common; fathers that passed when we were young, less-than-ideal relationships with our mothers, being only children. I wish there was something more positive that we could share."

"We both like beef wellington. And the color green."

She laughed and I found myself smiling at the sight. "I was thinking something more substantial than that but it's better than nothing."

We continued to talk, the conversation flowing with a surprising effortlessness. This was the most Aurora and I had sat and talked since we married, and it felt nice. Us being in a restaurant prevented (or highly lessened) the possibility of getting distracted by sex, which was a nice change of pace. Our union had been superficial but it finally felt like we were going deeper.

"Montrel," Aurora mused, putting down her fork. She finished chewing her pan-roasted haddock before turning her eyes to me. I could see the apprehension in them and I wondered what she was about to come at me with. "Do you think that...I'm not sure how to ask this..."

"Just say it."

"Is there anything I could do that would make you hate me?"

Reeling, I put down my own fork. "What would make you ask something like that?"

"I feel closer to you already, and I want it to continue. But I just...this is all so new to me, Montrel. I've never been great with relationships. And I don't want to ruin us with my mistakes. So I was just wondering what your breaking point would be."

What an odd question. But strangely, I appreciated her vulnerability.

Reaching over and taking her hand, I ran my thumb over her knuckles. Her eyes fell to the motion before sliding back up to me.

"It's hard for me to say, Aurora. I guess I won't know until it happens. But I wish you wouldn't worry about that. We'll *both* make mistakes; I haven't exactly been a savant with relationships, either. But we can help each other. I can't imagine you doing anything *that* heinous that would have me saying 'I'm done' just like that."

Her hand turned and gripped mine. "I hope not."

"I know one thing that might help us feel closer."

"What's that?"

"Pet names."

Her eyebrows shot up, clearly having never considered that. "Really?"

"I only call you 'Aurora' and you only call me 'Montrel.' Getting more cutesy and less stiff couldn't hurt. And things like this," I motioned towards our joined hands. "The only time we really touch each other is when we're getting down. We could hold hands. I could play in your hair. We could rub each other's backs. Just affection for the sake of it. I hear that's a good thing."

"I like the sound of that." Aurora's smile grew as she sat and gazed at me. The look in her eyes made me wonder what was going through her mind. "Yeah, I like that a lot...snookums."

"Uhh...we don't have to nail down the pet names right now. We can put a pin in that."

We shared a laugh, and I dared to think we were gonna be all right. Of course there'd be some bumps in the road, but we could deal with them.

Once we left the bistro, we went home and did something else we'd never done and watched a movie together in our seldom-used media room. We got a blanket and a bowl of habitual popcorn (I really didn't even like popcorn) and settled in, sitting close but not touching. As if suddenly remembering our vow to amp up the intimacy, she leaned over and rested her head on my shoulder. I put my arm around her. It didn't exactly feel natural, but it was nice. Part of me expected her hand to ease to my crotch at some point but to my surprise, that didn't happen. All we did was cuddle and watch the movie.

And when we eventually went to bed, Aurora laying on my chest, it was the first night in a while where I didn't dream about Claire.

Chapter 5 – Montrel

Aurora and I were going to see Monroe and I could tell she was on edge. Any pep talks and encouragement I'd tried to give fell on partially-deaf ears. I still wished I understood why she always got so anxious about visiting her stepfather, especially since she insisted again after our night at the bistro that he'd never abused or mistreated her in any way (I had asked her again in case our newfound attempts at closeness spurred any urges to confide). He just had high standards for her, but according to Aurora, so did her mother but she always mostly spoke highly of her. But I'd never heard her say anything positive about Monroe. They had a strange relationship, but I figured it just wasn't for me to understand.

"I really appreciate you coming with me, Muffin," Aurora said as we pulled up to Monroe's split-level house. That's the pet name she'd landed on for me; Muffin. I didn't love it but I appreciated the effort. "Maybe it'll be a more pleasant evening now that you're here."

"I'm sure it won't be that bad, Agave." That's what I'd chosen to call her. Mostly because I just couldn't think of anything else. Clearly I sucked at pet names, too.

"I wish I had a drink."

"You need more than the ones you had before we left the house?"

"Yes."

"Can you please chill out?" I reached over and rubbed her thigh, noting how she vacantly glanced down at my hand before looking out the window. "Look, when you reach your limit, just give me the signal and we'll leave."

"What's the signal?"

"Flash me the peace sign."

"Okay. Okay, that sounds good." She took a deep breath before reaching for the door handle. "Let's go; I don't want to hear any lectures about tardiness."

We headed up the walkway to the front door, and I could almost feel Aurora's nerves radiating off of her. I grabbed her hand before ringing the doorbell with the other.

Almost instantly, the door swung open and we were facing Monroe Dobson. A tall man who reminded me of one of those actors the ladies swooned over and put on dream boards. I guessed he was in his late fifties and as usual when I saw him, he was overdressed for the occasion. I liked being stylish but wearing a full suit around the house was ridiculous.

"Right on time," he greeted us, with the faintest possible hint of a smile. His light brown eyes dropped to me and Aurora's joined hands. "I like that. Come in."

We stepped inside and I could practically feel the dampness building on Aurora's palm. I absently noted the shiny hardwood floors, the crown molding, and the chrome sconces as we moved from the foyer to the living room, with Monroe striding over to the bar.

"Would you two like a drink?"

"Yes," Aurora immediately replied. She eased her hand from mine and ran it across her hips. "Brandy, please."

"Laird's?"

"Of course."

Monroe grabbed a decanter and poured a generous portion into a glass tumbler, setting it on the quartz bar top with a thump.

My brow arched at this. Monroe was apparently kind enough to keep Aurora's favorite apple brandy on hand. Either that or they shared a love for it.

"And for you, Montrel?" Monroe asked as Aurora scurried over to get her liquid courage.

"I'm good, thanks." I figured one of us needed to keep a clear head, since Aurora was intent on numbing herself.

"Very well." Monroe proceeded to fix himself a dry martini before rounding the bar as he took a sip, his other hand in his pocket. "Feel free to make yourselves comfortable. I need to go make a phone call."

"Sure." I parked it on the couch and Aurora followed suit, grasping her tumbler in both hands. Her leg started bouncing almost automatically and I eyed it but said nothing. Trying to keep her calm had already become an exhausting job and while I wanted to be supportive, I was also simultaneously trying not to be annoyed. Her level of nervousness still seemed irrational to me and I wished she'd snap out of it.

"Is it too early for the peace sign?" she whispered.

I looked at her, unable to tell if she was joking or not. "We just got here, Aurora."

"I know." She took a sip of her drink. "You think I'm being silly, don't you?"

Yes. "That's not for me to say."

"You can be honest. I get how it must look from your perspective. But I really am trying to calm down. The drink is helping some."

"Good." I was about ready to give my own peace sign.

Monroe re-entered the living room armed with a large charcuterie board full of various fruits, cheeses, crackers, and a small jar of honey. After setting it on the coffee table in front of us, he moved to the nearby armchair, crossing his long legs and glancing at his watch.

"I'm expecting someone else soon," he announced. "They should be here shortly."

Aurora's eyebrows lifted curiously. "May I ask who?"

"Just a lady I've been seeing. She's been asking to meet you so I figured now was as good a time as any. Her name is Bethany Penn."

I was surprised when Aurora grunted but when I glanced over at her, she just shrugged and took another swig of her drink.

"That's nice," I felt compelled to say. "How did you two meet?"

"At the barbershop, actually. She was there with her son. We got to talking about the best place in town to get a certain French press coffee we mutually enjoy and I ended up asking her out for drinks. We've been out a few times now."

"Is it serious?" Aurora inquired, her voice going soft again.

"I'm sorry; I couldn't hear you," Monroe smoothly scolded, sitting forward slightly. "What was that?"

Clearing her throat, Aurora put her drink on a coaster and picked up a cluster of red grapes from the charcuterie board. "I asked if it was serious, since you've been out multiple times. Is she your girlfriend?"

He chuckled as if her question was silly. "I'm a little advanced for that. We haven't directly discussed being exclusive just yet but I can see her becoming my woman. I think you'll like her."

Aurora popped a couple of grapes into her mouth. "You haven't dated anyone seriously since Mom died. At least, not that *I've* been aware of."

"True." Monroe rubbed his chin, his expression holding a hint of amusement. "But I think it's time for me to put myself back out there. It would be nice to have someone to share my life with. You know, like the two of you have in each other."

That seemed like sarcasm but I let it go because, whatever. Unlike Aurora, I didn't care what Monroe thought.

"Do you have an issue with me seeing someone?" he asked Aurora.

Taking her time responding, Aurora slowly finished chewing the grapes she'd stuffed into her mouth. "Not at all. I guess I can't expect you to be alone forever. As long as you're happy..."

"I am. Quite happy. So, Montrel, what's going on with you?"

Mildly surprised, I paused my action of reaching for a prosciutto-wrapped melon slice. I'd just planned to be a quiet fly on the wall for the rest of this obligatory tête-à-tête. "Actually, I've been thinking about getting into the workforce. I'm not sure what I'd like to do yet, but coasting along with no real purpose has lost its appeal."

"Really? That's commendable. I must say I didn't expect this from you; you always seemed perfectly content lounging on your inheritance and frittering your days away at the spa and the men's clothing store."

Okay, *that* was sarcasm.

"Um, there's more to my days than that," I retorted, a slight edge to my voice. "I spend a lot of time volunteering. Though admittedly not as much as I used to, at least at the nursing home, which was the main place I frequented. My favorite charge passed a few weeks ago and I haven't been able to go back there since."

"I'm sorry to hear that," Monroe stated, sounding sincere. "My apologies for my earlier comment, then. Aurora didn't mention to me that you did volunteer work. She only highlighted the constant spa days and incessant shopping."

I glanced at Aurora, whose cheeks were flushed and eyes were averted. What else had she said about me behind my back?

"'Constant' is a stretch," I replied. "I have a regular monthly appointment. As many people do."

"Hmm. Well, if you need help getting your foot in the door somewhere, let me know. I have a myriad of connections." He arched a brow. "You *do* have a college degree, right?"

My own brow arched. "I have a master's degree, Monroe."

"Do you? Well, that's good to know. I tried to convince Aurora to get one of those. Maybe then I wouldn't have had to help her get the job she has now."

I felt Aurora tense up next to me, and she reached for her glass of brandy, draining it. "You got me the *interview*; I earned the job on my own. *And* the promotion after that."

"The interview wouldn't have happened at all if it weren't for me. But true enough, you did manage to charm them into hiring you. And you've been there for several years now, so you must be doing something right." His eyes narrowed slightly. "Though I *have* been hearing rumblings about your performance declining recently. What's going on with that?"

"I..."

The doorbell rang, and Aurora's sigh of relief was noticeable. Monroe eyed her for another moment before standing and going to the door, his expression unreadable. Aurora got up to get more brandy.

Moments later, Monroe and a pretty lady with short dyed blonde hair and cat-eyed glasses entered the room. Her skin was a sunkissed brown, and the red ruched dress she wore really accentuated her ample bosom and rounded hips. Monroe was suddenly all smiles as he slid an arm around her shoulder.

"This is Bethany Penn," he introduced proudly, giving her shoulder a squeeze. "Bethany, this is my stepdaughter Aurora Chadwick and her husband, Montrel Burns."

"It's nice to meet you both," Bethany greeted, showing her dimpled smile. "Different last names, huh? How progressive."

I didn't know what to make of that statement so I didn't address it. Aurora hadn't wanted to take my last name when we married and honestly, part of me didn't want her to have it, anyway.

Standing, I moved over to shake her hand. "It's nice to meet you too, Bethany."

Aurora took her time addressing the guest, clearly opting to just wave from the bar. "Hi there, Bethany."

The rest of the visit could only be described as weird. Monroe almost seemed like a different person now that Bethany was there; gone were the probing questions and thinly-veiled criticisms and in their places were smiles and laughs and actually feeding the woman cheese and crackers and strawberries. Aurora suddenly started cozying up to me on the couch, sitting so close she was practically in my lap, placing her hand high on my thigh, even kissing my neck a couple of times. I wasn't sure whose benefit the show she was putting on was for, but I wasn't feeling it. Especially since she'd suddenly become lively and talkative when before she'd been nervous and antsy. Another one of her patented mood swings.

"Bethany, I hope you don't mind me saying how gorgeous you are," Aurora commented. "That hair color looks amazing on you. And I love those glasses. You have a great sense of style."

"I appreciate that, thanks!" Bethany beamed. "I've always loved clothes. And I'm constantly changing my hair; it might be fire engine red in a few weeks. It's fun to switch things up."

"Admirable. I've never had the nerve to color my hair. I can see why Monroe is so clearly taken with you."

"Yeah, we really hit it off. It's been a while since I've seriously dated anyone, honestly. But Monroe managed to break down my defenses." She placed her hand on Monroe's leg and smiled, and he grinned back at her, which almost looked foreign to me since he was usually so stern. Eying this, Aurora inched even closer to me. "He's even great with my son. They're like buddies already."

"Oh really? Somehow I can't imagine Monroe tossing around a football or playing video games."

Bethany's smile waned slightly. "Actually, my son is disabled so his interests are more along the lines of puzzles and reading. It's not every man who exhibits the patience that Monroe has with him. That's a big part of the reason I've been single for so long; a middle-aged woman with a disabled son isn't exactly first choice in most cases."

"Oh..." Aurora cleared her throat, clearly embarrassed. "I apologize for the assumption."

"It's fine."

The way Monroe was glaring at Aurora showed *he* didn't think it was fine, but he didn't comment on it. I could imagine she'd likely be hearing about that when they were one-on-one.

It was maybe ten minutes later when Aurora finally flashed that peace sign. Honestly, I was surprised it took her so long.

"We need to get going," I announced, standing. Aurora quickly followed suit.

"Aww, already?" Bethany moaned.

"What's the rush?" Monroe asked, though there was a knowing glint in his eye.

"No rush. It's just getting late and we have some things to do before we turn in for the night. Thanks for having us, Monroe. And Bethany, so nice to meet you."

"You too, Montrel. I hope to see you both again soon."

"Enjoy the rest of your evening," Aurora spoke up, hanging onto my arm as we started moving towards the door.

"I'll talk to you soon, Aurora," Monroe informed. It almost sounded like a warning.

She didn't respond. Just moved her feet faster.

We didn't talk much on the way home. I wanted to ask her about her attitude change after Bethany arrived, but I had a feeling she'd just act like she didn't know what I was talking about. Maybe seeing Monroe with another woman for the first time since her mom died was jarring for her and had her acting outside of herself. Which was understandable, I guess.

"That didn't go quite as badly as I thought," she finally said once we were almost to the house. "But I think the alcohol helped some."

"Well, I'd count that as a win, then." I pulled into our garage and killed the engine. Already over the whole visit, I turned to her and asked, "You hungry? Or did you somehow get full off that finger food Monroe provided?"

Her hand landed on my thigh again. "I am kinda hungry, actually. Hey, do you think Monroe is really into Bethany like that? I've never seen him smile so much."

I shrugged. "Seems so."

"Do you think they've been intimate? That maybe they started fooling around as soon as we left?"

Frowning slightly at the question, I scoffed, "I have no idea, Aurora. I'm glad to say Monroe's intimate habits have never crossed my mind. Why do you even care about such a thing?"

Instead of answering, she just started unbuckling my belt. In mere moments, she had my dick in her mouth, eagerly bobbing her head up and down and moaning loudly from the back of her throat. It was in the back of my mind to question her, but it was feeling too good...Aurora was undoubtedly the best I've experienced at giving head. And if she wanted to cap off the evening with that, I wasn't going to stop her.

Just like I didn't stop her when she stepped out of the car, lifted her dress over her head, tossed it aside, and asked me to fuck her on the warm hood of the car. I simply obliged.

And again when I bent her over the back of the couch.

And when she asked me to go down on her in the shower. Then fuck her again.

"Harder!" she cried out as I rammed her from the back like she liked it. Like she *demanded* it. "I want *all* that dick, Muffin."

Oh my god, I officially hated that nickname now. It sounded even stupider when we were having sex.

But I just grunted and gave it to her as she asked for like the good and willing husband that I was.

When she got into this kind of insatiable mode, I didn't question it; I just hung on for the ride for as long as I could.

And I'm not entirely ashamed to admit sometimes I had to tap out before she was done.

Which is exactly what happened that night. After the shower, she pulled me to the bedroom and mounted me. It was a wonder I even had anything left by then. I held her hips as she moved on top of me, her hands planted on my chest and her head thrown back. Her eyes were closed, as they had been for most of the time we'd been going at it. There was very little kissing, almost no endearing words, and as I mentioned, no eye contact. It seemed to be more about getting hers than about sharing intimacy with her man or mutual pleasure. I had only come twice while she'd had multiple rides to the mountaintop. I needed to find her stash of ginseng.

Eventually, though, my battery ran out. She drained me. I managed to hang on for her to get her latest orgasm before my body went limp and my eyes slid closed, my hands falling from her damp body onto the bed.

"Montrel? Montrel??"

She was shaking me but I was too zonked to respond. My eyes briefly opened to see her frowning face hovering over mine.

"Huh?"

"Montrel, wake up! What's wrong with you?"

"Tired..." I tried to turn away from her, but she yanked me back by the shoulder.

"We're not done! Get up!"

I heard her, but I was too gone. She shook both my shoulders and bounced on my lap but none of it made any difference. When she realized she wasn't going to wake me up, she slapped my chest in exasperation.

"Uggh!" I heard her scream. Then she was climbing off of me, then off the bed, then stomping out of the room. And I just rolled over and let sleep take over, finally.

I woke up hours later; the lights were still on and the other side of the bed was empty. I glanced at my wrist to check the time, but I never put my watch back on after getting out of the shower. And my phone wasn't on the nightstand. Rubbing my tired eyes, I gingerly sat up, glancing around the huge bedroom before swinging my legs off the side of the bed and standing up. I found my phone downstairs in my pants pocket where I'd left it after me and Aurora's couch session. My eyebrows shot up when I saw it was almost four o'clock in the morning.

"Aurora?"

The house was quiet. I roamed around, naked, looking to see if maybe she'd slept in another room. When I peeked into the garage, I noticed her car was gone. Mild alarm took over when I checked my phone and saw no messages from her. I didn't know where she could be that time of night, or why she'd gone in the first place. It wasn't really like Aurora to stay out all night. Well, usually.

I was just about to call her when I noticed a sloppily-written note on the kitchen island:

Gone to Mecca's.

Strange, but at least I knew where she was. I figured calling her at that point would be futile. She could explain her sudden departure when she got back.

Mildly relieved, I turned out all the lights, engaged the alarm, and went back to bed, fully expecting Aurora to be back by the time I got up.

She wasn't.

I usually got up no later than nine, since I'd never been one to lounge around in bed all day, but this particular morning, I allowed myself to sleep later, given all the energy I expended the night before. It was after eleven when I finally rolled out of bed, and Aurora still wasn't back yet. This time I did call her, and the call went right to voicemail.

"What the hell..."

She immediately sent a text letting me know she was still at Mecca's and would be back eventually, because she needed time to herself. Whatever the hell that meant. I was supremely annoyed. If I just up and left in the middle of the night with nothing but a raggedy note and a half-ass explanation, she'd probably throw a whole tantrum. But *she* got to do it, no problem. And I guess I was just supposed to deal with it.

I was banging around the kitchen fixing my breakfast when my phone rang. It annoyed me that I hoped it was Aurora calling to explain herself, but it turned out to be Forrest.

"What's up, man?"

"Hmph," I grunted, snatching a bowl from the cupboard.

"Damn, what's wrong with you?"

"Nothing."

"Man, I'm taking a break and don't have time to pull it out of you. Spill it."

"For what? You've already said that you don't want to hear about what's going on with me, remember?"

"So this is about Aurora. Look, I know what I said but if there's something going on with y'all that's truly bothering you, you know I'm here for you."

I hesitated in pouring my overnight oats into the bowl (I refused to eat them out of a jar). Part of me wanted to tell my boy everything while the other part didn't have the energy. Plus, I wondered how much I should tell, anyway; as Forrest himself had told me, some things between a man and wife didn't need to be broadcasted.

"I just feel like I'm on a roller coaster around here most of time," I finally admitted. "I honestly thought Aurora and I had reached an understanding...that we were both going to make the effort to improve this marriage. We were going to start spending quality time, have more in-depth conversations, being more affectionate, all that."

"And that's not happening?"

"Depends on the day. I go from having high hopes for us to not knowing what the hell is going on with her at the drop of a hat. She's constantly switching up. Like last night; we got home from visiting her stepfather and meeting his new lady friend, she ravaged me in the car and beyond, wore me the hell out, then I woke up to a message that she was at her friend's house because she needed time."

"For?"

"Hell if I know. And honestly right now, I don't even care. Emotionally, Aurora wears me out."

There was a pause. "I'm gonna ask you something and I need you to not get in your feelings about it."

"I can't promise that but go ahead."

"Why are you staying with her? You only married her so she could get her money; she's got that. You two clearly aren't in love. Seems like your main connection is sexual, which you can get anywhere. And given how much you complain, you're not happy with whatever arrangement the two of you have. Why not just divorce her and go about your business?"

Valid question. And not something I hadn't considered.

"She doesn't want a divorce. And for whatever reason, I want to try to make it work, too," I replied, absently swirling my spoon through my oats. "It might not be the deep, all-consuming kind but I *do* love Aurora. And I care about her."

"You might as well be talking about your aunt. You do realize you have more intensity whenever you talk about Ms. Debra – God rest her soul – than you do about your own wife, right?"

"I...those are two different situations."

"Could your reasoning for trying to force this marriage with Aurora to work be because you chose it over Claire and you don't want to have lost the love of your life for nothing?"

Conviction washed over my body like an ice cold shower. My hand dropped the spoon and rubbed my eyes. "Don't you have to go give a kid a checkup or restock your lollipops or something?"

"It's Saturday; I'm just going over some charts. And I must have struck a nerve. It's something to think about, man."

"This isn't about Claire."

"Uh-huh. Speaking of Claire, I heard Giselle mention that she's going to be around soon."

My back instantly straightened and I squeezed the phone so hard I was surprised I didn't crack the case. "When??"

"Not sure of the particulars. I only know that much from overhearing Giselle talk to their friend Chichi. If you want specifics, you'd have to ask her."

"As if Giselle *or* Chichi would tell me anything. Chichi hated me way before Claire and I even broke up."

"It's the only way you'll find out. And I know you wanna know."

Damn right I did. Knowing Claire was going to be nearby again filled me with an overwhelming amount of anticipation and excitement. I was tempted again to humble myself and go to Giselle for details, or at least, for some way to contact Claire myself. Just knowing what city Claire had moved to would be more information than I had.

But I had to pump the brakes. Even if by some miracle Giselle listened to me and believed I was truly sorry for how I treated Claire, she still wouldn't betray her friend's trust. I was sure Claire had made it clear she didn't want me knowing where she was or how to contact her. She didn't remove her social media and change her number for nothing. Access to that information would have to come from Claire, and I knew that. Really, that's what I preferred, because that would mean she wanted me to have it. Scheming was something the old me would've done and I wasn't going there.

Foolish as it was, there was a small part of me that still hoped that Claire would reach out to me whenever she came to town. I couldn't help hoping that she still thought about me and our relationship, even if it was the unpleasant parts. To me, that was better than her forgetting about me altogether.

Chapter 6 – Aurora

Montrel didn't have a lot to say to me, and I couldn't blame him. Especially since I wasn't totally honest with him about where I was when I skipped out in the middle of the night after he fell asleep on me.

I might have ended up at Mecca's, but that's not where I went first. When I left the house, I went straight to a club in the seedy backskirts of town, still buzzing and smelling like sex. I was restless and just needed to take the edge off. And two very willing gentlemen helped me do just that in the red light room. I didn't bother with the detail of their names, but one of them had a jaguar tattoo covering his right forearm.

It was just what I needed, but as soon as I was back in my car and caught a glimpse of myself in the rearview mirror, I felt that all too familiar shame. How had I ended up here? I'd been having a perfectly good time with my husband...until he ran out of energy for me, that is. Usually when that happened, I just dipped into my stash of vibrators and kept chasing the high. But for whatever reason, that wasn't going to cut it this time and I went outside of my house, again, to get what I needed.

Even though it had happened before, it *was* the first time since Montrel and I had agreed to give our marriage a legitimate effort. Knowing that made me feel even worse, and I knew I wouldn't be able to bring myself to tell him. He'd either get extremely pissed or deeply disappointed in me, and I wouldn't be able to handle either.

"It won't happen again," I told my reflection, determination in my red-rimmed eyes. "This...it didn't mean anything at all. Everyone's allowed a slip-up."

Though I didn't quite buy my own words, which is why I'd gone to Mecca's instead of going home. I needed that time to get my head together. I didn't even tell Mecca where I'd been. As far as she knew, I was reeling from another upsetting visit to Monroe's.

Montrel had been at his laptop when I finally got home Sunday afternoon, and when I ventured into his office, he glanced up at me and went right back to what he was doing. I opened my mouth to say something, but chickened out. When I started to slink back out of the room, his voice stopped me.

"Where've you been?"

My face immediately flushed. Making myself turn back towards him, I softly replied, "You didn't see my note?"

His eyes fixed on me and it took all of my strength not to squirm under his glare. I sensed that he didn't totally buy my explanation of my whereabouts, and I prepared myself for interrogation or berating.

But neither came. Several moments passed before he just leaned back in his chair and shook his head. "Whatever, Aurora."

He went back to his laptop and I went to wash the scent and sweat of those men off me.

The following day, I was at work in body but not in spirit. I sat in the morning meeting, half-listening, my eyes flitting around the long conference table. My mind automatically flashed to different scenarios when I focused on some of my associates:

Kurtis from Acquisitions: him sexing me against the wall of the bathroom stall when we were working late one night.

Parker from Marketing: him sucking my breasts in my car after he gave me a jump one rainy night.

Robbie, the guy that delivered the sandwiches (but was at the moment setting out doughnuts): finger-fucked me in my office and hooked me up with an extra bag of chips.

Lionel, whose title I could never remember: mutual masturbation and phone sex.

I never thought about these encounters afterwards; they each got shoved to the back of my mind as soon as they were over, the only repeats happening with deep-voiced Lionel and the phone sex. It was both shocking and thrilling to realize they were all in the same room. Part of me wondered if they'd told anyone about our dalliances, not that it mattered. I didn't try to swear any of them to secrecy. What's done was done. But since I hadn't heard any whispers or seen any sly looks or behind-the-hand snickering when I passed, maybe they'd kept it to themselves in hopes of a repeat. And a couple of them had extra incentive for discretion, considering the wedding pictures I'd seen on their desks.

"Aurora!"

My head snapped up to see Dan frowning at me from the head of the table. When I glanced around, all eyes were on me. Every part of me tightened at suddenly being the center of attention.

"Um, yes?"

"Have you been listening? Someone just asked you a question."

"Oh..." I suddenly wished my brown skin was darker because I was sure the flushing of my face was evident. "I'm sorry. Could...whoever asked...could you repeat the question?"

Dan's beady eyes narrowed at me and I knew he was pissed. Just like I knew he wasn't going to just let me off with a warning this time unless I pulled off some kind of miracle.

"Never mind," he snipped bitingly. Glancing at his watch, he snapped the laptop in front of him closed. "Let's wrap it here, everyone. The rest of the main points will be sent out via email. Aurora," he stood, those eyes back on me. "My office."

I ignored the wary or pitying looks from my coworkers as I gathered my untouched notebook and empty coffee cup from the table, making myself stride out of the room with my usual confidence. Tingles of both nervousness and anticipation danced across my skin.

After a quick stop to the ladies room, I headed for Dan's corner office. I gently knocked on the door, not waiting for his prompt before pushing it open and stepping into the plush room. My heels sank into the thick soft carpet, and I quickly took in the sleek shiny dark wooden furnishings, and wall that held his various diplomas and accolades. The morning sunlight beamed through the window that took up almost the entirety of the wall behind the desk. I used to muse about how I'd redecorate if I ever made it to the corner office.

Dan barely looked up once I entered the room.

"Close the door."

I did as I was told, then stood with my hands folded in front of me.

"Sit down, Aurora."

I would've preferred to stand, but I didn't protest. I just obeyed, again.

Finally, Dan looked up from whatever he'd been writing and sat back in his chair. His salt and pepper hair seemed almost iridescent in the sunlight streaming in behind him. I wondered how old he was; he'd recently celebrated his thirty year anniversary with the company. The certificate was right there on the wall. His papersack-brown face held a few wrinkles, but not that many.

"What the hell is going on with you?" he barked, snapping me out of my perusal. "You have been off your game for a little while now and my patience is just about *gone*, Aurora."

"Dan, I'm sorry," I felt I should say. My thighs pressed together, trying to quell my throbbing womanhood. "I know I've been rather distracted lately. I'll...I'll do better."

"That's what you said the last time I had to call you in here."

"Okay...Dan, can I level with you? I have some things going on at home that I clearly haven't done a good job of leaving at the door when I come to work. And I get it if that just sounds like an excuse or like I'm trying to garner your sympathy; I'd be skeptical of me, too. It's true, though."

His expression barely changed. I could only imagine this wasn't the first time someone had hit him with that particular sob story. "If that's the case, then you take time off and deal with it. If you're here, I expect you to perform as usual and do what we're paying you to do."

"I..." I sniffled and uncrossed my legs. "I guess I misjudged just how severe it was. Being here made me feel better; helped take my mind off of it. You can understand that, right?"

His eyes had dropped. My skirt was *just* at the length required by the company dress code, so it was easy for Dan to notice that I wore no panties underneath. Something told me removing them prior to this reprimand might be beneficial.

When he didn't speak for a few moments, I slid down a little in my seat to give him a better view. I noticed his breathing change.

"Dan?"

His eyes snapped to me. It was almost a reversal of the scene in the conference room earlier. "Yes?"

"Are you all right? You seemed to zone out for a minute, there."

Clearing his throat, he sat up straighter in his seat. I could tell he was fighting to keep his eyes above my waist. "My apologies. I need a drink of water; would you like some?"

"That would be nice, thanks."

Dan shot out of his chair and moved over to his mini fridge to retrieve a couple of bottles of Fiji, taking his time opening his with his back turned and taking a long gulp. When he finally handed me mine, his eyes flitted between my legs again as if he couldn't control it. All the while, my expression remained neutral.

Retaking his seat, Dan took another swig from his bottle before capping it and sliding it aside, lacing his fingers next to it on the desk. "Aurora, look...I don't want to be insensitive to whatever it is you have going on at home. So let's just consider this your last warning. If you need to take some time off, take it; that's what it's there for. But if you're here, I need you to be *all the way* here. Are we clear?"

"Absolutely. I appreciate the understanding. And you giving me another chance. I'll make sure you're pleased."

He just swallowed and gave a slight nod.

I opened my own water bottle and brought it to my lips, squealing when a tiny amount dripped between my cleavage. Scoffing at myself, I tried again, this time letting several drops land on my inner thigh.

"Oh my god!" I exclaimed, scooting forward and widening my legs a bit, dragging my palm along the wetness. "I'm such a mess today; I guess my nerves are getting the better of me. You wouldn't happen to have a napkin or anything, would you?"

When I glanced up at Dan, his face seemed a little paler than before. He silently reached into his inside jacket pocket and pulled out a handkerchief, handing it over to me. Smiling in thanks, I accepted it and proceeded to dab at the spilled water between my cleavage and my legs, being more thorough than called for. I knew I was pushing it, but I couldn't help it. This whole scene excited me, and I'd passed the point of controlling myself when I slipped off my panties in the bathroom.

Figuring I'd done enough, I finally ended my little performance and turned my attention back to Dan. He was gripping his pen so hard I half-expected it to snap in two. The shallow breaths through his nose and his clenched jaw indicated that I'd gotten to him, and I would've given anything to see just how big of an erection he was hiding behind the desk. The throbbing between my legs intensified, and before I did anything crazier like my imagination was taunting me to do, I needed to get out of his office.

"Thanks again, Dan." I smiled sweetly at him as I stood, gently pushing my skirt down. "Do you want your handkerchief back?"

"Please." He reached for it but didn't stand. I bit my lip, knowing why.

"Was there anything else?"

"No." His voice was rough, and he cleared his throat again. "Just remember what we talked about. I'd hate to...have to call you in here again."

"Of course. I'll leave you alone now, then. If you think of anything else you need from me, I'll be in my office."

I turned and sauntered towards the door, knowing he was watching me do so. Once I was back out into the hall, I pressed a hand to my chest, feeling my heart going a mile a minute. That had been more exhilarating than the time my friends and I broke into a neighbor's backyard and skinny dipped in their pool, especially after I noticed someone watching us with binoculars through the window.

The high had started to fade some once I was behind the closed door of my office. Seeing the computer and the files on my desk and the stack of messages Daria had left just reminded me that slithering out of that scolding meant I'd have to do the very work I had no interest in doing. Part of me went into Dan's office hoping he'd fire me. But thanks to resorting to my usual and practically automatic tactics, that didn't happen. And I still didn't want to just quit; the lecture from Monroe wouldn't be worth it. Though when I thought about it, it wasn't like he'd just let it go if I got fired, either.

With a resigned sigh, I figured I'd stop fooling around and get some actual work done. Disillusioned or not, I still didn't want the perception of me to slide to total incompetence. I checked my calendar and breathed a sigh of relief that I didn't have any client meetings.

Suddenly, the image of being almost eye-level with the top of my desk, moving back and forth as Boris Worthy banged me from behind flashed through my mind. My eyes squeezed shut, but I could still see it. I wasn't sure how in the world I would face him the next time he came in. It crossed my mind to refer him to another associate, but then I'd have to give reason as to why. I could always lie, but what if Boris decided to spill the beans on what we did? And that it happened thanks to my initiation?

I shook my head, putting it out of my mind. There was no use in worrying about that now.

Since I was still a little buzzed from the scene in Dan's office, I grabbed my silver bullet stimulator from my purse, sat in my chair, hiked up my skirt, and touched it to my clit, closing my eyes and releasing a shaky sigh. My head fell against the back of the chair as I brought myself to a quick orgasm, and was working on another when there was a knock on my door. Daria poked her head in right as I pressed the button to turn the stimulator off with my thumb, scooting my chair further under the desk.

"Your husband called while you were in with Dan," she informed, completely unaware that I was still stroking my clit under my desk. "He said he couldn't reach you on your cell phone, but when I let him know where you were, he said you didn't have to rush to call him back. Seems like he was worried about you and just wanted to make sure you were all right."

Or that I was actually at work like I said I was. "Okay. Thanks for letting me know, Daria."

She smiled and ducked out, closing the door behind her.

My thumb hit the button again, and I treated myself to one more silent orgasm before I finally got to work.

I ended up going into pre-trust fund mode and working overtime, strangely determined to get caught up on everything I'd been slacking on. I wasn't sure where the momentary surge of energy was coming from but taking advantage of it gave me the perfect excuse to delay going home.

Things were still weird between me and Montrel. I almost felt he'd be able to sense the things I'd done if I was in his presence for too long. The guilt of my weakness was getting harder and harder to suppress, yet even so, when I got that certain urge, it felt so delicious that I willingly gave in to it. It consumed me, and I wasn't satisfied until that urge was satisfied. It never seemed to enter my mind that I should restrain myself.

The fact that I'd slept with men outside of my marriage was certainly no secret to my husband. But he had no idea the level it had actually grown to.

I thought that I'd be okay after Montrel and I agreed to show more effort with each other and our marriage. But I suppose I should have known better.

Unwilling to face him just yet, I headed to the Prism Lounge for a drink. Out of courtesy, I did send Montrel a text letting him know I wouldn't be coming straight home. He read it but didn't reply. I couldn't decide how to feel about that.

I was at the bar, on my second Cosmo, trying to keep my eyes on the e-book I was reading on my phone to avoid any possible temptation. There were a few men in the place, and while I liked to think I had *some* self-control, I didn't entirely trust myself. The sensible thing would've been to just leave; it wasn't like that was the only bar in town. But I felt that if I just kept to myself, I'd be fine.

"Hello, beautiful."

My eyes squeezed shut as I tried to control my automatic reaction to the baritone voice in my ear. My womanhood clenched as it woke up from its forced slumber, and it only got more riled when the scent of Dior Sauvage Elixir made itself known.

You can do this, I silently told myself. *Resist.*

"Um, I don't mean to be rude, but I'd really rather be alone right now," I said, putting just the right amount of assuredness in my voice so he wouldn't think I was trying to be coy. I didn't even turn to look at him.

"You sure? I just want to have one drink with you."

"I'm absolutely sure. Please leave me alone; I don't need this distraction. Enjoy the rest of your evening."

The man continued to stand behind me and I wondered what was taking him so long to retreat. *All* of my energy was being used to tamp down my growing desire and I still couldn't resist turning my head just slightly enough to look down at his shoes. Shiny brown Prada. Him having such good style didn't help my condition any, and the ache to do sex-nasty things with this man I hadn't even looked at spread like a raging wildfire and had me squirming in my seat. I snapped my eyes back to my phone, kicking myself.

"All right then, since it's like that," he finally retorted, the smoothness in his voice now replaced with a razor-sharp edge and a suck of his teeth. "I came at you politely just trying to get to know you. It's not like I was asking you to meet me in the bathroom. You women always jump to conclusions."

I heard his footsteps click across the laminate floor as he walked away, and my eyes slid closed as I released a long sigh of relief. Potential crisis averted.

I resumed my reading, now feeling rather proud of myself. A couple months earlier I would have been all for some flirting and possible (probable) bathroom stall sex with a stylish, baritone-voiced suitor. The fact that I restrained myself made me smile, despite the heat of arousal that was still surging through my body. I flagged the bartender down for another drink, hoping it would help cool me off.

I'd managed to return my focus to my reading when I heard a somewhat-familiar female voice. Turning in my seat, I frowned slightly at the sight of three women coming through the door, laughing and talking amongst themselves. Two of them, I knew I'd seen before. Namely the thin one with the green eyes.

Claire.

The woman Montrel had been so in love with before he chose to marry me. And I certainly wasn't delusional enough to believe that those feelings were entirely gone. I'd overheard Montrel talking to his friend Forrest about how he still thought about her and wondered how she was doing. Apparently, she had moved away after he married me, so I wondered why she was back in town now, and if Montrel was aware of it. I could only imagine how quickly he'd arrive at the Prism Lounge if someone happened to tip him off that she was there.

I'd never met Claire directly. The only reason I recognized her at all was because Montrel had crashed her parents' anniversary party a couple of years earlier and had taken me with him. Even though she'd been there with another man, Montrel was clearly there on a mission to get her back, and was foolish enough to think I was oblivious to that. The both of them had disappeared for a little while, and then Claire left the party with her man, looking suddenly anxious. Of course, Montrel then had to leave too, rushing to drop me off at home so he could go handle something that had 'just come up.' It was almost humorous how transparent he was.

One of the other women with Claire had been at that party, too, though I didn't know her name. She was chocolate brown and thick with long pink and black braids, and was the loudest of the trio, animatedly flinging her hands around as she talked. The third woman looked to be biracial with a mass of long, curly hair and a pearly-white smile. But my eyes strayed back to the thin, green-eyed lady.

Claire looked different. Her hair was now shorter, and she wasn't as stick-thin as she'd been before. She looked so poised and polished in her gray sleeveless turtleneck midi dress and silver-heeled black ankle boots. I couldn't help but wonder if she'd recognize me if she happened to look up and notice me sitting there. Unwilling to find out, I swiveled back to the bar. It suddenly felt weird to sit and stare at her like that.

Reminding myself that I had to drive home, I closed out my tab and gathered my things. Suddenly I was looking forward to getting home to Montrel. I wanted to see the look on his face when he found out Claire was in town. Would he get excited? Upset? It didn't seem like they were still in touch, and I started to wonder just how much Montrel missed her. If there was any part of him that wished he'd married her instead of me. I knew he had intentions of committing to her before I used my feminine wiles to sway him towards marrying me instead. Honestly, I wouldn't have minded if he kept seeing her; it wasn't like Montrel and I married for love.

But now, things were different. My mindset had changed. I still couldn't say I was in love with Montrel, but I sincerely wanted to be. I absolutely loved him as much as I was capable of loving anyone romantically. And the thought of him pining over his ex caused an unfamiliar burn that most would likely categorize as jealousy. I wasn't used to this, and I didn't like it.

So when I got home and found him in the room he used for his yoga and meditation, I leaned against the doorjamb and watched him for a while. The room was cool and smelled of lavender and patchouli. If he noticed me there, he didn't acknowledge it; Montrel was super focused when it came to his yoga and it was almost mesmerizing watching him move effortlessly from one pose to another, displaying a deceptive level of strength. My hand clutched my top as I watched him go from Crane pose to a handstand with little effort, feeling a strange sense of pride.

As soon as he was done, I hurried over to him and threw my arms around his neck. I could tell he was surprised, but he thankfully didn't push me away or question it; he just hugged me back. I pulled back, gazing at his handsome, somewhat confused face, lightly running appreciative fingers around his features before pulling him in for a deep, needy kiss. I moaned as he obliged me, pushing my body even closer to his. I savored the feel of his arms, his faint Tom Ford cologne, his firm body. Montrel wasn't overly muscular because he didn't love lifting weights or anything else that would leave him sweating (sex being the one exception). He was a yogi and that's what sculpted his physique. Physically, he wasn't my usual type at all. Both his weight and his skin tone were lighter than I preferred. But I'd grown to love his body and his beige coloring. I'd grown attracted to more things about him, the important things. And it hit me that I didn't want to lose that. I didn't want to lose *him*, not to Claire or because of my uncontrollable actions.

Abruptly, I released him, running my hands down my hips and dropping my gaze. My face flushed as I stepped back and made my feet hurry out of the room. I could sense him watching me run; probably thinking I'd lost my mind.

By the time we were both getting ready for bed, we were at least speaking again. Thankfully, he didn't ask about my day. We got into bed and I curled my body into his, and he allowed it. Mild arousal simmered but amazingly, I didn't try anything.

Nor did I ever tell him I saw Claire.

Chapter 7 – Montrel

Mother did something she didn't usually do and called to ask if I could come over right away. She insisted it was good news, and that it apparently couldn't wait until the day of our usual visits. I'd been doing some research and didn't need or appreciate the disturbance, not to mention being exhausted from too many nights of restless and elusive sleep. My home life had started to weigh on me, and I spent an increasing amount of time agonizing over it.

But of course, Mother wouldn't care about any of that. She probably wouldn't even believe things were that bad, since she thought so highly of Aurora. Sighing heavily, I made myself get up so I could get myself together. Hopefully whatever she wanted wouldn't take too long.

Turned out that what she wanted was to introduce me to her new man. Blew my damn mind. I started to ask if she was punking me, but remembered she likely wouldn't even know what that meant. So I just tried to un-scramble my brain as I accessed this round bellied, gold-toothed gentleman whose arm my mother was hanging onto.

"Montrel, dear, I'd like you to meet James," she said proudly, grinning like she was standing there with Denzel or somebody. "James, this is my son, Montrel."

"Nice to meet you, young blood," James greeted, extending his fist.

I eyed it with an arched brow before Mother cleared her throat and gave me a pointed look. I finally barely touched my fist to his before retracting it. "You can just call me Montrel."

"Aye aye, Montrel," he playfully mocked, giving me an exaggerated salute.

Cutting my eyes at him, I turned my attention back to my mother. "What was so urgent?"

"You always said you wanted me to let you know immediately when I decided to foray back into the dating pool." She looked at James with an admiration I'd *never* seen from her. "Well, this is my foray."

I blinked. Was she serious with this? One, I barely even remembered telling her that. It had to have been at least fifteen years earlier, during a rare moment of vulnerability when Mother was feeling particularly lonely but claimed to be too scared to put herself back out there. She felt like no man would ever measure up to Father and didn't want to waste her time with anyone beneath her (which isn't what she said, but it's what she meant). It was so long ago that I figured she had either resigned herself to a life alone or she was keeping any dalliances she had to herself, which was just fine with me.

Secondly, I didn't have the time or energy for this. Whatever midlife crisis Mother was going through was her business. I had my own issues.

I still thought I was being punked. This James certainly wasn't anyone I'd have expected her to latch onto. He just seemed...regular. And he had a mischievous glint in his eyes that I didn't trust.

Apparently this little meet-and-greet included dinner, because Mother led us to her usually-just-for-show dining room for a meal of seared duck, truffle mashed potatoes, and cider-glazed roasted Brussels sprouts. Of course *not* made by her. But there were actually people there serving us, like this was a presidential state dinner or something. Mother was either really trying to show off or she was just sprung, and I didn't like the thought of either. I couldn't believe my eyes when servers filed out of the kitchen like a line of ants, armed with plates and side sauces they were available to drizzle on demand. Mother was really doing the most.

I was glad there seemed to be plenty of wine, even if it was red.

"Montrel, James owns his own business," Mother boasted once we were seated, kicking off her hype mission. "He sells insurance."

"That's nice," I droned, swirling my Malbec in my glass. I eyed my mother's suitor, who was already shoveling mashed potatoes into his mouth like he hadn't eaten in a week. "What type of insurance?"

"Oh I do it all, young blood. I mean, Montrel," James corrected with a sly wink. My face tightened. "Car, home, renter's, all that. Started my own business after that company that *claims* we're in good hands laid me off. After eight years, too. But I'm gonna build my own insurance empire."

"Interesting. And how are you going to do that, if I may ask? I'd imagine competing with that and all the other big-name companies would present a challenge."

"I ain't ever ran from a challenge, my man," James assured with another wink. I wished he'd stop doing that shit. "I've been building this for a while because I had a feeling they'd screw me over eventually. My strategy is practically foolproof."

"Is that right?" I glanced over at Mother, who was just delicately cutting into her duck. Apparently she'd heard all this before. "James...I didn't catch your last name?"

"Didn't toss it." He cracked up laughing. Even Mother covered her mouth as she tried to chew and giggle at the same time. I rolled my eyes.

"All right, I'll be more direct, then," I pressed, no humor in my voice whatsoever. "What's your last name?"

"It's Nylon. James Tyberius Nylon."

"Tyberius," Mother repeated, practically shuddering with excitement. "I've never even met anyone with such a name before. It's so..." Her eyes landed on James and slanted in a look I wished I didn't recognize, "*Enticing.*"

No I was not sitting there watching my mother get worked up over some guy's ghetto middle name. It took all of my restraint not to get up and leave right then. I didn't wanna see that shit.

(Okay, *ghetto* was harsh. My bad. But it certainly wasn't anything to get aroused over).

James continued to go on and on about how he was going to put his former employer and all the other top insurance companies out of business (or at least take chunks *of* their business) and Mother just sat there cosigning everything. Not to mention how closely she was sitting to him, and all the touches to his arm and shoulder, and I was sure there was some under-the-table touching happening, too. James winked at her a lot, also, and fed her slices of duck.

I actually had to rub my eyes because I could not be seeing this.

For the life of me, I didn't understand what it was Mother saw in him. I couldn't say I knew what her type was, since I hadn't seen her with anyone but Father. I'd never heard her lust or gush over celebrities, thank god. But I figured if and when she ever did decide to date someone, it would be some refined stuffed-shirt from old money with a mountain of accolades and titles and a shallowness that matched hers. I certainly didn't expect someone like James. At least he owned his own business. Or, he planned to.

After we (mostly they) had pear tarts for dessert, James steered the subject to real estate after we were in the living room. He stretched his arms along the back of the couch while Mother sat cuddled up next to him. I parked it in the armchair. My earlier desire to leave had been replaced by a curiosity about this man that was trying to mack my mother.

"You live in the area, James?"

"No, but I sure wish I did. Crystal Hills is one of those neighborhoods I always drove through and prayed while I pointed out houses I liked. But I'll make it over this way soon enough. I'm manifesting it."

"Hmm."

"Yes, James has big aspirations; I admire that about him," Mother claimed, resting her hand on his belly. "Just because we've reached a certain age doesn't mean we should stop dreaming."

They shared a smile and I tried to keep my dinner from coming back up. They were dreaming, all right.

"Any kids?" I asked, breaking up their googly-eyed gazing.

"I have a daughter but we don't really talk," James replied with an unbothered shrug. "To be honest, she's kinda stuck-up, like her mama. Both of them think they're better than folks."

And yet you got with my mother? I itched to say it, but refrained.

That *was* rather ironic, though. Mother wasn't exactly down-to-earth. She'd been floating in an air of superiority ever since I could remember. Hell, she never liked Claire because she thought she wasn't 'cultured' enough for me. And because she wasn't a supermodel with a fancy career. She was just a regular woman with a regular job, and Mother never understood what I saw in her.

That's why she pushed so hard for me to get with Aurora. Stayed on my damn back until I agreed to go out with her, then when I did and declared I wasn't interested (and I wasn't), she refused to accept it. She kept on me, chipping away at my defenses and my patience until I relented and gave Aurora another chance just to shut Mother up. And even then, I was ready to bail until Aurora seduced me so good that I forgot what my name was. It became harder to dismiss her after that.

And just like Aurora had clouded my brain with sex back then, James was clouding my mother's brain with something now (that I was choosing to believe *wasn't* sex). I almost didn't even recognize her, the way she was acting with him. It was possible that she had sincere feelings for this man; was still caught up in the new infatuation fog. As disturbing and foreign as that was, it wasn't my main concern.

There was something about James I didn't trust. Not just because he came out of nowhere and had my mother acting like someone I didn't recognize, but because his whole aura just screamed 'ulterior motive'. Not to mention, he was delusional enough to think he could actually put companies like AllState and State Farm out of business.

"Do you work, Montrel?" James asked me, his hand slithering down to Mother's hip. I made myself ignore it. "Let me guess; you're an Instagram model or something like that, right?"

"He's certainly handsome enough to be a model. But a *real* one; not just on that Insta-whatever nonsense," Mother spoke up, smiling at me. I forced a tight smile in return at the compliment.

"I'm not a model," I informed, not adding that I could've been if I wanted to. "Mostly I just do volunteer work. But I *am* looking to change that soon, though."

James's eyebrows lifted curiously. "Yeah?"

"What do you mean, dear?" Mother asked, her proud smile melting.

"I mean I'm looking for a job. More specifically, a career I'd enjoy. It's time I started doing something more with my life."

There's the stern expression I was used to seeing. Mother was looking at me like she wanted to fire off one of her dismissive, condescending comments, but one glance at James seemed to mute it.

"Interesting," she muttered.

"Hey, kudos to you, young blood," James commended with another salute. "A man *should* get his hands dirty and know what it's like to put in an honest days' work. Hey, if you want, you can come work for me. I could always use some young and hungries on my team to help me take over this insurance game."

I managed not to laugh in his face. "Thanks, but as I mentioned, I want to focus on finding a career I actually like. I doubt I'd enjoy selling insurance."

"Well, the offer stands," James replied, not put off by my dismissal at all. He seemed to be the kind of man that let things roll off his back. "Breaking into the workforce at your age won't be an easy task, though, young blood. Especially if you've never had a real job before. Lots of competition out there. You might have better luck starting your own business, like I'm doing. Of course, there's always OnlyFans."

As if.

"What's OnlyFans?" Mother asked, her eyes flitting between James and me.

"Never mind," I quickly replied as James opened his mouth to answer her. He could explain that to her after I left. "I'm not going there, either. I'll figure out what it is I want to do in time."

"Well, good luck to you," James said. He glanced down at Mother. "We're behind you a hundred percent, ain't that right, baby?"

Mother just looked at him before turning her gaze to me. I got all the response I needed when she busted out laughing.

"I'm sorry, dear," she sputtered, a hand to her chest as she tried to compose herself. "But the idea of you trying to have a career at this point is ridiculous."

Of course she'd say that. "Oh really?"

"Montrel, you're in your late thirties. You have never had a real job, *ever*, because you haven't had to. Your Father and I made it so you would never have to worry about money. You have it made. People would kill to be in your position. Why you'd want to waste time battling some desperate recent college graduates and single mothers and washed-up has-beens for a paycheck that wouldn't even cover the cost of one of your beloved sport coats is beyond me."

Well, damn. Tell me how you really feel, Mother.

I didn't expect her to be supportive but I didn't think she'd go in like *that*. Even James was looking uncomfortable. I wasn't even hurt, though; I was pissed. Supporting me just because I was her son was clearly something she still couldn't grasp, despite the love fog she was under. I didn't need her to agree with it. But even a passive 'good luck' would've been better than the shit she just said. Her new man had been more supportive of me than her and he'd known me all of an hour and forty-eight minutes.

And the comment about her and Father providing my comfortable life was a joke. Mother didn't do a damn thing. Father was the one that brought in all the money and made it so the both of us could have the lifestyles we did.

After a few beats of awkwardness, James excused himself to go to the restroom and I stood, ready to take my leave. I needed to get back to what I was doing before I was summoned but mostly, I just didn't want to be there anymore.

Mother actually looked up at me in surprise. "Where are you going, dear?"

"It's time for me to go."

"Why are you rushing off?"

"I'm not rushing. But I have things to do. Things I was in the middle of when you called me over here."

"At least stay and say goodbye to James."

"Give him my regards. Good night, Mother."

Without waiting for a response, I headed for the door, sure she'd scold me for being rude at some point, but whatever. I was already planning to ignore it when she called next.

To my surprise, Mother followed me outside, something she'd never done. Her eyes roamed over my Audi before turning her attention back to me.

"You're following me," I noted, as if I thought she was unaware.

"Yes. I wanted to see what you thought of James," she replied in a somewhat hushed voice. She looked up at me with expectant eyes. "He's wonderful, isn't he?"

Fighting the urge to roll my eyes, I unlocked my car. "I'm not sure if 'wonderful' is the adjective I'd use."

Her excited expression dimmed and she looked slightly affronted. "Meaning?"

"Meaning there's something about him I don't trust. I think he's hiding something."

"Oh," she scoffed and waved a dismissive hand, as if she'd been expecting me to come with something better than that. "That's ridiculous."

"It's not, Mother."

"What are you even basing this on, Montrel? You just met him this evening."

"It doesn't take long. Some people just give off a vibe, and he definitely does. I'm telling you, you should stop seeing him. Like, immediately."

"I'm not going to do that," she spurted defiantly. "James is the first man I've connected with since your Father and I'm not going to dismiss him just because you think you know something you don't. It's not like you're a master at reading people."

"I'm clearly better at it than you."

She gasped, her face registering pure shock. I hadn't meant to say it but I didn't try to walk it back. Truthfully, I held my tongue too much when it came to my mother; always had. I'd told myself that it was because I didn't want to bring her any more stress or strife after Father passed, but it's been over twenty-five years; the ship had sailed on that excuse. Really, it was just easier to let her think she was right than to try to sway her. I'd agreed to a lot of things over the years just to shut her up. It took way too long for it to register that I was just shooting myself in the foot by doing that.

Mother folded her arms and fixed her glare on me, and I knew she was waiting on me to apologize. She'd be waiting all night.

When she realized it wasn't happening, her jaw tightened and her back straightened. "Well. Just like you told me I could no longer comment on your love life, I don't need you interfering in mine."

"Right. The difference, though, Mother, is that you *asked* me my opinion about James. I've never once asked you for your opinion on any woman I've dated. You just felt you were entitled to give it anyway under the guise of motherly concern. Well, consider this concern from your son. James is going to end up hurting you. In fact, I'm not sure you should leave him in your house unattended."

"Duly noted. And you are certainly entitled to your opinion, dear. But you're wrong. And there will be plenty of time for him to prove it to you because he's not going anywhere any time soon."

With that, she turned and strutted back into the house, closing the door behind her harder than necessary.

Whatever. If she was intent on acting like some naïve teenager, I couldn't stop her.

I got in my car and headed back home, going from one tense environment to another.

Things between Aurora and I were...okay. There was still an undercurrent of tension that I'd become all too used to. We were speaking, but the conversations were empty. She seemed to have a lot on her mind and I only accepted her vague responses when I bothered to ask what was bothering her because I had plenty of my own shit to worry about. We were just maneuvering around each other, politely co-existing. Whatever affection we did share was sporadic and devoid of much emotion. Clearly, neither of us was in a hurry to acknowledge that our marriage had taken yet another dip.

One night I was in the kitchen, mindlessly staring into the open refrigerator when my phone chimed with a text. My brow furrowed when I saw it was from Aurora, asking me to come upstairs. Part of me wondered what she was up to but the other part was grateful for the distraction, and I closed the refrigerator, heading towards the stairs.

I found Aurora in our bathroom. The lights were out; there were just a couple of lit candles on either end of the vanity. Aurora sat between the two sinks wearing nothing but a short sheer robe, her thick hair falling over her face. I couldn't deny she looked damn sexy.

"What's going on, Bunny?" I asked, hovering near the doorway. I'd decided that was better than calling her Agave. And way more apropos.

She extended a hand towards me, eyes inviting. "Can you come here?"

Hesitating only for a second, I crossed over to her, putting my hand in her extended one. She pulled me closer as her legs slid open, her other hand caressing the side of my face.

"I need you," she whispered, her hand guiding mine to her wetness, shuddering when I made contact. "Touch me."

Maybe I should have resisted. But I didn't. In that moment, I just needed something good between us.

"Touch you where?" I asked, my own voice barely above a whisper against her lips. I retracted my hand slightly, making her whimper. "Where do you want me to touch you?"

"There." She winded her hips, causing my body to react. "Touch my pussy, Montrel."

My index finger barely grazed up her wet folds, making her eyes slide closed and she released a series of shaky breaths before my lips took over hers. She kissed me back eagerly, clutching me as my thumb began circling her clit.

"Yes..." she breathed between our kisses that were becoming increasingly intense. "Yes, baby..."

I eased a finger inside her, feeling how intensely wet she was. Then another. Then another. Each addition only ramped up Aurora's arousal.

"Montrel!" She wound intently against my hand, her head falling back momentarily as she kept her grip on my shoulders. She then quickly grabbed my face and tongued me down as I continued finger-fucking her to orgasm, feeling her clench and cream all over my hand.

Of course she wanted more. Aurora always wanted more. And she thankfully caught me on a night where I didn't mind giving it to her.

Before too long, I was on my knees, my face between her legs and my tongue where my fingers had just been, something I admittedly didn't do much but I was caught up in the moment. Aurora shrieked in pleasure, holding the back of my head as she enjoyed what I was doing to her.

"Fuck yes, just like that..." Her voice almost sounded as pleading as it did pleased. "Montrel, I love you so much..."

I didn't respond. I just continued savoring her, getting almost as much enjoyment from it as she was.

After she came a second time, then she wanted the dick. She shed her robe and I shed my clothes, entering her with an eagerness that matched hers. We both cursed loudly at how good it felt, wrapping each other up tightly and kissing deeply as I stroked her.

To an outside observer, it would seem like we were deeply in love. The romantic vibe, the intimacy. I knew it was all temporary. But I didn't care. I'd take the momentary closeness over what we'd been doing recently.

"You see what we're doing?" She ran her tongue up my neck and sucked my earlobe for a moment before leaning back slightly to look at me. "We're making love."

Were we? Okay.

"We're capable of that, you know," she continued, biting her lip. "I wanted to show you there's more to our relationship than you think."

Using sex to show that we were more than just sex. Made perfect sense.

I didn't bother mentioning that she was relying on her usual crutch yet again. I just pushed her back so I could help myself to her breasts, wanting to just enjoy the moment. She eagerly welcomed my diversion, her chest arching forward as she braced her hands on the counter behind her.

The talking was on pause as we continued to go at it. My hands pressed against her back as I slid my tongue between her breasts up to her neck, sucking her soft skin before tonguing her chin, then her lips. I pulled her back to where her chest was flush with mine, sliding her hips even closer to the edge of the counter as we moaned against each other's mouths. I'll admit that in that moment, I felt extremely close to my wife. If only it could last.

"I love you, Montrel," she panted again, her hips meeting mine in perfect synch. If we didn't have anything else, we had sexual chemistry. "You're in my heart, baby. You mean so fucking much to me and I don't wanna lose you. Do you love me?"

I could feel the desperation in how she clung to me and her eyes begged for an answer.

"Yeah, Bunny," I granted her, my eyes roaming her pretty face. "I love you."

Her hold on me tightened and her hips began to move faster. "Say it again."

"I love you."

Her skin squeaked against the marble countertop. "Again. Please..."

"I love you, Aurora!"

I started going harder, the moment getting to me. Pretty soon our skin slapping together filled the room, with our pants and grunts as the backdrop. Aurora's eyes never left mine and our previously-whispered words were now practically screams.

"Montrel baby...I'm so sorry!" Her hand clutched my face. "Tell me you forgive me!"

By then, I was willing to say just about anything. "I forgive you..."

"Please don't leave me, Montrel. I love you the best way I know how to. Tell me you won't leave." She stuck her tongue down my throat, her hips momentarily slowing down. "Tell me again that you love me."

"I fucking love you," I complied through gritted teeth. Not just because she was asking me to say the same thing over and over, but because part of me hated that it was true. I *did* love Aurora, and I cared about her, as much as I sometimes wished I didn't. And this was the most she'd said she loved me the entire time we'd been married.

Our bathroom counter sex continued, each of us making loving declarations that were foreign to the kind of relationship we had. It was nice for the moment, but sadly, it was all bullshit. It would only be a matter of days before Aurora had yet another one of her mood swings and this whole scene would be practically forgotten, even if a teeny tiny part of me remained that wished that wasn't the case.

Did I believe Aurora loved me? Sure. If only that was enough for me.

For the time being though, I just chose to be grateful for the temporary peace in the house.

"Just wanted to let you know about a change we made to Jenna's birthday party," Forrest announced when he called me a few days later. "Instead of renting out the room at the community center, we're just gonna have it here at the house."

"Okay. Thanks for the update. Why the change in plans?"

"She's turning two, not twelve. No need in doing all that when she's not gonna remember it, anyway."

"Understandable. I'm surprised Giselle agreed to that, though."

"I thankfully made her realize it isn't about the venue, but about celebrating our daughter's birthday with our loved ones. And we've both been so tired lately, it wasn't that hard a sell."

"Well, I'll be there loaded up with gifts for the birthday girl."

"You bringing Aurora with you?"

"And have Giselle even *more* upset with me? No. Besides, Aurora would probably have some convenient excuse to get out of it, anyway. I think there's something going on with her."

"Something like what?"

"I don't know. She's been acting rather strangely. Over the course of the past few days, she's gone from being unusually tender and affectionate to withdrawing and having next to nothing to say. And she doesn't seem angry, she seems saddened."

"Did something happen?"

"Nothing that I'm aware of. I tried to ask her what was going on but she muttered something about how I wouldn't understand."

"You think something shady is going on?"

I paused. "Shady...in what way?"

"Don't know, man. But it's clearly something. If you two didn't have a falling out, maybe it's something with her job, or that stepfather you said she doesn't get along with."

I'd forgotten about Monroe. It was totally possible that he'd said or done something to send Aurora into her current funk. I still wondered why she continued to deal with him, since he brought her so many headaches. I got the thing about respecting her late mother's wishes but, to me at least, that shouldn't take precedence over her own happiness. It was almost like she enjoyed the misery.

"Could be," I muttered, snapping out of my musings. "Truth be told, I don't have the energy to try and drag it out of her. Between this career stuff and the shit that Mother is getting herself into-"

"Wait, what are you talking about? What shit your mama is getting herself into?"

I told him all about my visit at Mother's where I met her suspicious new beau, including her dismissal of my warnings about James and her literally laughing in my face when I mentioned wanting my own career. I still wasn't over that.

"You think he's using her?" Forrest asked when I was done.

"Wouldn't surprise me. But of course, Mother insists she knows everything so whatever ends up happening is on her."

"You've got his name, right? Run a background check on him."

"That requires more effort than I feel like expending. And she'd just flip out on me for doing that behind her back, anyway, no matter what the findings were. I'm good on that."

"Could it be that you just don't want to see her with anyone else that's not your dad? Or that you're just used to having her to yourself and don't want her attention on somebody else?"

I broke out laughing, loudly. Was actually holding my stomach, I was cracking up so hard. "Thanks for that, man. I haven't laughed in a minute."

"I was serious but, okay."

"You can't be. You know more than anyone that Mother and I do *not* have that kind of relationship. I love her but I can't say I like the kind of person she is. Honestly, if she weren't my mother, I'd probably have nothing to do with her."

I paused, realizing that was the first time I'd admitted that. It was both refreshing and disheartening.

"Wow," Forrest sighed. "That's a damn shame but I get it. Hopefully this new man of hers is being straight up. On another note, there's something I wanted to tell you but I've been on the fence about doing it, since I know you'll trip."

I'd been just about to roll up the mat I'd used for my yoga and mediation session but his words stopped me. "What is it?"

A couple of moments passed before Forrest finally admitted, "Claire was here."

The mat fell to the floor. "What? She was at your house? You saw her?"

"She was in town. Giselle met up with her and Chichi a few nights ago. I'm not sure how long she was here."

"Why are you just now telling me??"

"Because I knew you'd try to go see her if you knew she was here. And I wasn't trying to have Giselle on my case for letting you know she was in town, 'cause she surely asked me not to."

I slinked over to the wall and flopped against it in disbelief. I couldn't believe that Claire was mere miles from me and I didn't know about it. My temper flared at everybody making decisions on my lack of deservedness. It was like they were all on a mission to keep me from her. Yes,

I messed up our relationship. Yes, I hurt her. But it wasn't anything I shouldn't be forgiven for. I was genuinely sorry for blindsiding Claire with my wedding announcement, which I would've gladly told her myself if given the chance.

"Montrel?" Forrest called out when I hadn't spoke for a few moments.

Part of me wanted to go off on Forrest for not telling me about Claire, but decided it was pointless. It wouldn't change anything. And he was probably still in the camp that believed that I was just getting my due karmic retribution. The thought angered me but I tried to keep it in check.

"Yeah," I grunted before clearing my throat.

"You mad?"

"I'm not happy. Not really sure why you told me at all if she's already gone. Kinda feels like you're taunting me, throwing it in my face like that."

"What? That is not what I was doing, Montrel."

"If you say so."

"Look...she'll be at Jenna's party."

That perked me up. I'd been wondering if she was going to come back for that and knowing she was gave me a shot of excitement. My grin spread the more I thought about the possibility of *finally* getting to see Claire in person. "Good to know."

"I'm sure I don't have to tell you this, but do *not* come up in here causing a scene. If she doesn't want to talk to you, respect that."

"Forrest, you don't have to tell me how to behave. I've caused Claire enough trouble. And besides, I'd never do anything to mess up my goddaughter's birthday party."

He paused. "Hmph."

"What?"

"Montrel...what makes you think you're Jenna's godfather?"

My grin faded. "Why wouldn't I be?"

"So you just appointed yourself?"

"Forrest, we've been boys for years. I'm the one that stepped to Giselle at that party back in college and introduced you two because you were too shook to do it yourself. I was best man at your wedding. I was right there for you all when you were dealing with all the infertility issues, helping you with the rift in your marriage that it caused, and I was the main person you vented to when you were all nervous about becoming a father. Was I not?"

He hesitated. "Yeah..."

"I camped out for hours in the waiting room while Giselle was in labor. Started Jenna's college fund. And I'd babysit if Giselle wasn't still holding a grudge. But I'm more than willing to help out any way I can, and you know that. So how am I *not* her godfather?"

"Man..." He sighed. "You're not wrong about any of that and I do appreciate all of it. But you're not Jenna's godfather; my brother is."

The frown took over my face immediately. "Excuse me? Why him and not me? Was I even considered?"

"Honestly...no."

Damn. So this was what getting drop-kicked in the chest felt like. "Wow. I knew Giselle was upset with me but I had no idea she'd take it this far. And, what, you went along with it to keep the peace?"

"Montrel...look. You're gonna feel some kind of way about this but I'm gonna be straight up. This wasn't all on Giselle. We talked about it and actually agreed that my brother would be a better choice. Don't take this personally, but we don't think you're mature enough to handle that kind of responsibility for our daughter."

"How the hell can I *not* take that personally??"

"Montrel, man-"

"Nah, I get it. You made your point. We're done here."

I hung up and tossed my phone to the floor, not caring if it broke. Irrational or not, I felt like I'd just been betrayed by someone I thought of as my brother. The realization of him basically admitting that he didn't trust me with his daughter had me sinking to the floor, and as angry as I was, raw hurt was the main thing weighing me down.

Chapter 8 – Montrel

I still had an attitude about the whole godfather thing several days later. All of Forrest's calls were sent to voicemail, because I had no more words for him. Not sure what else there was to be said, anyway.

Clearly, my past was being used against me. I'm sure most of Forrest and Giselle's judgment was based on how I treated Claire, which I felt was unfair. One thing didn't have anything to do with the other, in my opinion. They should've known I'd never do anything to harm their daughter, and if something were to happen to them and Jenna was put in my care, I'd be the best guardian I could possibly be to her. And as long as Forrest had known me, he should've known I wasn't an inherently bad person; I'd just made some stupid decisions. Decisions I'd owned up to and accepted my penance for. But I guess I didn't deserve credit for that.

It burned me that Giselle was still icing me out. She and I had been friends since college, years before she even met Claire. What happened in our relationship had nothing to do with Giselle. Yet *I* was the immature one. And I bet Forrest didn't even try to plead my case. But why would he, since he apparently didn't think any more of me than his wife did.

Nice to know how they really felt about me.

But hey; their daughter, their decision. Since there was nothing I could do about it anyway, I tried to put it out of my mind and focus on my career research. I'd been making a list of things I thought I'd like to do and had started narrowing it down. Had even taken a couple of online career assessments to see what clicked. Before Forrest kicked me in the teeth with his revelation, I'd been really excited about it. But now, every time I opened my laptop, I just felt exhaustion.

"Snap out of it, Montrel," I groused to myself after zoning out yet again. I scooted a little closer to the desk, scowling in forced concentration. "You can do this."

Mother's mocking laughter rang through my head. Aurora's lukewarm response came after that. The words on the screen in front of me started to blur as doubt began creeping in. *Was* this ridiculous? What was I trying to prove? So many people had aspirations from childhood about what they wanted to be when they grew up and I really had nothing of the sort. I'd always admired my father and his business acumen, but I couldn't say I wanted to follow in his footsteps. Outside of him, I didn't have any role models to speak of. I cared about getting good grades simply because I liked the sense of achievement. My focus growing up mainly centered around girls and clothes; I'd always been a clotheshorse. Even now, Aurora and I had to have separate closets because there was no way all of my things would fit into one with hers.

I rubbed my eyes with the heels of my hands, frustrated. I hated that my mother and my wife, two of the people you'd *think* were the closest to me, had me doubting myself. So what if they didn't see the point in what I was doing? It wasn't like I agreed with every damn thing they did, either. It wasn't about them, anyway; this was something I felt I needed to do for myself.

This latest pep talk rejuvenated me, and I managed to refocus on my list. James's assumption that I was a model had me considering that as a possible option, but I ended up nixing that. As handsome as I was, it wasn't something I really wanted to try to dive into at my age. I wouldn't have minded doing something with clothes, given my love for them, but the idea of standing behind a register didn't move me. A designer, maybe? I had no talent for that, but I could partner with someone who did. A buyer? Stylist? Merchandiser? All viable ideas.

Aurora came in as I was tapping my pen against the desk and chewing my bottom lip. I was so deep in thought that I didn't notice her at first.

"Just wanted to let you know I was here," she said softly, halfway over the threshold of my office.

I briefly glanced up at her, pen still tapping. "Okay."

"I don't feel like cooking anything."

Shrugging, I returned my attention to what I was doing. "Okay."

"We can go out, if you want."

I started to respond when my phone rang. When I saw it was Forrest calling again, I sucked my teeth and immediately declined it. Aurora looked at me curiously.

"What's wrong? You're scowling."

Was I? I just shrugged again.

"Was that your mother?"

I sighed and dropped my pen, wondering why she was suddenly in the mood to talk. She'd been in her own little world for days. Just as I predicted, after our impromptu night of 'lovemaking' in the bathroom, she went right back to her weird semi-aloof behavior a couple days later, and even though I knew it was gonna happen, I'd been holding out small hope that this time would be different. So I was as frustrated with myself as I was with her. I should have known better by then.

"It was Forrest," I informed her. "If you must know, he and I had a difference of opinion. And I have nothing to say to him for the time being."

Aurora looked intrigued, venturing further into the room. My eyes registered the fitted white tee and boy shorts she was wearing. "What's going on? I've never heard of you and Forrest being at odds before."

"Well, hearing that neither he nor his wife think I'm worthy of being godfather to their daughter surely put us at odds. He actually said I was too immature."

"That's surprising." Aurora stood over my desk, bracing her manicured hands on the edge as she leaned over. "As close as I thought the two of you were, I figured you'd be first choice."

"You and me both. But I was wrong, clearly."

"If Forrest thinks that about you, why are you even friends?"

My brow furrowed. "Good question."

"I'm sorry you're upset. I can see why you'd feel affronted by that. But if you ask me, Muffin, you should feel relieved."

I looked at her in surprise, not only at her statement but at the pet name. We'd both faded on our efforts to strengthen our intimacy (consistently, at least), and that had been one of the first things to go, save for the night in the bathroom. Especially the stupid ones I had for her. I'd gone from 'Agave' to 'Bunny' to not even bothering trying to think of anything else.

"Why do you say that?" I chose not to acknowledge the pet name that I still hated.

"Because taking on the role of caretaker for a child that isn't yours is difficult. *Extremely* difficult. And God forbid if it were to happen when they were a teenager. There's no telling how they'd react to you, especially if you don't already have a close relationship."

"I mean, yeah, I'm sure a period of transition would be necessary and it would take some patience, but that doesn't deter me."

"It would surely deter *me*. I've already told Mecca and Bron that I wouldn't want to be a godmother if they have any children. I'll be there to support them but I don't want that kind of responsibility."

Aurora's declaration didn't surprise me. She didn't want any kids of her own so of course she wouldn't want to take care of anyone else's.

I had to stop and wonder if Aurora being my wife had anything to do with Forrest and Giselle denying my godfather privileges. If I'd married Claire instead, would they have come to the same conclusion?

"Yeah, well," I straightened my Movado watch, dismissing the thought. No point in going there. "It's a moot point. The brother he hardly even talks to gets the honor instead of me."

"Can I do something to cheer you up?"

My temper instantly flared. "I'm not in the mood for a damn blow job, Aurora. That doesn't fix everything."

Something flashed in her eyes. She stood up straight, taking a step back from the desk. "I was talking about making you a sundae."

I only felt marginally bad for causing the hurt look on her face. It wasn't like my comment was unwarranted. Aurora had tried to use sex to comfort or distract me more times than I could count.

"Sorry," I felt compelled to say.

"I can't believe that's what you think of me."

"Let's not get overly dramatic, all right?" I said bitingly. "You know good and well that's usually your go-to. Just because it wasn't this *one* time doesn't mean you have room to go acting all insulted."

Tears started shining in her eyes and instead of feeling regretful for hurting her, I felt myself getting irritated. She was acting like I'd called her out her name or something, when all I'd done was told the truth. I didn't know why she was acting so sensitive but I wasn't in the mood for it.

"You can be really mean, you know that?" she practically whispered, still staring at me.

Sighing, I ran my hands down my face before letting them fall to the desk with a thump. "And you can be like a moody toddler. But this is what we signed up for, right?"

Her face tightening, she turned and stomped out of the room. So now she was mad again. It already felt like I was dealing with a damn child.

Whatever. I wasn't going to let another one of Aurora's mood swings bother me this time. I put that whole scene out of my head as I went back to what I was doing.

Truth be told, I kinda hated I didn't take her up on that sundae.

Somehow, Aurora and I still ended up going out to dinner together after that. Only this time, I didn't care about trying to make it romantic. I was just hungry.

"I'm still upset with you," she informed me as she looked at her menu.

I quirked an amused brow as I perused my own menu. "It's funny that you think I care."

"You *should* care. You made me cry."

"I didn't *make* you do anything. You chose to get in your feelings about something we both know is the truth."

"Why are we doing this?" She put down her menu, looking pleadingly across the table at me in our booth at Orange Pearl Bistro. "How did we get here?"

I started to shoot off a sarcastic response, but stopped myself. My shoulder lifted briefly. "Don't know."

"I thought we said we were gonna try."

"That's what we said. But neither of us are doing a very good job of it."

"I don't want to give up on us. I'm sorry for not doing my part. Let's just consider this our clean slate and start over."

I just looked at her, feeling anything but encouraged. Aurora was so wishy-washy that there was no telling how her feelings would change the next day, or the day after that. I wasn't going to make the mistake of getting excited about her momentary desire to act like my wife again.

"Aurora..." I tried to be mindful of my words, "Maybe we should just face facts. This doesn't work."

She actually looked surprised. "How can you say that?"

"Because I'm being real. Love had nothing to do with us getting together. We're not on the same page about most things. You do your own thing half the time. And I never know if you're gonna welcome me or push me away when I try to get close to you. Hell, you haven't even been sleeping in our bed that much the last few nights. Clearly something is going on with you but since we don't talk about anything significant, I have no idea what it is, and I know better than to try to ask. I'm just not sure what it is we're hanging on for."

"Just because we have some rough times doesn't mean we throw in the towel, Montrel. I'm not purposely trying to shut you out."

"So does that mean you're willing to be a hundred percent honest with me about why you do what you do? And don't give me any shallow, pacifying answers. I want the real, raw deal. Can you do that?"

"Montrel, I..." She sighed, as if suddenly exhausted. "I wish you could understand that it's just not that easy."

"It doesn't have to be easy. A lot of things in life aren't easy."

Before she could respond, a man approached our table, eyes fixed on Aurora. He didn't even acknowledge me.

"Hey there," he greeted, looking at her hungrily. "It's been a minute."

Aurora looked up at him, glanced at me, then back up at him. Her wide eyes only held faint recognition for this stranger.

"Um, hello..."

"I was wondering if I'd get to see you again. After we hooked up that time I never heard back from you."

"Uhhh..." Aurora's face flamed as she shot a bashful glance at me. "If you don't mind, I was in the middle of a conversation with my *husband*."

The guy finally looked at me, not looking put off at all by the revelation that Aurora was married. If anything, he looked amused.

"Okay then," he conceded, holding up a hand. "You know where I am if you need me again."

He turned and strolled off, hands in his pockets. Aurora took her time turning her eyes back to me.

"Who was that?" I asked flatly.

Her shoulders lifted slightly. "I, um, I can't quite remember his name."

"Wow. It's gotten to that point, huh?"

She released a long breath as she looked at me, then dropped her eyes. The server came over and asked if we were ready to order and Aurora told her we needed a minute, which didn't help my mood any. As I said, I was hungry.

"Montrel..." She placed a hand to her chest. "Does it *really* bother you when I sleep with other men?"

Her voice had gone soft again but I still heard her. How's that for a change in subject.

"I don't love it," I admitted. "But you established very early on that being faithful to me wasn't something you were interested in."

"This is going to sound strange, but that...my doing that is no reflection on you. It's not about trying to hurt you."

"Then what is it about, Aurora?"

Her mouth quickly opened, but just that quickly, she lost her nerve. She toyed with the edge of her napkin. "I...I wish I could explain it."

"What, are you some kind of sex addict or something?"

Her eyes snapped to me, blazing fire. "How dare you!"

My question had been partially facetious, but given how incensed she automatically got, I clearly hit a nerve. I sat back in my seat, eying her in a new light.

"Why are you getting so upset?"

"Because that was an insult, Montrel. Yes, I enjoy being physical. Perhaps more than most. But it does *not* make me a sex addict."

"What does it make you, then? Why is it that you can't be satisfied sharing your body with just me? It's not like I make a habit of denying you. Hell, I love sex, too. But as willing as I am, I'm still not enough. So make me understand why that is."

"Some people are just wired differently. Just like you love buying new sport coats every other day, I enjoy the feeling that comes with touching and being touched. And yes, you're usually very willing. But let's not act like your stamina always matches mine."

The server appeared at that moment and my nostrils flared, knowing she'd heard my wife basically say I couldn't hang. I didn't even look at her as I waved her away, indignation now taking over my previous hunger.

"So you're gonna go there, huh?" I hissed, the edge of the table pressing into my chest as I leaned forward. "You're taking shots now?"

"Like you told me earlier, there's no need in getting insulted." She sat up defiantly. "You and I both know it's the truth, right?"

"One or two times in two years doesn't mean anything, Aurora. I fuck you over and over, and you know it. Just because you can never get enough doesn't mean there's anything wrong with me."

"Is it that I can't get enough, or that you can't satisfy me?"

My jaw clenched so hard it hurt, and I could feel the blood rush to my face. In that moment, I hated this woman.

Without another word, I slid out of the booth. I stood there and glared at her for a moment, but didn't trust myself to say anything else. I abruptly turned and headed for the door.

"Montrel!"

I kept walking. Went straight to my car, got in, started it, and pulled out of the parking lot without a second glace. I didn't care that we rode there together. Let her unsatisfied ass find her own way home.

I couldn't remember when I'd been so angry, not to mention insulted. Yes, I could; just a few days earlier when Forrest told me I wasn't fit to be godfather to his daughter. This topped that. I wasn't sure if Aurora meant what she said or if she was just lashing out at me for suggesting she might be a sex addict, but either way, my blood was still boiling.

As a further blow, I didn't even have anybody I could call and vent to. Forrest could still kiss my ass. Giselle still had her damn grudge. Ms. Debra was gone. Mother wasn't even an option. The realization that my circle of loved ones was so miniscule caused a hollowness to form in my chest. It never occurred to me just how few friends I really had, or people that I felt like I could turn to in critical moments. Can't say it was a good feeling, knowing I had no one.

I went straight home, resisting the urge to go to a bar or somewhere else. I was still buzzing with emotion, and I didn't want Aurora to think I was avoiding her. Part of me couldn't wait for her ass to get home so we could go for round two. The urge to cut her as much as she'd cut me had me furiously pacing around the house. She did call, but she hung up before it went to voicemail. Not that I was going to answer it, anyway. I wasn't worried about her safety. Her ass had more than enough money for a rideshare.

Finally, I heard the front door open. By that time, my stomping around had carried me upstairs. My hands wrung in anticipation; whether she was going to ream me out for leaving her at the restaurant, try to lay a guilt trip, threaten me, toss out some more emasculating comments...I was ready for whatever she had. I felt wired, like a boxer counting down to a fight.

When she appeared in our bedroom doorway, she just stood and looked at me. I could see her eyes were a little red, but the fire of anger in them blazed at me from across the spacious room. My back straightened as I faced off with her, chest heaving, blowing air out of my nostrils, glaring so intensely my eyeballs actually ached.

She walked right up to me, getting in my face. Our chests heaved practically in tandem. Her chin quivered as her eyes bored into mine, as if searching for something.

Then she hauled off and slapped me.

It was a firm hit but not enough to move me. The shock from the suddenness of it threw me off for a moment, and my hand itched to return the favor. She almost looked like she was silently daring me to do it. But no matter how angry I was, I couldn't bring myself to raise my hand to a woman.

When her hand lifted to hit me again, I caught it by the wrist and held it between us for a few moments before she snatched it away.

"I *hate* you, Montrel," she spat.

I chuckled snidely. "It's mutual, sweetheart."

In the next second we were slobbing each other down. Our hands immediately started tearing at each other's clothes, tossing them aside like nuisances. I clawed at her luscious nude body as our tongues wrestled against each other's, and she jumped into my arms, wrapping herself around me. I tossed her onto the bed and stroked my dick as I stared at her, ready to punish. I felt like I'd had a case of Red Bull, I was so wired. She sat up on her elbows, eying me with anticipation.

There was no foreplay or teasing. Once I was inside her, I started banging as hard as I could, gripping her lower legs and maneuvering them like joysticks as I fucked the hell out of her. She looked at me in mild surprise as her jaw hung open, releasing pants and noises with every hard stroke.

When I dropped her legs and hovered over her with my hands braced over her shoulders on the bed, she tried to pull my head down for a kiss but I knocked her hand away.

"You don't deserve any more of that," I informed her through gritted teeth.

"Please..."

"Shut the fuck up and take this dick."

"Oh I want it. I want *all* the dick, Montrel."

"I said shut up!"

Just moments later, she was quivering with an oncoming orgasm. Her nails dug into my back as she screamed into my ear, her head digging into the pillow. Again she tried to pull my head closer by the back of the neck, but I was having none of it.

"Turn your ass over," I whispered, roughly shoving her onto her stomach. When I jammed into her from behind, she glanced over her shoulder at me in approval before moaning and dropping her head, her thick hair flying back and forth as I rammed her. This was the one instance I *could* slap her, and my hand hit her ass several times in a row as I stroked, each time harder than the last. She screamed with each hit, loving it.

"God, *yes*!" she screamed.

I watched myself going in and out of her before my eyes traveled up her sweaty back, and when I felt my own orgasm coming, I didn't warn her. I just went harder, my fingers digging into her hips, before I suddenly pulled out and unloaded all over her back. She shuddered, whispering how much she loved feeling my cum on her skin.

"More," she whispered.

Still wired, I grabbed her shirt from the floor and hastily swiped my cum from her back before tossing it aside, snatching her up, and slamming her against the nearest wall, entering her as her legs wrapped around my waist. Her eyes were locked on mine as we went at it, her brow furrowed as if in concentration and mine in a deep scowl. We ended up changing positions several times, each time with her almost eerily focused, throwing it back at me as hard as I was giving it to her. Sometimes she whispered pleas, sometimes encouragement, sometimes taunts, with a lot of screams and groans in between. I didn't have any words; I just wanted to fuck.

I had her braced on the corner of the dresser, on her knees on the hardwood floor, against the window facing the street. My hand squeezed her throat. I pulled her hair. Bit her skin. Squeezed her breasts like stress balls and pinched her nipples. Had her ass literally red from all the slaps. I wanted to hurt her in the most acceptable way possible. But to my immense frustration, turned out she loved all that shit.

I don't know how long it was before we eventually ended up on the floor, sweaty and panting. We laid close but not touching. Her hand drifted up and absently began tweaking her nipple as she looked up at the ceiling but then, as if catching herself, she lowered it to her stomach.

"Do you really hate me?" she asked, her voice almost timid.

My anger wasn't totally gone, but I was too tired to be as cruel as I wanted to be. Sighing, I turned my head away from her. "I don't know."

She whimpered. "I'm so sorry." Her hand landed on my hip, unsurprisingly close to my crotch. "I'm sorry for everything."

I just shook my head. How had this even become my damn life?

"Yeah. I bet you are."

Chapter 9 – Aurora

"This what you wanted?"

"Yes..."

"I told you you'd be back," he taunted, still moving in and out of me. My breasts were mashed to his dark muscled chest as I grinded on his lap, my hands clinging to his shoulders. I avoided his eyes and instead focused on the painting of the faceless Black couple on the wall behind him, just wanting to enjoy the pleasure that had overtaken my body and mind. But unfortunately, he kept talking. "You know you can't stay away from me."

I didn't respond not only because I wasn't in the mood for his usual sexual banter, but mostly because he was right. There had been several times where I said I wasn't going to end up back at his house only for that uncontrollable urge to land me right back on his doorstep. This time, I showed up at three in the morning after Montrel left me hanging.

I'd come home from work and went looking for him, needing a release. I'd had another meeting with Boris Worthy that day and had managed to keep things professional, despite my womanhood throbbing so intensely I literally couldn't keep still in my seat. The way he eyed me made it clear he remembered what happened the last time he was in my office, and I was sure he wouldn't have resisted if I asked for a repeat performance. But I managed to keep it together. And I felt I deserved a reward. So when I found Montrel out on the back patio about to get into the hot tub for one of his post-yoga soaks, I went straight over to him and briefly grabbed his dick through his swim trunks before yanking them down and out of my way, dropping to my knees on the travertine pavers and taking all of him into my mouth. Gosh, how I loved Montrel's dick...he was always so clean and well-groomed, too. Something I couldn't say for all the men I entertained.

Montrel didn't say much as he obliged me a few rounds, and that was fine with me. But then he suddenly cut me off, pulling out of me after we finished intensely sexing on one of the patio chairs and striding into the house, ignoring me when I asked him to come back. I could tell he wasn't tired; he was just punishing me.

I tried to go on about my evening, telling myself I'd had enough, but my body wasn't listening to my mind. After masturbating in the shower then going to bed early to try to sleep the urge away, I tossed and turned, frustrated beyond belief. When Montrel finally came to bed, he barely even glanced in my direction. He was kind enough not to push me away when I yanked him around and slid my mouth over his dick again, but after he ejaculated down my throat, he just pushed me off of him and rolled over before I could mount him like he *knew* I wanted to. I just sat there, buzzing and fuming.

So that's what led me to...what was his name? We can call him Brian.

"You love me, don't you?" he panted, licking his lips as I leaned back, bracing my hands on his knees as I snaked my body, letting my head fall back. His hand slid up and grabbed my breast, his calloused thumb stroking my nipple and earning a long, tortured groan from me. "Damn, you are fucking sexy."

Thankfully, he stopped asking me questions and just gave me what I came for. At almost five a.m., I peeled myself off of his sculpted body and ran both hands through my disheveled hair, my wedding ring momentarily getting caught in it, letting my head hang for a moment before I stood and reached for my clothes.

"You can stay."

I didn't even turn around as I slipped my nightshirt over my head. "You know better."

"Clearly your man isn't handling business. Quit wasting time with him and come get what you really want." I heard the bed shift, then felt his tongue on my bare ass. Despite myself, I shuddered automatically, which only egged him on. "I promise you, baby, if you were with me, you wouldn't *ever* need to go running to somebody else."

Glancing at him over my shoulder, I wondered if he could see the amusement in my eyes in the darkened room. He really had no idea.

"I have to go," I announced once I slid on my mismatched shoes and hastily tied the drawstring on my shorts. I hadn't even worn any panties. "It was nice knowing you. I won't be back."

He laughed at me. "We both know you will." He pushed himself from the bed and I had to avert my eyes from his muscular frame. It was easy to focus on his face because it wasn't much to look at. His physique was definitely the best thing he had going for him.

Grabbing my chin, he leaned in and ran his tongue around my lips. "Like I said, you can't stay away. You can't help it. My door is always open, baby; come get this dick whenever you want it."

I just clenched my jaw and walked out.

By the time I was in my car heading home, tears were streaming down my face in sheets. I banged my hand against the steering wheel, furious with myself for getting caught up yet again. And now I looked like some pathetic weakling for going back to him when I repeatedly declared I wouldn't.

This was all Montrel's fault. If he'd just kept going earlier instead of trying to punish me, I wouldn't have had to go anywhere else. A husband was supposed to please his wife as much as she wanted, right? He could've just laid there and I would've done all the work. But he wouldn't even oblige me that.

Montrel didn't stir when I finally got back into our bed. I didn't even bother taking a quick shower first. I just pulled the covers up to my chin, turning by back to him like his was to me.

"Hope you enjoyed yourself," he muttered.

I just squeezed my eyes shut as a fresh batch of tears overran the dried ones.

Unsurprisingly, things between Montrel and I didn't exactly improve after that. I admit I'd lash out at him out of frustration from trying to force myself to resist my natural urges with anyone other than him. It might have been easy for some people but it was anything but for me, and it left me rather irritable. Not only from having to refrain from the pleasure my body naturally craved but because I sucked at it. It wasn't like it was the first time I'd committed to sharing my body with Montrel and no one else only to succumb to a weak moment shortly after. And I hated that my resolve was weakening yet again; as much as I wanted to, I just wasn't sure how much longer I could hold out.

But that still didn't make me an addict.

I was thankful when another Saturday rolled around and I could take my time getting out of bed. Montrel got up early and went on about his business. I figured he had his overnight oats as usual, did his mediation, showered, and left for his monthly spa day. He used to at least let me know he was leaving but not this time. I wasn't sure how things had gotten so strained between us. We'd said some things in anger the night he left me stranded at the bistro, but I'd hoped that we could move past it and get back to working on our marriage. But he didn't seem to be interested in that anymore and the realization had me feeling like a rejected failure.

And if I wasn't mistaken, I could've sworn I heard him mutter Claire's name in his sleep. More than once.

It wasn't supposed to be like this. I was making a mockery of marriage, and I wasn't proud of that. If it wasn't for the stipulation that I had to be wed to get my trust fund, I would have taken the time to find the man that I was madly in love with before walking down the aisle. But my dad ruined that when he succumbed to my mother's bitching and added that caveat. It's because of them that I had to settle for Montrel.

Not that I didn't love him. I did. But he wouldn't have even been on my radar if it weren't for my situation. He became ideal when I met his mother Annie at some function and she began singing his praises, showing me his pictures and letting me know how wealthy he was. And when I had an acquaintance dig into him and his background (for the payment of a hand job), verifying that his mother wasn't just blowing smoke, I was sure he was just the man to get me what I wanted expeditiously.

Yes, it might have started out as basically a business deal but my feelings for Montrel started to grow fairly early on. Which was why it never felt good when I disappointed him. I wasn't heartless. I just had urges I couldn't control sometimes.

Did that make me a bad person?

Knowing Montrel would likely take his time coming back home, I tried to busy myself with reorganizing my closet, moving the furniture around in the sitting room, and some of that meditation that Montrel always did, but being in the house alone got to be too much. The antsy feeling was overtaking me again. It actually crossed my mind to call Monroe, only because I knew he would give it to me straight. But I realized I wasn't in the frame of mind for the barrage of questions I'd have to endure to get his advice, so I dismissed that idea. I tried to call Mecca to see if she was available, but she texted me shortly after letting me know she'd gotten called into work. Huffing in exasperation, I called Bron.

"What up," he greeted. It sounded like he was outside.

I breathed a sigh of relief. "Hey, Bron. Please tell me you're not busy today."

"Not really. I'm just leaving the court; got a few games in with my boys. I have to go pick up my aunt's prescription and run it over to her but that's about it. Why, what's up? You need to get out of the house again?"

"I do, yeah." I shifted my weight from side to side anxiously.

"Bet. You can meet me at my spot. I should be there in about thirty or forty minutes."

"Great. You have any alcohol at your house?"

"There's some Hennessey in the kitchen."

"Perfect."

I hurriedly got showered and dressed and headed over to Bron's, wanting to be gone by the time Montrel got back. But there was no trace of him by the time I pulled my car out of the garage. And of course, no messages. I bit my lip at his indifference, blinking back the tears that started to sting and shaking my head so hard my hair flung around my face and got stuck in my lip gloss. I didn't want to cry again. I wanted to stop caring like he seemed to.

My mind forcibly ran down all of Montrel's faults as I drove. He was spoiled. He could be incredibly childish. He wasn't very self-sufficient, since he hired people for just about everything. His aversion to sweating. He had no plan for his life. With all the money he had, he could've been traveling, exploring, experiencing things people only dreamed of. But he just puttered around town, doing nothing worth mentioning. He'd probably try to say he stayed around for his mother, but I knew he borderline hated her. Or at least, it seemed he did.

I was still scraping together things to add to the list as I pulled up to Bron's duplex. By then, I'd accumulated a good amount of resentment towards my husband, and just wanted to put him and our disaster of a marriage out of my mind for as long as possible.

Bron's car wasn't out front but I had a spare key, so I let myself in. I immediately felt better just being there. I wandered to the middle of his modestly decorated living room and released a long, cleansing breath, not even minding the faint hint of Black and Mild in the air. It was actually strangely comforting, likely because it was so opposite of the scents Montrel usually had flowing through our house. He was *so* metrosexual (which also got added to my list).

By the time I poured a double of Hennessey, Bron was walking through the front door. He smiled when he saw me, his signature backward Braves hat perched on his head.

"I figured you'd beat me here," he greeted, placing his duffle bag near the door and kicking off his sneakers.

I nodded as I took a long swig of my drink. "Thanks for letting me come over."

"You know you don't have to thank me. What happened?"

I hesitated, not really wanting to get into it. "Nothing in particular. Just...need a friend right now."

"Well, that's me." He flashed his dimpled wide, white smile, revealing the tiny gap between his front teeth. He used to hate it but had grown to accept it over the years. "Make yourself at home. I'm gonna go take a shower real quick."

"Okay."

I was flipping through Bron's family album by the time he finished his shower about twenty minutes later. He flopped onto the couch next to me, smelling like baby oil and deodorant and wearing a loose tank top and sweats. His dark skin was still moist when his arm brushed mine.

"I forgot you have such a big family," I commented, turning a page. There were pictures of family reunions, weddings, birthday parties, casual gatherings, as well as solo shots of Bron through the years. Everyone looked so happy, the camaraderie and family bonds evident through the pictures. It was actually fascinating that he grew up in such a big, loving family like he did. It was just me and my mom until Monroe came along, and while it was far from a miserable life, it wasn't like the loving family sitcom Bron had grown up in.

"Yeah, there's a lot of us but I love it." Bron leaned over, looking at the pictures with a small smile. "Nothing like having a tribe."

"I hope you realize how fortunate you are, Bron."

"Oh, I do." He gently reached over and closed the album, pulling it from my lap and setting it on the end table. His eyes bored into my profile. "Tell me what's up."

I so wanted to confide in him about everything; to get it all off my chest, finally. Holding it all in was becoming an increasingly heavy burden. And, of my friends, Bron was the ideal person; as much as I loved Mecca, I didn't feel she'd have the empathy for me that Bron would once she heard everything.

But being totally transparent required strength that I didn't have yet.

"I just..." I sighed, rubbing my hands back and forth along my thighs, "I haven't been making the best decisions lately. Work isn't enjoyable anymore. My marriage is a mess. I've been missing my mother..."

His arm slid around my shoulders. "Things really that bad? I love you but you know you have a tendency to over-dramatize."

"I am not over-dramatizing. I've seriously thought about getting in my car and just...leaving. Going somewhere no one can find me and just starting over."

"Don't do that." He squeezed me closer to him. "We'd miss you too much."

"*Some* of you might."

"What you mean? I thought you said things were going so good between you and Montrel."

I instantly regretted not being more forthcoming with my friends, at least in part. I'd always portrayed my marriage to them as some kind of fairy tale love story when it was far from it. They still didn't know the real reason we married. And now I couldn't even confide like I wanted to without having to explain why I lied in the first place and making myself look foolish.

"They were," I replied softly, repeatedly pinching Bron's sweats between my fingers. "But things have gone off the rails recently."

"Y'all fell out?"

"I guess you could say that. We're hardly even talking."

"Did he mess up or did you?"

I pulled my bottom lip into my mouth. "We both made mistakes. But I think he's starting to regret marrying me. In fact, I'm all but sure he wants to go back to his ex."

Bron sat forward, immediately angry. "He what?"

"He misses his ex. I know he does. And I'm sure there'll come a day when he gets fed up with me enough that he'll finally leave and try to go back to her. Then I'll be alone again."

I only felt partially bad for embellishing like I was. Sure, Montrel probably missed Claire, but I didn't think he'd actually leave me for her. Not that he could, anyway, since they still weren't on speaking terms, to my knowledge. I guess I just wanted someone to get as mad at Montrel as I was, even if it was for falsified reasons.

Mission accomplished. Bron looked like he wanted to get up right then and find Montrel to beat his ass.

"You mean to tell me he'd actually leave you – *you* – for somebody else? What did he even marry you for if he was still hung up on her?"

My shoulders hunched. "Who knows."

"Say the word and I'll make him regret it."

His scowl was turned on full force, and I knew he'd make good on that promise if wanted him to. Bron was no stranger to fighting; he'd gotten into plenty back in the day. He calmed down as he got older but he was still fiercely protective of people he loved.

My hand briefly brushed his face before landing on his arm, gripping it lightly. I felt that familiar throbbing ignite at his willingness to go to bat on my behalf. I told myself to ignore it. "I love you for that. But it's not necessary. This situation is messy enough as it is."

"You sure?"

"I'm positive. Just knowing you have my back is good enough."

"I don't like seeing you sad like this."

"I'll be fine." I forced a smile. "I don't want to spend my day worrying about this. Do you have anywhere you have to be?"

He shrugged. "One of my boys said something about going to watch the game later. But I don't have to go."

"Good. Then you're all mine today. Come on, let's have a bunch more drinks, watch some movies and forget about everything else."

So that's what we did. That bottle of Hennessey he had didn't last long and we ended up ordering more, along with a bunch of Thai food. We fired up a marathon of Samuel L. Jackson movies, who was Bron's favorite actor. I threw my hair in a ponytail before I curled up next to him and he wrapped a comforting arm around me, our eyes locked in on his fifty-inch screen.

"Bron, it's only because I appreciate you spending your Saturday with me that I'm sitting here watching *Snakes on a Plane*."

He sucked his teeth. "Y'all always try to clown this movie."

"Because it's ridiculous. I know you think Samuel can do no wrong, but..."

"You just like to act like you don't think this is funny. Every movie doesn't have to be *Citizen Kane*."

"A classic."

I was messing with him but I really didn't care what we watched. It just felt good to be around him and his positive, supportive energy. I wasn't thinking about my situation at home, my work frustrations, my irksome relationship with Monroe. None of that existed at the moment and Bron being the catalyst for that made me want to thank him however I could.

A long comfortable silence stretched between us as we continued to watch the movie. My head was on Bron's chest, his hand resting on my side, and the throbbing ache between my legs hadn't gone away, but I was managing it pretty well, considering.

"I'm gonna go to the restroom; be right back," I said, pushing myself up.

Bron's eyes stayed on the screen. "Okay."

I padded across the carpeted floor to the small half bath and closed the door. I just needed to take the edge off. Perching myself on the sink, I slid my hand down my shorts and circled my fingertip around my clit, biting my lip as I tried to suppress my moans. I worked myself over quickly, my other hand pulling at my nipple through my shirt, taking the quickest route to release. When the orgasm washed over me, I shuddered and rode it out, my hips still grinding against my hand and huffing relieved breaths through my nose.

"That helped," I whispered to myself, turning to wash my hands. I looked at my reflection in the mirror and swiped my fingertips underneath my eyes before smoothing my hands over my ponytail. The stress lines on my face and the slight bags under my eyes were evident and I was surprised Bron hadn't commented on it. Physically and mentally, I hadn't exactly been feeling stellar of late, and it was starting to show outwardly. But I pushed all of that out of my mind because I just wanted to enjoy my day with my friend.

Taking a deep breath, I forced a smile and told myself everything would be just fine. *I* would be just fine. After making sure my clothes were straight, I opened the door and headed back to the living room.

Bron just glanced up at me as I retook my seat on the couch, his hand absently running along his low-cut black hair.

"You want the last of this Ciroc?" he asked, nodding towards the almost-empty bottle.

"I'd better not. I don't want to overdo it. I *do* still have to drive home at some point."

"You could crash here if you needed to. Plus you know I wouldn't let you drive if I thought you were even a little bit drunk."

"I know you wouldn't." I smiled, looking up at him. "You're always looking out for me."

"Damn right."

I returned my head to his chest, noticing his dark nipple through the wide opening of his tank top that had shifted over. Without even thinking, I snaked out my tongue, grazing it lightly.

His breathing changed, but he didn't say anything. I did it again, this time swirling it around the nipple slowly. My hand that was resting on his stomach clenched, taking a handful of his shirt.

"Aurora."

I sat up, my hand sliding slightly towards his waistband. "Is that your way of stopping me?"

He just looked at me, an unreadable look in his eyes. I pursed my lips, my back straightening.

"Why didn't you tell Mecca about us fooling around?"

His brow furrowed a little. "What?"

"When we were at Prism Lounge. You broadcasted how she and I messed around that one time but didn't say anything about what you and I did. Why is that?"

His expression clearing, he shook his head, actually looking like he was contemplating the answer. "I don't even have an answer for that. Best I can say is that it's always easier to call out other folks' shit instead of your own."

"Are you ashamed of it?"

"No." His response was quick. "Never that. We're grown, we were both down, and neither of us tried to make it more than it was afterwards. Nothing to be ashamed of."

"I'm so glad you said that. I feel the exact same way. And it felt like we got so much closer after that first night."

"That's good. Part of me was worried that you would start feeling some kind of way at some point but you never did. Sex can ruin friendships sometimes but I'm glad that didn't happen to us."

"Me, too. I don't ever want to lose you as a friend, Bron. Your friendship is everything to me, especially now."

He tweaked my chin, the corner of his mouth lifting in a smile. "I'm not going anywhere."

I leaned in and pressed a light kiss to his cheek. "Promise?"

Our eyes locked as he nodded. I had an up-close view of just how good looking Bron was. His high cheekbones, goatee, dark thick brows, thick lips that always looked as if they'd just been moistened.

"Yeah, girl. I promise."

"So if I do this..." My hand slid and grabbed his partially-erect penis through his pants, "You'll still be my friend, right?"

His eyes closed briefly before he nodded.

"What about this?" I whispered, going behind the waistband of his sweats and briefs and gripping his warm bare dick, which was growing by the second. My lips were brushing his. "Would we still be friends then?"

"Yeah." His voice was gruff as he began slowly pumping into my hand. His bottom lip was pulled between his teeth. "Hell yeah, girl. Best friends."

"Good. That's what I hoped you'd say." I continued to slowly stroke him, my own arousal multiplying at super-speed as he moaned and cursed under his breath. "I love the look on your face right now. Oh my god, Bron..."

My own hips started undulating all on their own. Bron's hand eased behind the waistband of my shorts and gripped my ass.

"I need you right now," I breathed, grabbing his other hand and placing it on my breast, which he immediately squeezed. "Let's get rid of these clothes so you can *really* touch me."

He hesitated.

I almost panicked at the thought of him rejecting me right then. "Please?"

Without waiting for a response, I withdrew my hand from his pants, earning a frustrated groan from him, and lifted my shirt over my head. My bra was next to go. Bron looked at me hungrily before he stood and began removing his own clothes, to my delight. I quickly shimmied out of my shorts and panties, kicking them across the room. Standing, I grabbed Bron behind his head and pulled him to me for a deep, hungry kiss. I gushed when he responded to me, both hands grabbing my ass and pulling me to him. He kissed so differently from Montrel. Bron's kisses were more authoritative, more demanding. I loved it.

We stood there making out and grinding against each other before he suddenly stopped, taking a step back and giving me a regretful look.

"What?" I panted.

"We shouldn't be doing this," he grunted, though I could tell it was forced. His erection was still jutting out at me. "It was different when we got down before; you weren't married then. But now-"

"Bron, are you forgetting about the second time? I was as married then as I am now."

He stilled, apparently having forgotten about that. I told myself not to feel affronted.

"Okay, I was drunk that time," he finally acknowledged. "We both were. But still-"

"Still, I might be married but I'm far from happy," I blurted, closing the distance between us. My hands rested on his chest. "And I already told you what I was dealing with. You have no idea what it's like to share a house with someone who pretends that you're not even in it with him. Please don't think you're ruining anything. You're helping me."

I placed a soft kiss to his nipple before following it up with a slower, wetter one. Bron had super sensitive nipples. He groaned, pulling off the elastic band holding my ponytail and dropping it to the floor before sliding his hand into the back of my hair.

"Don't make me beg for it, baby." I pressed closer to him. "We both want this, so we shouldn't deprive ourselves. You're all mine for today, right?"

His breath hitched as I continued to tongue kiss one nipple, pinch the other with one hand, and stroke his hardness with the other. I could almost feel his defenses breaking down as the time ticked by, the forgotten movie still playing around us. When his fist tightened in my hair and he pulled my head up for a kiss, I hoped we were finally on the same page.

"Fuck me, please," I kept whispering between kisses. He released a long grunt.

"Shit, Aurora..."

"I want you, Bron." I swiped my fingers between my legs and shoved them into his mouth, which he greedily accepted. "That's all for you."

I didn't have to do more convincing, thankfully. We ended up in his bedroom, going at it on his king-sized bed. The bliss that I felt was indescribable. Bron was so expressive, and not shy about getting loud. I held him to me as he sexed me in that firm, smooth way of his that I loved.

"You feel so good, girl," he panted, looking down at me. "Fuck, you feel good."

I pulled him in for another kiss. "You have no idea how much I needed this, Bron. Please don't stop, baby. Please, *please* don't stop."

"I'm here for as long as you want."

"I'm gonna hold you to that."

And I did. It was dark outside by the time I finally rolled off of Bron, sweaty, sore, and satisfied. I couldn't even count the number of positions we did; ones I'd wanted to do with Montrel but didn't think he'd indulge me, thinking they were too wild. Bron was down for anything, and I absolutely loved it. He had actually managed to tire me out, which didn't happen often.

"You staying?" he asked drowsily, his hand sliding to my stomach. "Or you have to dip?"

"I don't have a reason to rush off. I'll just crash here, if that's okay."

"Stay as long as you want."

My hand landed on top of his. "I appreciate you, Bron."

His eyes opened and he gave me a small smile. "You know I got you."

We shared a lingering kiss before we both started to doze. I threw my leg over his and fell into the most peaceful sleep I'd had in a while.

And when I woke up to Bron sucking my breasts and fingering me, I had the most pleasant wake-up call I'd had in a while.

He brought me to a lazy orgasm, just by enjoying my breasts while gently playing with my clit. I grabbed his hand when he started to pull away after I came, silently letting him know I wasn't done.

"More," I whimpered, my hips still winding. "I need more, please..."

"Damn, girl," he muttered, easing a finger inside of me and biting his lip when I moaned and began grinding against his hand. "You're even greedier than you were last time we got down."

He was right. My sexual appetite had grown leaps and bounds since the time we slept together years before, and even more so in the months since our recent romp. It was almost like it matured or strengthened over time all by itself. One orgasm only made me want another. The high that came with bringing my body that level of pleasure was hard to get enough of.

We fooled around for a while longer before we dozed off again. When my eyes slid open the next time, I had no idea what time it was but the sun was shining through the blinds of Bron's bedroom window. I eased myself up, my body aching from the hours of intense sexual activity. Bron was still sound asleep, his head turned away from me. My eyes traveled down his naked body before I looked away, and pushed myself off the bed.

When I found my phone in the living room, it was almost dead but I saw it was also close to noon. No messages from Montrel, asking where I was. I sucked my teeth.

"Whatever," I muttered, snatching my clothes up from the floor.

I went to the bathroom and washed up before getting dressed. When I peeked back in on Bron, he was still knocked out. I rounded the bed and knelt down next to him, gently placing my hand on his warm cheek.

"Bron."

He grunted before his eyes eased open. "You heading out?"

"Yeah. I should."

"Okay." He started to get up, but I placed a gentle hand to his chest.

"Don't get up. Stay here and rest. I'll let you know when I get home."

"Girl, stop." He grabbed my wrist as he sat up and stretched before swinging his legs over the side of the bed. "You know better. Just give me a minute."

I waited as he quickly went to the bathroom before strolling into the living room, now semi-erect again, and grabbed his sweatpants from the floor. Not bothering with a shirt, he slid his feet into his slides and followed me outside.

"Make sure you get you something to eat soon," he told me, unlocking my car door. "I'd offer to make you a sandwich or something but I have a feeling you'd decline that."

I smiled at him. Sometimes I forgot how well Bron knew me. At least, relative to other people. He always accepted me the way I was and that urge to tell him everything flared again, but that would have to wait. I needed to quit while I was ahead.

"Next time," I assured, sliding my arms around his neck. He wrapped me in a tight hug, burying his face in the crook of my neck. When he pulled back, we shared a long deep kiss, with him pinning me to the car with his body. It felt so delicious and naughty to kiss him like that out in the open, in full view of his neighbors. The idea of them possibly seeing us spurred me to tighten my hold on him, feeling the press of his erection.

"I thought you had to leave," he muttered between kisses. He lifted my leg so he could get closer.

"I do." My hips began to move against his. "In a minute."

We grinded against each other as our kiss continued. Part of me imagined Montrel driving by and catching us, even though I knew the chance of him coming to Bron's neighborhood was practically nonexistent. It wasn't the slum or anything but it wasn't the affluent part of town that we lived in, and Montrel wouldn't go there without reason. Still, the idea of it had me increasing my intensity, and thankfully, Bron indulged me. He discreetly pinched my nipple, bringing me to one last yummy release, moaning rapidly against his mouth as it overtook me.

"Oh my god, yes," I panted softly, opening my eyes. I so hated that I had to leave. Everything in me wanted to pull Bron back inside and just spend the Sunday holed up with him. He'd made me feel better than I had in months.

"You good?" he muttered, his forehead resting against mine. He gently lowered my leg back to the ground.

"Yes. I'm great." I smiled as I glanced at the houses around us. "You think anybody saw?"

He shrugged. I loved that he was unbothered. "Probably. People are nosy as hell."

"I apologize in advance if I get you into any trouble."

"Trouble for what? These folks know not to bother me. And anyway, it's not like we were fucking out here. They'd better *not* come at me with any bullshit."

I felt that throb again and I knew it was *really* time to go.

With one last peck, he eased his hand between us and adjusted himself before stepping back. Once I stepped aside, he opened my car door for me.

"Let me know when you get home," he instructed.

"I will."

I got in my car and glanced at Bron, who just stood there with his hands in his pockets. I flashed him a grin and waved, pulling out of his driveway. He stood there watching me as I took off down the street.

The grin was still on my face as I danced to the Mary J. Blige song blaring through my satellite radio, both hands gripping the steering wheel. I didn't have a care in the world and I just wished I knew how to hang onto that feeling.

Well, I'd have to figure it out another day because my little bubble was instantly punctured with a call from Monroe.

"Ugh, what the hell does *he* want?"

Sighing, I went ahead and answered it, choosing to think positively. Maybe he wouldn't be too much of an asshole this time.

"Good morning, Monroe."

"It's after twelve-thirty," he corrected. "I'd hope you aren't still lazying around in bed."

"If I was, so what? It's Sunday, I'm off work, and more importantly, I'm grown and can do what I want."

The line went quiet. It wasn't often that I snapped at Monroe like that. But he was already on my nerves and I just wasn't in the mood after the great eighteen hours or so I'd had with Bron.

"Speaking of work, I heard through the grapevine that your performance has still been taking a nosedive," he retorted, that all-too-familiar hard edge in his voice slicing through the good vibes in my car. "You recall that Dan is my frat brother."

"Yes, I'm aware. You keep reminding me."

"And yet you keep fucking up. If you don't care about your reputation, that's *your* foolish choice. But I'm the one that recommended you for that job and convinced them to be patient with you when you first started falling off, so your shit reflects on me, Aurora. If it weren't for me, you'd have been out of there months ago."

"Nobody asked you to do that, Monroe. I didn't ask you to help get me a job or plead my case to anyone. Frankly, you're more than welcome to butt out."

Another pause. I was throwing him for a loop with all this backtalk, but the adrenaline was pumping hard.

"So you think you've got it all together, I guess," Monroe retorted. "You don't need me? Well, how many times have I heard that? Only for you to come running back, apologizing. So spare me the tantrum and get your shit together ASAP."

"Whatever." I was determined not to let him get to me this time.

"Yeah, whatever." Monroe chuckled snidely. "You know your mother would be ashamed of how you're behaving. It's like everything she taught you is going to hell, with how you're blowing it at work *and* at home. You're failing in your marriage, and you're delusional if you think folks can't see it. The marriage, I don't care as much about. But you're not gonna keep sullying *my* good name, too."

He hung up and I hated that tears were now streaming down my face. He played the one card he *knew* would knock me down a few pegs: my mother. I didn't know why Monroe chose to still be so stern with me after all this time. But I hated that he'd ruined my good mood, especially since he wasn't wrong. While I had improved some at work, I still wasn't exactly hitting it out of the park. And Montrel and I had never been in a worse place, though I wondered how Monroe knew how bad things had gotten. I couldn't imagine Montrel had confided in him.

That was the least of my concerns right then, though. I could feel myself sliding back into that dark place I was in when I arrived at Bron's the day before. The urge to turn around and go back to his house and take refuge almost had me doing a U-turn in the middle of the street, but I knew I'd have to go home sometime.

At least Montrel wasn't there when I arrived. Part of me was worried and hoped he was all right but the larger part was relieved. I'd take any peace I could get.

Chapter 10 – Montrel

Can I complain about my life again?

I was sinking, hard and fast. Ever since the disastrous dinner date with Aurora where she ever so gently intimated that I was less than satisfactory in bed, my mood, my energy, and my desire to do much of anything was in the toilet. Any productivity I did have required exhausting effort, which only left me snappy and disgruntled. That statement just kept blasting over and over in my head:

"Is it that I can't get enough, or that you can't satisfy me?"

And this wasn't about my ego. I'd never been anything less than confident in my bedroom capabilities. But Aurora was clearly an anomaly. And given her apparently bottomless sexual appetite and the fact that she had absolutely no problem throwing it in my face just further confirmed that I had absolutely married the wrong woman. I knew it already but had told myself that I could make the best of it; that just because we started out one way didn't mean we couldn't change. We liked each other. Had love for each other, I felt. It wasn't impossible that could blossom into something deeper.

But it wasn't happening. Aurora didn't want that; her actions proved she didn't. She was still stepping out on me after all of her declarations of wanting us to have a 'real' marriage, and wasn't even trying to be discreet with it. Slipping out of the house after she thought I was asleep, staying gone for hours, easing back into the bed with the stench of her liaisons permeating my bamboo viscose bedsheets. I was insulted, disgusted, but most of all, disheartened.

The main reason I'd agreed to marry Aurora - sex - was the very thing that was making me hate her.

Aurora wasn't the only source of my growing depression. The feeling that I was wasting my life wasn't helping any. Yeah I had money, but you know what I also had? A mother I didn't like, a best friend that didn't seem to think very much of me, no other friends to speak of, and almost zero idea of what I saw my life like even a month ahead, let alone years. And of course, a wife that I had no business marrying in the first place.

I ached to talk to Claire. I missed her more with every day that passed. The more I thought about our relationship, the more ashamed I was for how I treated her. That woman genuinely loved me, and I knew that, but I took it for granted. Breaking up with her (one time on her birthday), slinking back when it looked like she was trying to move on, only to punk out and dump her again. And when she did get into a relationship with someone else, a serious relationship, I didn't respect it; because in my mind, she belonged to me. I honestly felt like I could do what I wanted and she'd just wait for me to get my shit together. I hurt her, wasted her time, cost her the relationship with someone that loved her like she deserved, and then went off and married someone else. I wouldn't even share my spa time with her; wouldn't even tell her which one I went to, which is damn ridiculous. It wasn't lost on me that all my bullshit was now biting me in the ass. But still, every part of me wanted Claire back, even if it was just platonically.

As I'd done a few times since we parted ways, I scoured social media for any traces of her; yes, it was desperate and sad but I couldn't resist. I knew she'd closed her accounts from before, but I thought – hoped – that she'd maybe opened new ones. But again, I came up empty. She clearly didn't want me to find her.

And yes, I knew it wasn't impossible to find her if I *really* wanted to go there; I was the king of paying people to get things done and could've easily hired someone to track her down. I had the means and the desire. But that wasn't the way to go about it, and I knew that. Desperately and repeatedly scouring for traces of her on social media on my own was already doing too much.

After the night Aurora came home in the wee hours from her latest creep session, I stopped sleeping in our bed. The house had three guest bedrooms, and I claimed the one furthest from her. I certainly had no interest in sleeping with her anymore. The reality that my cutting her off sexually would only affect me and not her was just another blow. Regardless of how fucked up our situation was, I couldn't bring myself to do what she did and find pleasure outside of our marriage. With all my faults, I'd never been a cheater, and I wasn't going to let Aurora's actions drive me to that.

Thoughts of just getting in my car and leaving became more and more appealing as the days progressed. There really wasn't anything keeping me in Terston, where we lived. Starting over fresh and getting my life together somewhere else might be just what I needed. And since I wanted to be free of this joke of a marriage I was in, I called my attorney and told him to get some divorce papers drawn up for when

I was ready to finally pull the trigger. Aurora and I had a prenup so we'd each be leaving with whatever we came with. I just hoped that she didn't try to continue this charade and put up a fight about it.

Mother wouldn't be pleased, but I didn't give a fuck.

Speaking of Mother, I was actually surprised when she called me one afternoon. We hadn't spoken since the night I met her new man James, and honestly, I hadn't given it a second thought. Part of me wondered if she was calling to get onto me for skipping my weekly visits, but as far as I was concerned, she didn't need me now that she had Mr. James Tyberious Nylon.

I sent her call to voicemail, having nothing to say to her. But of course, she called right back. With a heavy sigh, I yanked the phone up and snapped, "Yes?"

"Montrel?" she confirmed as if she didn't recognize my damn voice. She was clearly taken aback. "Since when do you answer the phone that way?"

Rolling my eyes, I droned, "What is it, Mother?"

"Why do you sound like that? What are you doing?"

"I'm in bed."

"In bed? It's almost two o'clock in the afternoon."

"I know what time it is."

"Hmm. Well, I called because I wanted to share some good news."

No question about why I might be in bed in the middle of the day or concern if something might be wrong or not. She only wanted to talk about her shit.

Resisting the urge to say I didn't care, I dutifully asked, "What?"

"I'm entering a new business venture. More specifically, I'm going into business with James."

I chuckled sarcastically. "It's not with that insurance nonsense, is it?"

"It's not nonsense, Montrel. He has a legitimate plan and he wants me to build his empire with him. I'm excited about it; getting to build and grow with my man is thrilling."

"So he finally swindled you into that, huh? I knew it would only be a matter of time."

"Don't be churlish, Montrel. No one swindled me into anything. James has an actual business plan, and I looked over all of the information myself. It's all on the up and up."

"Sure."

"Why aren't you happy for me?"

"Because, frankly, this is idiotic. You don't know the first thing about the insurance industry. This man has you so sprung that you're willing to give him...how much?"

She hesitated. "I don't want to say. But I'm not *giving* him anything; it's an investment."

"Uh-huh. Well, however much it is, I hope you're prepared to not get it back. Because I'd be willing to bet my kidney that this is going to crash and burn faster than you can sing '*like a good neighbor.*'"

She scoffed in the haughty way only she could. "I don't understand why you're being so negative, Montrel. It's bad enough that I haven't heard from you recently; now when I share something I'm genuinely excited about, you respond with nothing but negativity. That's not how I raised you to be."

I laughed out loud at that. "Right, Mother. Give *me* decorum lessons when you never ask about what's going on with me, never come visit, never show any concern for me in the slightest. The only reason you called was to talk about you, which is the only reason you *ever* call other than to try to tell me what to do."

"That is not true!"

"Yes it is. You hear I'm in bed this time of day and what do you do? Just skim right over it and go into your shit. You care more about that man than you do your own son."

She gasped. "Montrel! I take offense to that. And since when do you speak to your mother with that kind of language??"

"You don't behave like a mother so why should I treat you like one? And why are you telling me about this stuff anyway?"

"Because I wanted to share my good news and I *thought* you'd be as excited about it as I am."

"I don't know why. I told you from the beginning that I don't trust James, but you dismissed that. As I'm sure you'd do if I were to tell you that I think this decision of yours is a bad idea, which I do. You're gonna do what you want, anyway, so why do I need to know? Clearly what I think doesn't matter."

"Montrel." She had the nerve to try to sound saddened. "I really can't believe you're speaking to me this way."

"Yeah, well. I've listened to you speak to me any kind of way for almost thirty-six years and I put up with it. So you'll be all right."

"Your father would be so ashamed. Regardless of whether you agree with me or not, I am still your mother-"

"Let's not try that again, all right? Look, I'm going on record as saying that you involving yourself with James's business venture is a terrible idea, but if you choose to proceed anyway, you deserve whatever you get. And on the slim, miniscule chance that it *does* work out, it's not like you'd share any success with me, anyway; you'd just gloat. So either way, I'm out."

"You're out?"

"All the way out. Now, I have to go, Mother. Enjoy the rest of your day. And for the record, you *still* haven't asked how I'm doing."

Before she could respond, I ended the call and dropped the phone onto the bed next to me before turning over and staring out the window into the woods behind the house. It felt good to finally get some things off my chest to Mother that I'd been holding in for years, but at the same time, I didn't expect for it to change anything. Mother was never great at admitting when she was wrong. The realization that my already subpar relationship with my mother was now even more splintered drained me of what little energy I had left, and I ended up staying in bed the rest of the day.

The day of Jenna's birthday party rolled around and I seriously debated if I should even go. Forrest and I still weren't speaking; I eventually responded to a couple of his texts, but they were succinct responses. And I wasn't eager to be around Giselle and her attitude towards me, either.

The only reason I didn't make up an excuse and skip it altogether was the knowledge that Claire would be there. She's the reason I rolled out of bed and took a long (and frankly, much-needed) shower, went to get a haircut, and even treated myself to an impromptu massage, hoping to ease the anxiety and nervousness over seeing Claire again and also from being around Forrest for the first time since our gut-kicking conversation. I went home and anxiously took another shower, using my best body washes and oils, and took extra time deciding what outfit would be eye-catching but not like I was doing too much for a two-year-old's birthday party. My hands were actually shaking. I so wished there was a way I could just send over little Jenna's gifts and get some time with Claire somewhere else.

I was standing in front of the mirror in the guest bath trying to decide if I should change my shirt a fourth time when Aurora ventured in. I didn't even know she was home and I wasn't exactly glad to see her.

"Yes?" I asked impatiently when several moments passed with her not saying anything.

She gently rested her head and hand against the doorjamb, looking at me tentatively. "May I ask where you're going?"

"Why do you care?"

"Because I was hoping we could spend some time together."

"Oh, this is the point in the cycle that you're paying attention to me again? I'm good."

Her hand dropped. "Can you not be like that?"

"Aurora, as you can see, I have plans. Jenna's birthday party is today."

She frowned. "You're going to see another woman?"

I chuckled as I adjusted my collar. "That's funny. Even if I was, so what? As much as you go off and fuck other men, there wouldn't be anything you could say about it. But I'll leave the adultery to you. Jenna is Forrest's daughter."

"Oh...right. I'm sorry." Her expression cleared and she stood up straight, shooting me a hopeful look. "Can I go?"

"No."

"Why not?"

"Because you weren't invited. It's a wonder *I'm* even allowed there, given how pissed Giselle still is at me. The woman that I left her friend high and dry for is certainly not welcome. And I'm not in the mood to get cussed out."

"Did you even try to plead my case? I've never even met Claire; it's not like I did anything to her directly. Speaking of which, is she going to be there?"

"From what I hear."

"So my husband is going to a party without me where the ex that he still has feelings for will be, and I'm not allowed to join him. How are we ever going to get back on track, Montrel, if we keep ignoring each other?"

Was she serious? We'd been doing just fine acting like the other wasn't there, and I had no desire to change it. The fact that she just up and decided she was ready to spend some time with me wasn't flattering, it was frustrating. I never knew what the hell I was going to get from Aurora from one day to the next, and I was over it.

Aside from that, she looked like shit. Her weary eyes revealed that she hadn't slept in days, her hair was a mess, her skin was screaming for moisturizer, and she was dropping weight. I wasn't sure what she could possibly be so stressed about, but whatever it was was taking its toll on her physically. A few weeks earlier, I'd have cared what that was. But since it was evident she wasn't worried about me (at least, until she happened to be in the mood to do so), I wasn't going to expend any concern about her.

"I think the ship has sailed on us 'getting back on track', Aurora. Although to even say that would imply that we were ever on track to begin with. You're going to do your own thing regardless so I wish you'd spare me on trying to act like you want the real deal with me. Clearly, that was bullshit and I've learned to accept it."

"Montrel, no!" She lunged for me, gripping my shirt in her hands. The look in her slightly-sunken eyes was pleading. "I'm so sorry; I'm sorry for how I've been acting and how I've treated you. All the terrible things I said that night in the restaurant, and when I said I hated you...you don't deserve any of that. Please, I...I just need you to bear with me. I really do want to be the wife you deserve but I need some help."

I stared at her for a moment before gently prying her hands off me and smoothing the wrinkles she'd created in my shirt with the flat of my hands. "I don't believe you, Aurora."

And here come the tears. "Montrel..."

"I'm tired of looking like a fool for you. I've given you the benefit of the doubt so many times only to have you spit in my face. You're draining me, Aurora. Can't you see that??" I stepped back, holding my arms out to my sides as I looked at her intently. "You're draining me! And I don't have anything left to give you."

"Please don't give up on me!" She grabbed me around my waist, pressing her tear-stained face into my chest. And sealing the decision as to whether I should change my damn shirt. "Give me *one* more chance. Please let me go to the party with you. I swear I'll be on my best behavior. Hell, I'll even stay in the car. I just...please don't leave me here alone. I really shouldn't be alone, Montrel."

Her words and what they might mean didn't even register. My mind just automatically went to denying her.

"It's not happening, Aurora." I grabbed her arms. "Now, please let me go so I can finish getting ready and get out of here."

She looked up at me, sniffling and silently pleading for me to change my mind. When she saw I wasn't going to budge, she finally hung her head and stepped back.

"I wish you'd change your mind," she whispered.

"And I wish you'd kept your word when you said you were going to give our marriage real effort. How many other men have you slept with since you told me that?"

Her chin quivered before she looked away, tugging at her oversized t-shirt.

"Right." I stepped around her, hating the ache I was feeling in my chest. "But you want us to work, huh?"

I slammed my hand on the light switch, leaving her standing there in the dark fiddling with her wedding ring.

That whole scene now had me running late, and I forced it out of my mind as I went to change my shirt before grabbing my keys and leaving the house, only marginally hurrying. It wasn't like anything hinged on my being there on time. Giselle didn't really want me there in the first place. I was in no hurry to see Forrest. And yes, I looked forward to seeing Claire, but I had to be real about the possibility that she probably wouldn't want to talk to me.

Why the hell was I going to this, again?

I was a man of my word, so I got in my car and headed to Forrest and Giselle's house. There were already several cars in the driveway and along the street in front of their house, and it took me a minute to find somewhere to park, which ended up being a little ways down the street. I turned off the engine and tried to steel myself from whatever nonsense that may await, and reminded myself that the day was about little Jenna and not any drama. And giving a silent promise that I'd respect it if Claire wanted to keep her distance, but putting in a prayer that she wouldn't.

I grabbed Jenna's gifts from the backseat and got on out of the car, locking it before trudging up the street towards the house. I could hear music and people talking from outside. My eyes searched the cars in the driveway and in front of the house for Claire's, but I didn't see it. So either she hadn't arrived yet or she'd also changed her car since I last saw her.

I knocked on the front door a couple of times before realizing it was open, and eased inside the house, automatically looking around the room. There were a few people in the living room, some of whom I recognized as Forrest and Giselle's family. They greeted me with smiles and waves, which put me at ease a tiny bit. I could hear kids playing in another part of the house. I was putting my gifts for Jenna on the gift table in the corner of the room when Forrest approached.

"I was wondering if you were going to show up."

Silently reminding myself to behave, I turned to him, keeping my expression neutral. "Said I would."

"Still no words for me, huh?"

"Man...I'm not here for all that. Just want to help celebrate Jenna's birthday, that's all."

Forrest's droopy eyes fixed on me for a moment before he gave a slight shake of his head. "All right, Montrel. Hopefully we can hash all this out at some point, but I agree, now isn't the time. The party is in the backyard. Drinks and food in the kitchen."

"All right."

I left him standing there and headed towards the kitchen, which led out to the backyard. Giselle and another woman were in there, arranging cupcakes on a platter and pouring juice into plastic cups. Giselle looked up when she saw me and the smile she'd been sporting moments before flattened slightly.

"Hello, Giselle," I greeted, not wanting to be rude. I *was* in her house, after all.

"Montrel," she nodded, lips in a straight line. Her wild curly hair was piled on top of her head. "Nice of you to come."

"Sure." Not knowing what else to say, I continued on to the backyard, easing the sliding door open. There were several adults out there on the deck, with kids running around on the grass, enjoying the inflatable bouncy house and other toys and games that had been put out there. The birthday girl Jenna was on the lap of an older White gentleman, and a salt-and-pepper haired Black woman sat next to them, playing with her. I knew those were Giselle's parents, and I waved to them politely as I moved to the corner of the deck, already feeling out of place.

I was starting to rethink my decision to be there. On the outs with the hosts, only marginally acquainted with some of the other guests. At least if Aurora had been there I'd have someone to talk to. But I ended up just standing off in the cut and watching the kids play, checking the time every couple of minutes.

When some woman came over and struck up a conversation, I welcomed it, even though I usually abhorred small talk. At least now I wasn't looking like some lurking stranger.

"Are you from around here?" she asked me, sipping from her cup of red juice.

"Yeah."

"How do you know Forrest and Giselle?"

"We all went to college together."

"Oh okay, great. So you all have been friends for a while, then. Wait, are you Jenna's godfather?"

My lips immediately curled in. "Nah. That's Forrest's brother."

Who I had yet to see, I might add.

The woman (whose name I didn't even bother remembering) continued asking me questions and I continued answering them, grateful to at least have a distraction. When she excused herself and headed into the house, I glanced at my watch, wondering how much longer this was going to last. But those thoughts evaporated when I looked up just as Claire stepped out onto the deck.

My breath immediately caught in my throat. She looked delectable. Her thin brown hair was cut shorter now, showcasing her pretty face. She looked like she'd picked up about twenty pounds and she was carrying it beautifully; she never did love how thin she used to be. Mother actually thought she was anorexic. Just like she thought her green eyes were fake. She never missed an opportunity to take a dig at Claire and I knew if she were to see her now, she'd just conjure up something else to criticize.

Claire was talking to Giselle's parents and I got the first sound of her voice when I heard her laugh. My eyes were transfixed on her as she knelt down in her olive green belted jumpsuit to kiss little Jenna, the short sleeves showing off toned arms and the buttons opened just enough to see a hint of cleavage. Chocolate brown wedge sneakers were on her feet, and wooden jewelry adorned her ears, neck, and wrist. She looked so bohemian and sexy and confident. Her whole aura was different and it made me wonder just what she'd been up to since she'd been away.

My hopeful expression faded when her friend Chichi stepped out from the kitchen and joined her, her set of triplet sons running past her towards the yard. Her voice carried across the deck; she'd always been loud as hell.

It didn't take long for her to start looking around, and when her eyes landed on me, they instantly narrowed and her face morphed into a sneer. I refused to look away, because she wasn't about to think she was intimidating me.

When I lifted my hand in a polite wave, she just turned up her nose and rolled her eyes.

Some things never changed.

She nudged Claire's arm and jerked her head in my direction, muttering something under her breath. That's when Claire finally noticed me.

She stood up straighter, those green eyes roaming over me from head to toe. To my delight (and honestly, surprise) she didn't look displeased to see me. Her glossed lips actually stretched into a small smile, and she nodded graciously at me. I nodded back.

Just when I was about to venture over to her, Giselle and Forrest emerged from the kitchen announcing that it was time to sing happy birthday to Jenna. Giselle put a large plastic bib on Jenna while Forrest placed a small individual cake on the round deck table before grabbing his pigtailed daughter and placing her on his lap. Everyone gathered around and sang and took pictures as Jenna dug her tiny hands into the cake, stuffing her mouth with it, getting pink and white frosting everywhere. I couldn't help smiling at how cute it was. I was just glad I wasn't the one that was going to have to clean up the mess she was making.

Giselle, Chichi, and Claire started bringing out cupcakes, pizza, and trays of juice. I got something to drink but refrained from everything else, having never been much of a pizza fan and I didn't need any cupcakes. I got caught up with Forrest's mother as everyone ate and mingled and took more pictures, the kids shooting back out into the yard as soon as they scarfed down their food.

I was waiting for a good opening to try to approach Claire, but as time wore on, I started to lose my nerve. She hadn't wanted to talk to me in two years; why would it be any different now? The fact that she had at least smiled at me instead of flipping me off was enough of a victory. I needed to just take my leave and quit while I was ahead.

Instead of just leaving without a word like I was tempted to do, I waited until Forrest was mid-conversation with a couple of people before I briefly butted in and let him know I was heading out, not giving him much chance to respond as I continued towards the door to the kitchen. He looked a little disappointed, but he thanked me for coming before resuming his conversation, though I could feel his eyes on me as I walked off.

Thankfully, I didn't see Giselle as I made my retreat. I was sure she wanted me out of her house, anyway. I muttered polite goodbyes to whoever was milling around the living room as I passed through, and actually breathed a sigh of relief once I stepped onto the front porch.

"You seem like you're in a hurry."

I was halfway down the front steps as I whirled around at the sound of Claire's voice. She was sitting on the cushioned porch swing, gently rocking back and forth with her feet on the ground and looking cool and comfortable, her even gaze fixed on me.

"Oh," I cleared my throat. "Kind of, I guess."

"So I don't suppose you'd have time to shoot the breeze for a minute, huh?"

I cocked my head, confused. "Are you serious?"

"Sure." She shrugged a shoulder, stretching her legs out in front of her before lowering them. "It'll be nice to catch up. If you want."

Still not sure I wasn't being pranked, I slowly ascended the couple of stairs back up to the porch and eased over to her, looking at her warily. She noticed my apprehension and chuckled.

"You can sit down, Montrel," she insisted, patting the space next to her. "I'm not gonna splash my drink in your face or anything."

"I guess I'm just a little thrown, is all. I wasn't expecting you to be so...nice to me."

"Two years is a long time to hold a grudge. My life is great; I don't have time to dwell on the past. I swear, there's no ulterior motive here. Come on and sit down."

I relaxed some as I sat on the swing, leaving respectable space between us.

"I, um, I heard about Ms. Debra," she commented softly. "I'm so sorry; I know how much you loved her. I can only imagine how devastating that was for you."

Emotion stung my eyes automatically and I willed myself to hold it together. I still wasn't anywhere near over Ms. Debra's passing. "Extremely. Sometimes it still doesn't feel real, her being gone. I miss our talks more than I can say."

"You can still talk to her. I know it's not exactly the same but she's still with you. Do you ever go to her grave?"

I shook my head, looking absently out towards the street. "I tried once but...I couldn't take it. Seeing the dates on her tombstone just made it so...*final*. I know that might sound silly but-"

"No, no; it's not silly at all...I get it." She briefly touched my arm. "You grieve however you need to, Montrel. I was certainly emotional myself when I heard the news. I felt guilty for not going to see her before I moved, and not doing better about staying in touch after I left. Between you and me, I actually wrote her a letter to get my feelings out."

My entire body warmed upon hearing that Claire not only felt it when Ms. Debra passed, but that she'd coped in one of the same ways I did by writing her a posthumous letter. I started to mention that commonality but refrained, unsure if she'd believe me.

"She understood, Claire," I assured her. "And believe me, she got onto me plenty for driving you away. She thought as highly of you towards the end as she always did; actually asked about you a few days before she passed."

Claire's smile was sad but her relief was evident. "That's great to know."

We sat in silence for a few moments, gently rocking back and forth on the swing. Part of me was still marveling that I was actually sitting there with her. Finally.

But I figured I'd better start talking before she found an excuse to end our time together.

"How have things been going?" I asked after mentally whirling through a list of questions. Apparently that's the best I could come up with.

"Everything's great. I moved over to Brodence, in a cute cozy bungalow. Started my own little garden. I'm a school counselor at the new high school out there, and I've started working towards my PhD in Counseling Psychology."

"Oh really?" I was impressed. She'd mentioned wanting to do that a couple of times back when we were together but I honestly never thought she would. "That's great, Claire. I'm proud of you."

"Thanks. It's going to be a long road and a *lot* of work but I'm excited about it. What's been going on with you?"

My smile faded as I looked at the ground, leaning forward to rest my elbows on my knees. It was harder for her to see the shame on my face in that position. "Not much, really."

"How's Mrs. Burns?"

I rolled my eyes as I played with my freshly manicured nails. "Mother is Mother. As insufferable as ever."

"How's your wife?"

There wasn't any bitterness in her voice so I figured she wasn't trying to be snide. Still I said, "We don't have to talk about her, Claire."

"I'm not trying to be slick, Montrel, for real. I'm sincerely asking."

"There's nothing good to tell. Things are pretty much a mess with Aurora, with me, and with Aurora and I together. I don't even like going home half the time and when I do, I'm never sure which version of her I'm gonna get. It was the biggest mistake of my life, marrying that woman."

I could practically feel her shock behind me. I hadn't expected to unload like that but it just came out.

When she didn't speak after a few moments, I glanced at her over my shoulder. She blinked, still stunned. "You can gloat if you want to. I wouldn't even blame you."

"I'm not gonna do that, Montrel, come on. It's no victory to hear you're going through that."

"Really?"

"If this were a year, year and a half ago, yeah, I'd have been dancing upon hearing that things weren't going well for you and Aurora. But thankfully I've moved past all that anger and resentment I had towards you. It doesn't make me feel good to see this look you have on your face. Really, you haven't looked very happy since I first saw you outside. You've barely smiled."

"Yeah, haven't been doing a ton of that lately. It's not just my home life that's jacked up. I feel aimless, like I'm just kinda...drifting through life. Forrest and I aren't exactly rock solid right now. And Giselle hasn't wanted anything to do with me since I foolishly hurt you. And don't even get me started on what's going on with Mother."

"I'm sorry about Giselle." Claire sighed. "I tried to tell her that she needed to let that go. You two were friends before I even came into the picture."

"Yeah, well..." I sat back, heaving a sigh of my own. "That apparently doesn't matter. Her loyalty is solely with you now."

"Montrel...I really am sorry things are going so badly for you. Is there anything I can do?"

I glanced at her in surprise but she looked sincere. "Claire, that's very big of you but even if I thought there *was* something I could ask of you right now, I wouldn't. Believe me, I recognize that I brought all of this on myself with my stupid decisions."

"We all make mistakes. Doesn't mean we should be punished for them forever. Especially if we own what we did and are willing to make amends."

"Hmph. Well, I'm just trying to grin and bear it. Take my lumps; lord knows I caused you plenty. It *does* give me some comfort knowing you're thriving like you are, though. That I didn't jack things up for you to the point where you spiral into a soul-sucking abyss that leaves you bitter and living off of ice cream and peanut butter and hating everything with a dick."

"*Damn*, Montrel!" Claire burst out laughing. "Your dramatic ass needs to be writing novels or something!"

I couldn't help but chuckle. "I can keep that on the backburner, I guess."

"No, but for real," Claire said, looking over at me as she calmed herself down, "Things are going to get better. Like the song says, trouble don't last always."

"That's mildly comforting. I need to find that song and keep it on repeat. Claire, I...I want to apologize to you."

She straightened her large wooden circle earring. "Yeah?"

"For how I treated you when we were together but especially for how we parted ways. It's shameful how long it took me to realize how insensitive it was to invite you to my wedding to Aurora but when I did, I was actually embarrassed. You didn't deserve that and I sincerely apologize."

"Thank you for saying that. I was surely embarrassed, too, especially since I thought you were coming over that day to try to get back together. And I would have been foolish enough to jump at it, since I thought things were over with me and Warner, the guy I cheated on with you. I was desperate and willing to take anything, which is never good. In a warped way, you kind of did me a favor."

"How so?"

"Montrel, I didn't realize my value when I was with you. When you dumped me on my thirtieth birthday, the night wasn't even over before I was wondering how I could get you back. I'd convinced myself that us ultimately being together would be my reward if I just stayed loyal and patient, regardless of what you put me through. I let you have too much power over me, and it took something as devastating as what you did to realize it. So yeah, it hurt in the short term, but it was a much-needed lesson in the long term."

"Is that why you moved away?"

"Yeah, I needed to get my head together, and I knew I couldn't do that if I was going to be paranoid about running into you and your new wife around town, not to mention Warner, who dumped me after I cheated with you. Then with Chichi and Giselle progressing and thriving in their marriages...it was just too much. I felt myself sinking and I knew I had to make some kind of move before I lost myself completely."

"Wow. Did you know someone in Brodence? Is that why you chose to move there?"

"Didn't know a soul. A colleague referred me for the opening at the high school, and I jumped at it. Since it's only a couple of hours away, it's close enough where I can still get back here to my parents and my friends when I want to and still have my space. I started feeling at peace as soon as I got there and I knew it was the right thing for me."

"Well..." I forced a smile. "I'm glad that you had such an epiphany but I hate that I had to hurt you so badly for you to reach it."

"See, *that's* how I know you've changed," she stated emphatically, sitting forward slightly while pointing a finger at me. "The old Montrel I knew would have been patting himself on the back and taking credit for the positive turn in my life instead of feeling remorse for all the stuff he did prior to it."

She had a point. I could totally see myself doing some bullshit like that. "True enough."

"Montrel, I know it sucks, dealing with everything you're dealing with right now. And I'm sure I don't even know the half of it."

"You're right about that," I muttered.

"But you're going to be all right. Believe me. Just like I came out on the other side of my shit, so can you. You just have to be willing to do what's necessary to get it going. It's not for me to say what that is but I have a feeling you know exactly what you need to do; you just haven't been able to pull the trigger yet. But you'll get to your breaking point and then nothing will be able to stop you from making that move. And there won't be any doubts or second-guessing. But for the time being, you just have to go through."

I looked over at her in wonderment. "They should just go ahead and give you that PhD now."

She laughed. "Hey, we live and learn."

I slid my hand over, briefly touching it to hers. "Thank you, Claire. For the encouragement, for not hating me...just, thank you."

Her hand grasped mine, and I felt the electricity immediately. Her brown skin was warm and smooth. "Of course I don't hate you. Anymore."

We shared a laugh at that. I actually felt a little better. It felt good to know that someone was in my corner, which was a feeling that had been foreign in the previous weeks.

"So I guess if I asked if we could keep in touch..." I ventured, looking at her.

She smiled at me good-naturedly, giving my hand a little squeeze. "I'm not sure that would be the best idea. I don't think we're at that point yet."

Surprisingly, I wasn't dejected to hear this. It wasn't like I was actually expecting her to say yes. But I figured it wouldn't hurt to try, anyway.

And maybe she was right. I needed to focus on all the shit I was dealing with, and I didn't want to risk trying to use Claire as a sounding board for my problems. I wanted us to at least be friends at some point, but I knew I needed to get myself together first.

"I understand."

Just then, Chichi came outside. When she saw me, she frowned so hard I'm surprised she didn't cramp up.

"What the hell is this?" she spat, motioning towards our joined hands. "Claire, *please* don't tell me you're still letting him get to you. After two years, all it takes is seeing him one time before you lose all your common sense again? Didn't we exorcise this demon??"

Claire shook her head. "Chichi, stop. It's not anything like that."

Releasing Claire's hand, I stood. "You ladies enjoy the rest of your day. I'm going to head out. Claire, have a safe drive back to Brodence. It was really good to see you again."

"You too, Montrel. Though I hope you're not letting Chichi run you off."

"No, it's got nothing to do with Chichi. It's just time for me to go."

Chichi sucked her teeth and folded her arms across her ample bosom, glaring at me. I wanted to hang on to the positive vibes I'd garnered from my conversation with Claire, and I didn't want them sullied with Chichi's negativity. She was just another person who refused to let go of the past when it came to me and I was out of energy for that.

So I guess my leaving *did* have something to do with Chichi. Oh well.

I didn't even look at her as I brushed past and descended the steps towards the driveway. Knowing that Claire had forgiven me and was no longer cursing my name put a little more spring in my step. I still wasn't sure how or when, but I knew I would come through everything I was dealing with at some point. I'd actually started to believe I wouldn't; that my relationships with my wife and mother and friends were payback for how I treated Claire and others in the past. That I didn't deserve to have a wife that loved and respected me and I'd better just be happy with what I could get.

But thankfully, I now knew that wasn't the case. Like Claire said, I just had to go through.

When I made it back home, the house was empty. There was no note or text from Aurora letting me know where she was, not that I was surprised. She'd stopped giving me that courtesy a while ago. And sadly I didn't even care where, or with whom, she was.

When I went to our bedroom to grab some clothes, I paused in the doorway when I saw what a mess the room was in. Aurora's clothes and shoes were all over the place, not to mention several things knocked over on the dresser. What was really strange was her wedding dress laid out on the bed like she'd been getting it ready for wear. Curiosity led me to peek into the en suite bathroom, and I slapped a hand over my mouth and nose as soon as I opened the door. The strong smell of various perfumes thanks to several broken bottles in one of the sinks almost made my eyes water. There were various colorful dots and streaks on the white vanity thanks to open tubes of lipstick that looked like they'd just been tossed down after use. Strands of her long brown hair littered the sink and vanity and floor surrounding it.

I couldn't help but wonder what happened there. Aurora used to freak out if I left even the smallest drop of mouthwash or body oil on any of these surfaces, but clearly that hadn't been a concern when she was making this mess. It was actually a little disturbing. Even more so when I happened to glance over and see the hot pink dildo and some other silicone toy shaped like a rose in the shower niche. I knew Aurora had sex toys – we'd even used some together – but seeing them out in the open like that made me wonder. Had she had another man in my house? I'm not sure why my mind went there, but it did. I'd like to think she wouldn't go *that* far, but I clearly couldn't put much past her. I just had a gut feeling that there was more to it than just one of her marathon masturbatory shower sessions. Especially since she never left her toys sitting out before.

My head was starting to hurt, and not just from the strong perfume stench. I was even more sure something serious was going on with Aurora, as she never left things in such disarray. Did she throw a tantrum because I wouldn't take her to the birthday party? She'd been pretty emotional when I left earlier. My mind recalled her telling me she shouldn't be alone, and I'd glazed over it at the time but now I wondered just what that meant.

And when I reentered the bedroom, I noticed another silicone vibrator on the nightstand, along with a bottle of warming oil and some lubricant. When I glanced at the window, there were some weird streaks and fingerprints that I was pretty sure weren't there before. I frowned, wondering what the hell was going on.

I eased out of the room, not touching anything as if it was some kind of crime scene. Closing the door behind me, I rubbed my temples that were now throbbing with a pounding headache. If it wasn't one thing with Aurora, it was another.

You just have to go through.

The encouraged feeling I experienced after my talk with Claire not even an hour earlier had been extinguished, though her words remained. Just being in the house Aurora and I shared sucked all my mental and physical energy.

Since I hadn't eaten anything at Jenna's party, my stomach was starting to growl, but I didn't have the energy to go all the way downstairs. My head felt like it was swimming with all the events of the day as I trudged to my appointed spare bedroom and crawled onto the bed, burying my face in the pillow and putting another over my head. I wanted to just forget about everything for a while, and at some point remembered I still had a couple of the pills left that I stole from Mother's. I reached under the mattress where I'd been keeping them, then popped them dry, not having the desire to get up for any water. Then I rolled onto my back and waited for them to take me away.

Chapter 11 – Aurora

"I'm just gonna be honest with you, girl...you look like shit."

I downed the rest of my subpar Vodka Cranberry and cut my eyes at Mecca. "Thanks."

"I'm just saying. When is the last time you did your hair? And you could use a facial."

"I didn't ask you to meet me here so you could critique my appearance."

"Is there something going on?" Mecca peered at me from across the booth in the dive bar we were sitting in. I wasn't even sure of the name of it; I just recalled passing by it a few times and noticing how unimpressive it looked. But what made me turn my nose up at it then made it perfect for me now, because I wanted to go to a place as run-down as I felt. I didn't deserve nice things.

Mecca was still looking at me intently, waiting for a response. I knew I couldn't tell her everything, or even part of it. She would never understand. What's worse, I knew our friendship would be over if she heard some of the things I'd done. I didn't want her looking at me differently, like Montrel was already doing.

"I'm just dealing with some stuff, that's all," I responded lamely, swiping my fingertips under my tired eyes. I knew I had bags under them from lack of sleep. Even when I got in the bed at a decent hour, the little voices in my head and the flashbacks of all the things I'd done over the years haunted me so much that rest wasn't possible. Drinking rarely helped, but that didn't stop me from trying. I went to bed with a bottle of tequila more than I did with my husband lately.

"You know you can talk to me, right?" Mecca asked, reaching over to grab my arm. I could see the flash of concern in her eyes when she noticed how dry my skin was. Grooming hadn't exactly been at the top of my priority list lately. "Whatever is happening, you don't have to deal with it by yourself."

"Mecca..." I shook my head, eyes on my chipped nail polish. "You really have no idea. I wish I could unload all of this that I'm going through but...I can't."

"Aurora, girl, we've been friends for years. We've been through a lot of shit together. You're going to be matron of honor in my wedding. You know I would *never* judge you."

If only that were true. The Pope would judge me after the shit I'd done.

Three nights before, when Montrel refused to take me to the baby's birthday party with him, something came over me. I told myself I was going to get back at him, despite the voice in my head reminding me that he wouldn't care one way or the other, and that it would only make things worse. I made a mess getting ready and invited someone over, part of me hoping that Montrel would come home and catch us. I had that man in our bedroom. In our shower. We used my sex toys, vigorously. I was on all fours in my wedding dress as he ate and sexed me from the back. Made him fuck me against the window of our bedroom that faced the street, *wishing* that Montrel would pull up as we were going at it. But my spiteful husband couldn't even do that for me.

The next day, I had another marathon fuck session with Bron...and some other woman.

The day after that, Monday, I faked like I was sick so I could leave work early, then went trolling. I somehow ended up in the back of some middle aged White guy's Toyota 4Runner, letting him bang me from behind while I watched the kids on the playground at the school across the street through the tinted windows.

Tuesday, I called in sick and stayed in bed for half the day watching porn and masturbating, and having cyber sex with a couple of my standbys. I was purposely loud; even kicked a lamp to the floor. But Montrel didn't even notice. So the rest of the day consisted of crying and drinking. But that sadness morphed into a resentful anger and I threw on my shortest, tightest dress and headed out, cursing Montrel's name the whole time as I went straight to the sex club, aching for release. And two hours later, I had my fill in the red light room.

Wednesday, I went to back to work but it was a serious struggle. I managed to get through the work day without incident, but having no desire to go home and get ignored, I called Mecca and asked her to meet me. On the way, I got a well-timed dick pic text from the guy I named Brian and I rerouted to go get what he was offering. I didn't care that he would gloat that I'd gone back on my word about not going over there anymore yet again. I just needed him to help me feel better; help me forget, however momentarily. My pride was pretty much out the window by then. Mecca had no idea that I'd been ten minutes late because I was having anal sex on his recliner. Something Montrel wouldn't even try with me, the asshole (pun kinda intended).

Yeah, there was no way Mecca wouldn't judge me for any of that. Especially since that was just a sample size.

But if Montrel had just taken me to that party with him, this latest binge wouldn't have even happened.

I managed to get Mecca to change the subject to her pending wedding, which wasn't a much easier subject to talk about but at least it wasn't about me and my issues. As she talked about her and her fiancé Toronto's plans, I felt myself getting more and more tired. Hearing about her excitement for their marriage was like a siphon to my energy. When my phone buzzed on the table, I snatched it up and turned it over, then grabbed my purse with my other hand.

"You're leaving?" Mecca asked, startled.

"Yeah, it's Montrel; he's texting me, asking me where I am. He's worried and doesn't want me to be out too long, knowing I haven't been getting much rest lately."

"Well, that's sweet of him. But I hate you have to go."

I should've felt worse for lying to my friend like that. There was no text from Montrel; it was just a random email. But it was the perfect avenue for me to get out of there. I wasn't in the mood to hear about Mecca's blissful relationship, nor did I want to keep resisting the urge to throw cold water on her happiness. She'd learn for herself that marriage wasn't all people made it out to be, especially when you had a selfish, uncaring husband like I did.

I gave Mecca a quick hug before hurrying out the door. I'd only had two slightly watered-down drinks, but I planned on having plenty more strong ones when I got home. And

I was proud of myself for *going* straight home instead of somewhere I could try to forget my issues for a while in the most pleasurable way. I deserved some credit for that, I felt.

Montrel's car was in the garage, and I stood there eying it for a moment before sliding my key about an inch through his custom paint job, near the back. I couldn't resist. With as much pain as he was causing me, he deserved to get some of that back.

He was in the kitchen eating some Chinese takeout at the island when I walked in. When he glanced up at me, I could see something shift in his eyes as they scanned up and down my body, then roamed over my face and hair. The judgment was almost as potent as the aromas of his lo mein.

"Hey," he greeted evenly.

I tossed my keys onto the counter haphazardly and reached for the mail. "Hello."

"I have some extra wonton soup, if you want some."

"I ate already," I lied.

He put down his fork. "Are you okay, Aurora?"

"Why do you care if I'm okay or not? Oh right, you don't."

"I never said that."

"You show it by sleeping down the hall from me. Ignoring me for days on end. Not taking me with you when I ask you to. Not touching me or sexing me or even giving me so much as a fucking high five when we pass each other around here. So you didn't *have* to say it with words; your actions have shown me everything."

"Oh, you think *your* actions have been any better?" Montrel countered, all forced pleasantries gone. He stood up from the cushioned highback chair and braced his hands on the veined quartz island, eyes shooting daggers at me. "At least I'm consistent with my shit. You're all over me one day and then ignoring me the next. There was a time *you* weren't sleeping in our bed, either. And let's not even talk about what you do when you're out of this house. But you wanna throw a tantrum 'cause I didn't take you to a child's birthday party that you weren't even invited to? Give me a damn break."

"You see there, Montrel??" I threw the mail on the floor and stormed over to him, facing off over the island. "You see how you're so dismissive of my feelings? You *never* put me first! Maybe I wouldn't *need* to do anything outside of this house if my husband gave a damn about me!"

"I find it really interesting that you like to throw that 'husband' label around when it suits you. But you damn sure don't treat me like I'm your husband. Like I've said a hundred times, this marriage is a joke. You don't know the first thing about what it takes to commit to someone and consider them in your decisions, consider their feelings, put *them* first! You act like I've been so awful to you but you conveniently forget how you've treated me!"

"Excuse me for not being the model wife right out the gate. We're supposed to be there for each other, faults and all, Montrel! I still come home to you every night but I guess that doesn't count for anything, does it? *I'm* willing to dig in and work through our issues. But you're so freaking judgmental and ready to give up at the slightest-"

"Save it, Aurora, all right? Just save it!" Montrel yelled, swiping his arms through the air. "Spare me the bellyaching and whining like it's poor Aurora against the world. You are *not* blameless here! And I'm not saying I am, but at least I'm willing to acknowledge that. What, am I supposed to run up behind you, begging for your damn attention? Wait for my turn like a good little boy while you go out and do what you want? This whole damn marriage, you have been disrespecting me, Aurora, and I took it because I figured it was what I signed up for. But you know what I realized? It isn't. This is not the kind of marriage I want. I deserve better." He heaved a breath, clamping a hand on the back of his neck as he looked down at the floor for a few moments, his other hand braced on the island edge. When he finally looked back up at me, I could see the glassiness in his eyes. "I deserve better, Aurora. And you do too, but you have to want better for yourself."

His words doused some of my fire. I stood there, chest heaving, convicted.

And frustratingly, aroused.

Going at it with Montrel like that had lit another kind of fire, and it was one time I resented it. What the hell was wrong with me? Montrel's question about my being a sex addict rang through my head, but I refused to believe it was as dire as that. My being highly sexualized didn't make me an addict.

Did it?

"I get it, Montrel," I finally responded, my voice strained with trying to tamp down my unwanted desires. "I'm a terrible wife. A terrible friend. Just a terrible person all around."

He sighed, dropping his hand. "Can we not, with the pity party? That's just another way for you to make things all about you."

Running a tongue around my dry lips, I just gave a swift nod and adjusted the cardigan I'd worn over my plain white blouse and black slacks. I tucked a stray lock of hair behind my ear as my eyes fell to the floor.

"Right," I croaked. "We can't have that, can we? Oh, and you might want to check your car; looks like somebody keyed it. Probably some reckless child."

With that, I turned and shuffled out of the kitchen as Montrel rushed out to the garage, cursing loudly.

I had just put my purse into my desk drawer at work the next morning when Daria let me know that Ms. Barkley wanted to see me. Ms. Barkley was the bigwig everyone feared, and I had a feeling it was only a matter of time before she summoned me. Though I'd at least hoped to be able to get a cup of coffee first.

I quickly checked my appearance in the hand mirror I kept in my desk, glad that I'd actually put a little more effort into my appearance that day. I'd finally washed and deep conditioned my hair the night before and used some of the expensive facial care products that were littering my side of the vanity; for days, I'd been doing little more than splashing water on my face and slapping on some moisturizer. Light makeup, a red wrap dress, and leopard print Dolce & Gabbana pumps had me feeling a teeny bit like my old self, at least outwardly. I was still a mess on the inside, but I didn't have to keep walking around looking like it.

Ms. Barkley's office was on the other end of the floor, opposite from Dan's corner office. I wondered if he knew what this was about, or if he had passed the issue along to Ms. Barkley so he wouldn't have to deal with it. He hadn't been able to fully look me in the eye since I was last called into his office; maybe he didn't want to risk a repeat performance.

Her secretary who sat adjacent to her office door was on a call when I approached but she waved me ahead, silently telling me to go on in. I lightly tapped on the door as I opened it slightly, stepping inside and closing it behind me. Without even thinking about it, I locked it.

"You wanted to see me?"

Ms. Barkley swiveled around from where she'd been getting something from the large built-in cabinet behind her desk. Her sepia brown eyes gave me a quick silent assessment before motioning towards the seat in front of her desk, removing her stylish reading glasses.

"Sit."

Obeying, I crossed over and eased myself into the cushioned chair that was similar to the one in front of Dan's desk, but in a different color. Ms. Barkley reached into her desk drawer and pulled out a file, tossing it on the desk in front of me.

"You want to explain what the hell that is?" she asked coolly, nodding towards the folder.

I hated that my hands were trembling as I opened the folder and I wondered if it was noticeable. It wasn't fear; it was more a nervous excitement that was coursing through me.

"Um, these are the projections I submitted for the Walton merger. Is there a problem?"

She shook her head as if wondering if I were serious, her long black hair falling across her face. "Yes, Aurora, there is a problem. These numbers are totally off. What did you do, just bang on the keys until you filled up the page?"

Really, all I'd done was reversed a few numbers. But I didn't think it was *that* glaring. "Of course not."

"Then what's the reason for this incompetence? You know, Aurora, when we hired you, we had such high hopes. We honestly thought you were going to be running this office before it was all said and done. But lately, you've let something throw you off your game..."

Her voice faded into garbled white noise to my ears as I began really paying attention to the woman sitting in front of me. She looked to be around fifty or so. Her skin was smooth and clear and coppery brown, without a blemish in sight. I could only hope to ever apply my makeup as flawlessly as hers. Her full black hair hung past her shoulders in large waves, one falling over her right eye. And from the looks of her cleavage that was jutting out from the white fitted button-down top she was wearing, she looked to be about a 40D. My hands gripped the arms of the chair all on their own.

"Aurora."

My eyes lifted to hers. How had I never noticed how gorgeous she was before? Probably because she was usually so unpleasant.

"I'm sorry?" I breathed, running my fingertips through my hair.

"You seem distracted."

I felt myself stand and move over to the teal loveseat on the far side of the office without invitation, moving around the small round coffee table that was in front of it and dropping onto the soft cushions, running my hands along my thighs.

"Is this what you've always wanted to do with your life, Lovita?"

I could tell she was taken aback, by my addressing her by her first name and also by the subject change. She frowned as her head tilted slightly. "I beg your pardon?"

"I'm sorry; do you mind if we talk over here? It'll be easier for me to open up if it's a little less...what's the word? *Stiff.*"

Her face tightened slightly at the adjective that had been used to describe her on more than a few occasions since I'd been working there. People felt like they couldn't approach her, that she had no empathy. She sometimes tried to loosen up, but it never lasted very long. After I initially met her, I had vowed to stay on point so I'd never risk getting on her bad side.

But clearly, that ship had sailed. So I felt less inclined to keep kissing her ass.

After several moments of what I'm sure was internal debate, she finally stood from her desk and rounded it, heading over to me. She looked to be about five-eight, though the nude stilettos on her feet gave her a few inches.

Her rounded hips swayed in the rust leather skirt she wore that stopped just above her knees.

Once she was seated on the couch facing me, she fixed that stern look on me again, though I could see the hint of curiosity this time.

"What is going on with you, Aurora?" she asked me. "Do you know how many people would love your job? You do realize we gave you a chance even though you were slightly under-qualified, don't you?"

I chewed the corner of my lip, knowing that was thanks to Monroe. He certainly never let me forget it.

"I'm aware," I replied, turning in my seat. My knee almost touched hers. "And I *do* appreciate it. I guess I've just been feeling...restless. You know? When you like what you have but you still feel the urge to shake things up?"

"All right, Aurora, I'll play." Ms. Barkley, or Lovita, leaned against the back of the loveseat and rested her cheek on her fist. "Because I don't want it to be said that I didn't show concern for my employees-" her eyes narrowed, "-while they're still here."

I looked at my hands, glad I'd finally given myself a manicure the night before, too.

"What is it you feel you're missing, Aurora?"

"Excitement." The answer was almost automatic. "I used to love coming to work but lately it just hasn't been the same. Or rather, it *has*. It doesn't excite me anymore and clearly, it's affected my work."

"And that's our fault?"

"No, I'm not saying that...ugh." I buried my face in my hands. "Clearly I'm not explaining this right..."

I kept my face covered for several moments before I finally felt Lovita's warm hand gently grab my wrist, lowering it back to my lap. When I looked at her, I was surprised to see genuine compassion in her expression.

"I'm not a monster, you know," she said, lowering her voice as if she didn't want anyone to hear her admitting that. "Believe it or not, I understand what you're saying. I can't say I haven't felt it myself at any point during my time here."

"What did you do?" I asked, silently noting that she was still gripping my wrist. "When you felt that?"

"I had to take stock and reassess what it was I really wanted out of life. Took some time off and a step back."

"And it led you right back here?" My free hand covered hers, my fingertips lightly stroking her skin.

"Actually, it led me to hand in my resignation."

My eyebrows shot up. "That's a surprise."

"Dan wouldn't accept it. He said I was too much of an asset to lose and suggested I just change positions instead. Turns out he was right. A new role and a fresh outlook was just what I needed."

"Hmm. That's interesting, Lovita. Nothing like being in the right position. It means a lot that you would share that with me. I know you didn't have to."

She gently retracted her hand, as if just realizing it was still under mine. "Like I said, I'm not a monster. We're all human and we all go through things. But unfortunately, Aurora, you've been given several warnings at this point. Your time to reassess would have been months ago, when you started feeling this restlessness."

"You're right."

"We simply can't keep giving you passes for doing subpar work."

"True."

"So you understand what's about to happen, then."

I sure did.

"Yes. But before we get to that, I *have* to ask...is that Fenty?"

Thrown yet again, Lovita's matte brown lips parted slightly. "What?"

"Your bra." I ran a fingertip along my own cleavage to indicate where I could see the lace trim of her bra. "I was just curious if it was Fenty or not. I love those."

Glancing down at her chest before looking back up at me slowly, she nodded. "As a matter of fact, it is."

"Can I see it?"

Shock registered on her face. "Aurora-"

"Come on, Lovita, it's just a bra," I whispered, sliding closer to her. I smiled at her as I smoothly undid the top button of her shirt. "Don't make it a bigger deal than it is."

"Are you trying to distract me?"

"From what? Like you said, I understand what's about to happen."

She looked like she wanted to respond as I continued undoing the buttons on her shirt, but the words weren't coming. Once her push-up bra was exposed, I smiled approvingly.

"Wow, that is nice," I muttered. I was now outside of myself again and my urge had taken over. "And I like that it's the kind that snaps in the front."

Lovita gasped when I deftly undid her clasp, her hands automatically trying to hold her cups to her breasts. She looked at me like she hadn't expected me to actually do that.

"Aurora, I'm not sure what you're up to-"

"Yes, you are." I got onto my knees on the loveseat and crawled closer, slyly undoing the side of my wrap dress and letting it fall open. My flesh-toned bra and panty set was now on display, too. "You're too smart of a woman not to know. And certainly strong enough to have stopped me by now if you really wanted to."

"I like men."

"Is that what you're worried about? Honey, believe me, so do I. That's ninety-nine-point-five percent of what I go for." I gently lowered her hands, and she let me. Pushing her bra cups open like drapes, I gave her a reassuring wink. "Sometimes getting to where I'm trying to go requires a different route, that's all."

Her breath hitched when I ran a thumb over her nipple. Lovita had gorgeous breasts. I always thought I had a nice rack, but hers had mine beat, I had to admit. Heavy and full, still sitting up with just the tiniest amount of hang. Large areolas with thick nipples. Whether they were real or fake, it didn't matter.

"Lay back," I instructed in a whisper.

She only hesitated a second before she did as I told her.

"I'm gonna go ahead and take this off," I informed her, lowering the side zipper to her skirt. "Wouldn't want it getting all bunched up. It looks pretty expensive."

I was only marginally surprised when she didn't protest. She lifted her hips as I shimmied the skirt down her hips and legs, carefully laying it on the coffee table next to us. After removing my dress and laying it on top of her skirt, I eased my leg over her hips, straddling her. She bit her lip as I took both her breasts in my hands.

"I shouldn't-"

"Shhh," I stopped her, placing a finger to her lips. "You already are."

"My secretary is out there."

"Now Lovita," I reached back and undid my own bra clasp, removing it and tossing it aside. "Don't tell me you have this big beautiful office and have never fucked in it before?" I grabbed her hand and placed it on my breast, feeling her squeeze ever so slightly. My hips started a slow grind. "My office is half this size and I've surely fucked in mine."

Her eyes widened slightly as I leaned down and took her nipple into my mouth, running my tongue around it. She moaned softly, not bothering to try to put up any more resistance. Her hand slid into my hair as she arched into me, writhing. I could smell – and faintly taste - her perfume. Her skin was so soft, and warm. I continued to suck and lick her breasts as our bodies moved against each other's, the intensity growing.

Before I knew it, we were both naked on that loveseat. I mean, she had on a white shirt; couldn't risk getting my lipstick on it, right? It was just after nine o'clock in the morning; she had the whole rest of the day to go.

She was on my lap, grinding against me, her hair falling across her face as she held my head to her breast. I hungrily sucked as I matched her moves, every nerve on my body lit to full blast. This was something new for me. Outside of that drunken experience with Mecca back in college and the threesome with Bron and whatever-her-name-was, I only dealt with men. But really, Lovita being a woman didn't matter. She was a body that was bringing me pleasure. When it came down to it, that was all I cared about.

There was no kissing. The only thing my lips touched on her body were her breasts and fingers, which I licked for her before she began fondling herself. She clearly needed this as much as I did, with the reckless abandon she'd let herself fall into. So the way I saw it, I was doing her a favor.

She had just pushed me onto my back when there was a sudden knock at her door. She froze, her eyes widening in panic as she looked down at me.

"I locked it," I mouthed to her, dragging the tip of my tongue around her nipple.

She closed her eyes in relief, which quickly returned to the immense pleasure from moments before.

"Yes?" she managed to call out in a clear voice, our bodies resuming moving against each other's.

"You have a call on line two. It's a representative from Barringer."

Barringer was one of our biggest accounts. Or, theirs. I grabbed her ass, pulling her against me harder.

"Please let them know I'll have to call them back; this meeting is running longer than expected." Her voice gave absolutely no indication that she was naked and hunching someone as she spoke. "And please offer my apologies."

"Yes ma'am."

"I don't know why she doesn't just use the intercom," Lovita whispered, pushing her hair from her face.

"Looks like I'm not the only one who's incompetent."

Her hand grabbed my breast before gently tugging on my nipple, earning a slight whimper. "I *do* have things to do, Aurora. As much fun as this is..."

"Then we should concentrate so you can come, then, shouldn't we?"

And that we did. It was a hot, intense, concentrated hump session, and it was all we could do to keep our voices down. Our legs scissored, our slick breasts rubbing together as we held each other close, the friction driving us both wild. Our hands were all over each other and Lovita's lips hovered over mine, her hot pants mixing with my own. We locked eyes as we urged each other on. I almost felt like I was in a porno and partially started performing as if I was. It was *so* deliciously erotic. The practical newness of it all left me so heady I felt like I was floating.

I'd already had two orgasms by the time Lovita got her first, her body seizing as her head fell back in restrained ecstasy. I sucked one breast and fondled the other before whispering dirty encouragement in her ear, urging her through it as I careened towards orgasm number three, myself. Her hips were still winding out of control when she suddenly grabbed my chin, sticking her tongue in my mouth in an erotic finisher. I let it happen. After everything we had just done, one kiss was nothing.

When she finally calmed down, she looked at me, her chest still heaving slightly. She finally disentangled herself from me and sat there a moment before standing, and I wasted no time getting up and reaching for my clothes. I had a feeling I knew what was coming; regret, and possibly shame, on her part, for losing control like she did. Embarrassment for calling me into her office for the purpose of firing me only to end up naked and grinding on my lap. It was going to gradually overtake her as time went on, and there'd be no way she'd be able to look me in the face after that. I was all but sure of it.

Sure enough, her eyes stayed averted as she snatched up her undergarments and clothes, not saying a word to me as she stomped to her small adjoining bathroom. What a perk. Since I figured she wouldn't let me join her in there to fix myself up, I just got myself together best I could without the benefit of her amenities, using a few tissues from the holder on her desk to dab my face and chest. My hair was just the tiniest bit damp and limp, and I could just imagine how my makeup looked. At least my clothes weren't wrinkled, thanks to my forethought of getting naked.

I didn't bother saying anything to Lovita; I just left her office, strutting out with my head held high. Her secretary gave me a slightly curious look as if she was trying to place what was different about me, but I just grinned and kept walking. I didn't care about possible gossip because I was sure I wouldn't be seeing her again, anyway.

Sure enough, I got the hammer not thirty minutes after getting back to my office. Dan informed me, by email, that I was terminated effective immediately, thanks to gross incompetence and as a kicker, sexual harassment. That was hilarious. Lovita had been more than willing, but I guess it was easier to blame me than to admit to a weak moment.

Whatever. I didn't even acknowledge the email. I just left my access badge on my desk, grabbed my purse, and walked out, giving Daria a bright smile and a wave as if I was heading out to another meeting instead of leaving for good. I could see the confused look on her face, but I was sure it wouldn't take long for word to spread. Gossip was notorious for that.

I felt as free as a bird when I stepped out of that big stone and glass building and into the morning sunlight. I actually turned my face up to it and smiled. I'd worked for that company for thirteen years; it'd been fun. On to other things now.

My high was only mildly dampened when I realized Monroe would likely be hearing about my termination before the day was over with, and would no doubt have an earful for me. But oh well. I'd cross that bridge when I got to it and anyway, when he was done tearing me a new one, I'd still have gotten what I wanted, which was to no longer work there. And I needed to stop being such a punk when it came to Monroe, anyway.

Too wired to go home, I texted Mecca and Bron, asking when was the soonest they could meet up with me. Seeing as how it wasn't even eleven a.m. yet and they still *had* their jobs, both said it wouldn't be until after five. Undeterred, I entertained myself by going shopping, getting a pedicure, treating myself to a luxurious lunch, going to a movie, and just driving around, feeling like I didn't have a care in the world. It didn't even cross my mind to call Montrel. I wasn't 'giving him what he deserved' anyway; so I was sure he wouldn't be interested in my menial updates. He didn't care, so I shouldn't care.

Never mind that a big part of me wished he did, though.

Bron and Mecca were both starving so we all decided to meet up for dinner. As soon as they entered the restaurant, I gave them both big hugs and kisses on the cheek, which I could tell had them confused.

"What's going on with you, girl?" Mecca asked cautiously, taking her seat. "This is a far cry from how you were when I saw you yesterday."

"Yeah, you hit the lottery or something?" Bron joked, holding my chair out for me before taking his own seat. "That's that 'I hit the jackpot' smile."

"I kinda feel like I did," I replied, scooting my chair closer to the table. "I got fired this morning."

Their heads snapped to me, shocked.

"And you're happy about it?" Mecca marveled.

"Extremely."

"I don't get it..."

"Yeah, I knew you weren't exactly happy with the job lately but I didn't expect you to wind up fired," Brod added.

"Oh? I didn't know you were feeling like that about your job, Aurora," Mecca noted, looking back and forth between us. "How come Bron knows that and I don't?"

I was sure Bron was glad for that dark skin of his, because I could see the moment he realized his slip-up. His knowledge about my recent job apathy came via pillow talk after our latest sex marathon, after what's-her-name had left. I'd actually forgotten that I hadn't told Mecca about that, as well. But it's not like it was the only thing she was in the dark about.

"It's no big deal, girl," I smoothly assured her with a wave of my hand. "I just happened to tell Bron when we were hanging out solo one night, when I was feeling extra whiny and bitchy about it. I certainly wasn't leaving you out on purpose."

"Oh okay." She thankfully was satisfied with that explanation. "Why didn't you just resign, though? What did you have to do to get fired?"

"Gross incompetence, they said," I stated, of course leaving out the other accusation. "I'd been slacking off for a while and just ran out of chances. Really, I just quit trying. It wasn't as if I forgot how to do the job. I just no longer cared about it. But I didn't want to just up and quit for what seemed like no reason."

"What are you gonna do now?" Bron asked.

Our conversation paused as the waitress came over to take our drink and appetizer orders. Once she was gone I replied, "For the time being, nothing. I just want to be lazy for a little while."

"You've got some ends stacked then, I take it. Or is Montrel going to float you while you do your thing?"

I scoffed as I took a sip of my water. "Montrel has his money and I have mine. I'm more than prepared for this transition."

"So you must've been planning this for a while now, then," Mecca surmised.

"I've always been saving and investing, anyway," I replied, which was true. "That's been a thing since I got my very first job, at my mother's insistence. You never know what might happen so regardless, that was a given."

It was tempting to just go ahead and tell them about my trust fund. The larger part of me didn't *really* expect them to start treating me differently because of it, though I did recall their flippant comments when they learned that Montrel was a trust fund child and didn't have an actual job. I could only imagine what they'd say (or at least think) about my intentionally getting fired from a perfectly good job I'd been at for years just because I got my trust fund – which was the real reason Montrel and I married, not love, as they thought – and I wasn't interested in finding out.

I steered the subject to them, asking about their respective days at work and other things going with them. It felt so good to sit and laugh with my friends; it felt like I hadn't laughed much lately.

Mecca was taking a bite of her stuffed chicken breast when her phone buzzed. She glanced at it, a bright smile taking over her penny brown face.

"What's up?" Bron asked, nodding towards her phone as he cut into his steak.

"It's Toronto. Letting me know he's pulling up. He'll be in here in a minute."

I took a long gulp of my chardonnay. I wished Mecca had given us more of a heads-up that she had invited her man to crash our little threesome. I'd been having a great time and now my vibe was dampened a little bit. Toronto was all right but I didn't feel entirely comfortable around him. But I knew I couldn't tell Mecca that without it turning into a whole *thing*, so I just tried to keep my happy face on.

Before I knew it, here came Toronto. Tall and vaguely resembling late actor Merlin Santana, he tended to draw attention wherever he went. A couple of the female restaurant patrons kept their eyes on him as he strode over to our table.

"Hey guys," he greeted, bumping fists with Bron and leaning down to peck my cheek before giving Mecca a kiss on the lips, his fingertips under her chin. He snagged the extra chair, smoothing down his tie as he slid a little closer to his grinning fiancée. "I see y'all are already throwing down."

"I thought you were coming straight from work," Mecca commented, sliding her plate closer to him.

"Traffic. There was some accident down the street from the office and everything was at a standstill for a while." He slid her plate back over to her and looked around for the waitress. "I'm not gonna take food off your plate, babe. I'll order something for myself."

"How are things at work, man?" Bron asked him.

"I'm still adjusting. Being in the corporate office is definitely a different arena than being on the sales floor, but I'm enjoying it."

"It's a good thing you got that promotion before you and Mecca got married, though, huh? Is that what you were waiting on to propose?"

"I wouldn't say that." Toronto took a sip of Mecca's water as the waitress appeared to get his order. I checked updates on my rarely-used social media pages. There was already one missed call from Monroe, but I was in no hurry to return that.

We continued our dinner, though my appetite and energy had waned since Toronto showed up. It felt less like a celebration now that he was there. And when they all started talking about hitting up the Prism Lounge for some after-dinner drinks and hookah, I knew it was time for me to call it a wrap.

"That sounds like so much fun, y'all, but I need to get home to the hubby," I stated, motioning to the waitress for my check and avoiding Bron's pointed look. The truth about the lack of happiness in my marriage was the price I had to pay for unlimited access to his dick, and at the time I was glad to pay it, but now I could only pray he didn't call me out. Mecca would surely pitch a fit over yet another piece of information that I'd shared with Bron and not her.

"What?" Mecca whined, sinking down in her seat a little. "You sure you can't hang with us for a little while? This is the second time in a row you've invited me out and then suddenly rushed off."

"Sorry, girl." I hadn't even realized that and felt the teeniest bit guilty. "It's just that I've been out all day and my man deserves some time."

"All right. I guess I'll be doing the same thing once I'm hitched myself." She tweaked Toronto's chin before pulling him in for a quick kiss. I just hurriedly held out a hundred dollar bill to the waitress to pay for my meal, not even caring to look at the check, telling her to keep the change. She brightened, scurrying off.

I stood and grabbed my purse, going around and giving them all quick hugs and kisses (including Toronto, forcibly), and hightailed it out of the restaurant to my car. I was just unlocking the door when Monroe called again. Figuring I might as well, I went ahead and answered.

"Yes?"

"You know I'm pissed, right?"

I chuckled sarcastically as I tossed my purse in ahead of me before lowering myself into the car. "So what else is new, Monroe?"

"Where are you?"

"Don't worry about where I am."

"I know your ass isn't at work. How could you let yourself get fired? And sexual harassment, Aurora, really? You're lucky they're not suing your dumb ass."

"Whatever, Monroe. I'm no guiltier of that than you are of being kind."

"Feeling yourself now, huh? Well you know who *was* kind? Your mother. And she-"

"Yeah, that's not gonna work this time." I pulled out of the parking lot. "Try something else."

"Get your ass over here, Aurora." His voice was practically a growl, and usually it would send my nerves into overdrive when he took it there. But now, practically no effect.

"Can't. I think I'm done running every time you snap your fingers, Monroe. Maybe if you added a little sugar to the invitation, I might consider coming to visit. But my days of willingly getting berated by you are over. I don't deserve that," I added, using Montrel's words. He was good for something.

I wondered if Monroe had hung up or if I'd hit a dead spot, since there was nothing but quiet for several moments.

"Fine," he pushed out. "Look, I get that I'm a little intense. But you know I promised to look out for you."

"And you did, but I'm thirty-four now, Monroe. I don't need you the same way I did when I was twenty, when Mama passed. I'd like for us to have a relationship but this dynamic we have now isn't going to do it anymore. So either you start treating me with more respect like the grown woman I am, or we can just part ways and not talk at all. Because just like how you're always claiming that Mom would be ashamed of stuff I'm doing, she'd be just as ashamed of how you talk to me. I'm sure of it."

"All right, all right." He sighed. "I'll concede that. And I'll improve on it."

"Good. Thank you. And for the record, I *am* sorry about making you look bad to your frat brother. But I was unhappy there. And I just want to be happy, Monroe."

"Fine. I still don't love the way you went about it, but I get it. I won't keep holding it over your head."

"I appreciate that. Oh, how's Bethany?"

"I haven't seen much of her lately. She travels a lot for work, too. I'm just heading back from the airport, myself. Why don't you meet me at the house? See, I'm asking nicely. I'll order some dinner."

"I just ate. But I wouldn't mind coming by for drinks."

"Excellent. I should be there in about thirty or forty minutes, depending on traffic."

"See you then."

Glancing at the time, I knew I'd get to Monroe's house way before he would if I went straight there, so I headed home to shower and get out of my work clothes. I could still faintly smell Lovita's perfume on me, and I shook my head at the memory of us in her office hours before, pushing it out of my mind.

Montrel wasn't home, thankfully. I showered, changed into a casual off-shoulder top with matching leggings, ran a flat iron through my hair, refreshed my makeup, and headed out. Montrel's car was coming down the street as I pulled out of the driveway, and we barely acknowledged each other.

Oh well. It looked like I was actually going to end my evening on a high note, and nothing was going to mess it up.

Chapter 12 – Aurora

As much as I told myself that I didn't care what Montrel did, I was worried about him. He had grown even more despondent than he'd been before that birthday party for Forrest's daughter. In fact, speaking of Forrest, I never heard Montrel talking to him like I used to. I couldn't help but be a little curious if Montrel was still ticked about not being named godfather for Forrest's daughter or if there was some other reason.

Since the night of our latest fight, Montrel had retreated back into his shell again. He stayed holed up in the guest room for days, and when he did come out and I dared to address him, he either brushed me off or snapped at me. But his eyes seemed empty.

"Montrel." I entered the hallway when he tried to ease out of his room.

"Aurora, I don't wanna fight with you, all right?" he droned, not even looking at me as he held his hands up. "I just need to get something from downstairs."

"What is it and where did you leave it? I'll get it."

"That's not necessary. I can do it myself."

"Montrel, please let me help you. Not just with whatever it is you need to get but with whatever is going on with you. You're clearly not yourself."

"Oh, is this your caring week?" He cut his slightly-red eyes at me. "'Cause just the other day, you were going off on me and acting like I was the worst person you'd ever met. I wouldn't be surprised if you're the one that keyed my damn car."

Heat crept up my neck. I felt guilty about that but not enough to admit it to his face. "Can we at least be civil, if nothing else?"

"Tried that, remember? Then you got into one of your moods and that was shot to hell. Now, if you'll excuse me..."

He tried to continue past me but I grabbed his arm, pulling him to me for a hug. When he yanked his arm free, I grabbed his shirt, pushing him against the wall with a little more force than intended. He looked at me like I'd lost it.

"What the *fuck*??"

"I'm sorry, but we need to stop this push and pull. We've been doing that too long now." My grip remained on his shirt as I stepped directly in front of him. "Look, we're both stubborn and difficult and a pain in the ass to deal with, but we care about each other. Regardless of what either of us might say in anger, we love each other. Maybe not in the ideal way, but it's there. I'm still your Bunny and you're still my Muffin. So while we're still here under one roof, we need to be here for each other, Montrel. Why not make things as pleasant as they can possibly be?"

He stared at me for a moment. "All of that sounds lovely. But let's see if you're still feeling the same way a few days from now. We'll revisit this then."

Prying my hands off him, he stomped off down the hall. I noted his sweats and plain tee, which was not his usual attire, even around the house. Montrel *always* looked pulled together, so seeing him in wrinkled sweats and with days-old stubble was throwing me for a loop.

I wasn't blind to the fact that I likely had a large hand in Montrel's surly mood. He'd tried many times to get closer to me, to do his part towards our marriage being for love and not just on paper, and I disappointed him over and over. I lashed out at him. Shut him out. Tried to hurt him because I was hurt. Cheated on him repeatedly. I'd even stood him up for a funeral, which I was ashamed of. Then vandalized his property out of spite. I still couldn't believe I'd been so selfish and inconsiderate towards him.

My conscience burned when I remembered yet another thing I'd kept Montrel in the dark about. The morning after he agreed to go to Monroe's with me and I woke him up by putting my head between his legs, my lashing out when he tried to keep me in bed with him was out of panic that he'd somehow discover I'd caught Chlamydia. I'd been kicking myself for being in that position in the first place, feeling stupid for being so incredibly careless. That was why I didn't try anything with him when we were cuddling watching a movie later that night after our date where we agreed to try to be more romantic with each other; I wasn't about to risk passing it to Montrel. I still had a couple more days of antibiotics at that point.

As I usually did, instead of facing it and dealing with it, I tried to push that shameful memory out of my mind. Like if I went long enough without acknowledging it, it was almost like it didn't happen.

Since Montrel had been living on junk food and takeout for days - even more proof that he wasn't himself – I decided to cook him a nice dinner. It had become my mission to take care of Montrel, and since I didn't have to worry about work stressing me out, I had more time to do that.

I rinsed off some shrimp in a colander in the kitchen sink as I thought back to the last few nights. Montrel had started talking in his sleep, and I could hear him despite him being down the hall. When I got out of bed and moved closer to the guest room door, I could hear constant rustling of sheets, like he was tossing and turning. I was sure he was because he'd been doing that when he was still sleeping in our bed with me, though it wasn't every single night. But now it was, and I couldn't help but wonder what triggered it.

I knew he missed Claire. But it didn't hit me just how much until recently. He must have seen her at Forrest's, at the birthday party. Did she reject him? Tell him she missed him, too? Did they touch, hug, kiss? I didn't know anything about Claire, but I knew Montrel pretty well. And I certainly never heard him call out *my* name in his sleep. He wanted her back, and the fact that he couldn't have her was turning him into this disheveled mess that was stomping around and isolating himself, not wanting to be bothered.

And I'm sure I hadn't helped things with the way I'd treated him. The fact that I was essentially a consolation prize didn't matter; he tried. Montrel sincerely tried to make our marriage work and I just let him down over and over. I could just imagine what my mother would say, if she were still alive.

Short of getting Claire to take Montrel back, I wondered what I could do to better things. I'd clearly failed in my mission to fall in love with him the way he wanted, and I could only imagine it was mutual. Maybe we just weren't built for that, or at least, I wasn't. I still maintained that I loved him as much as I was capable of loving anyone. But I couldn't expect that to be good enough for him long-term. Maybe some men would have been just fine with our arrangement, but I hadn't chosen any of them; I'd chosen Montrel. And now, while I had my money, I'd also repeatedly hurt someone I cared about.

And what's worse, he *still* didn't know the depths of everything I'd done.

Maybe he was right; maybe we needed to just let this go. My shoulders sagged at the thought, and tears stung my eyes.

My phone chimed with a text, and when I saw it was a message from an unsaved number, I ignored it. It was likely from someone I'd met when I was in one of my zones, and I didn't want to be tempted.

Once I'd finished preparing a meal of shrimp and grits and toasted French bread with honey butter, I cut up some fruit, drizzled it with agave (I actually sometimes missed him calling me that), put it all on a tray with a bottle of sparkling water, and headed upstairs. I could hear Montrel moving around behind the guest room door as I approached.

"Montrel," I called out, gently knocking with the side of my elbow. "I made you something to eat."

The movement stopped. I braced myself for him to send me away, but to my relief, he quietly opened the door, eying the tray. He took it from me, his eyes barely reaching my face.

"Thanks," he mumbled.

"You're welcome. Do you mind if I sit in here and keep you company? We don't have to talk if you don't want to."

He sighed, but shrugged as he carefully placed the tray on the bed. "Suit yourself."

I entered the room, perching myself on the opposite side of the bed. I didn't try to get too comfortable, for fear he'd think I was pushing it and kick me out. Montrel ate his food in silence, finishing most of it and the water before wiping his mouth and sitting against the headboard.

"Thanks, Aurora."

I gave him a small smile. "My pleasure."

"I was thinking about what you said," he continued, his hands on his stomach and his legs stretched out in front of him and crossed at the ankles. "I don't think we should stay married, Aurora. We're just making each other miserable, and for what? You've got your money, so you don't need me. And I'd like to end this before we get to where we hate each other. *Truly* hate each other."

I looked down at my finger tracing a design on the tan bedspread. "You're right."

"But like you said, while we're both here, we might as well try to be civil. I'm just...I'm exhausted, Aurora. I feel crushed in this house, in this marriage. And that's no way to live. So if you're willing to agree to keep it together for however much longer we're in this, I will, too."

Sucking in a long breath, I looked over at him. He was already looking at me intently.

"That's fair," I softly conceded. "And I'm not sure how long you had in mind, but would you be willing to stay until my birthday?"

"That's three months away."

"Yeah. I'd just like to at least have that with you. Then, if you still feel you need to leave, I'll respect it and won't try to stop you."

He quietly pondered my request before eventually shrugging. "That's reasonable, I guess."

"Thank you."

I took his tray back down to the kitchen before rejoining him in his room. We just sat on the bed and talked. I told him about my breakthrough with Monroe. He told me what was going on with his mother and her new beau. Then the conversation strayed to outside things, even though there were plenty more issues related to us that we could have used that opportunity to dive into. But I sensed that he didn't want to touch on anything potentially volatile at the moment, which for the time being, I was on board with.

When Montrel started to yawn a few too many times, I suggested we call it a night.

"Would you consider coming back to sleep in our room?" I asked him. "We don't have to do anything. I just hate you sleeping way down the hall from me."

"I suppose, yeah."

Smiling, I gently grabbed his hand and led him out of the guest room. He opted to take a shower, and I kept my distance, despite the mild urge to ease in there with him. But I waited until he was done before taking mine, and then we climbed into bed.

I placed a hand on his arm, waiting for him to look over at me. "I love you, Montrel. Sincerely."

He gave some semblance of a smile. "I love you, too."

Instead of kissing his lips like I started to, I just lifted his hand and kissed that instead. We laid there just staring at each other, and I noticed that the earlier lines on his face had eased. He didn't look as tense. Since we'd agreed to end our marriage amicably, that heaviness had clearly been lifted from his shoulders. It hurt to know that I was causing him so much stress, but there was no need in acting like I hadn't. I had not been an easy wife to have, or even just an easy person to live with.

But at least we had three pleasant months to look forward to. I wasn't worried at all about messing things up before my birthday deadline. It finally felt like we were on the same page, even though there was still a lot more that needed to be admitted to and purged. I wasn't exactly looking forward to the idea of Montrel knowing the down and dirty about me, but I knew I'd have to cross that bridge before I burned it.

We both drifted off to sleep, our fingers touching in the middle of the bed. I wanted to cuddle, but I hadn't been getting the sense that Montrel was trying to amp up the affection, and we hadn't talked about any physical parameters during this last three months in the house together. I'd need to venture the subject, though, because I knew trying to go that long without any kind of sexual touch was going to be pretty close to impossible for me. Especially since we were trying to be pleasant to each other. And I wanted to refrain from going elsewhere for pleasure, for once, so hopefully Montrel would oblige me. A sexually frustrated Aurora was *not* fun to be around; I knew that better than anyone.

It was still dark in the room when I felt Montrel start to rustle in his sleep some time later in the night. My eyes eased open to see him moving around, his legs tangled in the sheets, a deep frown on his face as he grunted in frustration.

"Claire."

My eyes widened.

"Claire," he groaned, a little louder this time. He flopped onto his back, his hand sliding diagonally down his chest before his fist pounded into the bed. "Claire!"

My lips mashed together, watching him. He looked like he was in complete anguish.

Sitting up, I quietly removed my nightshirt, dropping it off the side of the bed to the floor. I was naked underneath. Carefully pulling the sheets from around and between Montrel's legs, I placed a hand to his chest, running it gently back and forth.

"Shhh..." I soothed, leaning close to his ear. "I'm right here, baby."

"Claire?"

"Yes, Montrel, it's Claire. Try to calm down, okay? I've got you."

His hand grabbed my arm and held onto it, as if afraid I'd disappear. His other arm snaked around my waist, pulling me closer.

"I missed you so much, Claire."

"I know." I felt the emotion start to pelt like hail on a car hood. "I missed you, too."

"Come closer." He squeezed me. "I need you to be closer."

I snuggled my body as close as possible, lifting my leg over his. He moaned, and I could feel his dick stir against my shin. His hand that was holding my arm slid up to my shoulder, and he turned to face me. His eyes never opened. It really seemed as if he felt he was dreaming.

"Kiss me."

I obliged him. Gently at first, and then I felt his tongue begin to search for mine. The urgency built quickly, and in no time he was kissing me desperately, one hand clawed to the side of my face. He clutched my body, his hips beginning to move. I moaned, unable to help it.

"You like that?" he whispered against my lips. "I still remember what you like. I remember everything about us, sweetheart."

I hastily swiped at my tears before caressing his face. I needed to keep myself together, because this wasn't about me. This was about giving Montrel, the man I cared about, something he so clearly needed.

"Can we make love? It's been so long, Claire."

"Of course, baby." I slid his shirt up and over his head before easing his pajama bottoms down. His body writhed, eager and ready. I stroked his hardness a few times before mounting, sliding down onto him and releasing a shaky breath. "Like this?"

"Yes, just like that." He dug the back of his head into the pillow as he bit his bottom lip, moving in rhythm with me. "Fuck yes, just like that, Claire."

We continued to make love, with Montrel thinking I was Claire and me pretending to be her. I indulged him for as long as he wanted until he finally drifted into a peaceful sleep for the first time in probably a long while, holding me tightly and blissfully unaware of my silent tears.

The next morning, I woke up around nine o'clock in bed alone. I looked down and frowned, temporarily forgetting why I was naked, then I remembered. It felt strange, what Montrel and I had done the previous night. That was definitely something I hadn't experienced before, and while on one hand it was hurtful to hear him call out for another woman and think he was touching her like I wanted him to actually touch me, on the other, I was glad that I could give him that peace. I at least owed him that.

When I noticed some delicious aromas coming from the kitchen, I figured Montrel must have ordered breakfast.

"Good morning," Montrel greeted cheerfully when I made my way down to the kitchen. I had to wonder if I was still dreaming when I saw him cooking. Like, actually *cooking*, not just pouring his overnight oats into a bowl like he usually did. He smiled at me, a genuine smile. "How'd you sleep?"

"I slept great," I replied, returning his smile. "What about you? You certainly look more refreshed than I've seen you in a while."

"I am. Last night was just what I needed."

I paused. Did he know that it was me making love to him and not Claire? I wasn't about to ask, in case he didn't. Nor did I want to outwardly question if he was so happy because we'd agreed to end our marriage. The last thing I wanted to do was anything that would bust up this good mood.

"Um, what's going on, Montrel?" I eyed the omelet he was tending to as well as the blueberry waffles and turkey bacon that were already plated. "You...*you* made all this?"

"I did." He casually flipped the omelet. "You're welcome to some, if you want."

"Since when do you know how to do all this? I thought you couldn't cook."

"I never said I couldn't cook." He grabbed a plate with his left hand and slid the omelet onto it with his right, as if it was the most natural thing in the world. "I *don't* cook. Doesn't mean I can't."

I just stood there with my mouth open, in clear shock. Learning that Montrel could cook floored me. What else didn't I know about him? I felt both closer to him and...also like I didn't quite know who I was married to.

And it wasn't lost on me that he felt this urge to display his hidden culinary skills the morning after what he thought was dream sex with Claire.

"Aren't you going to be late for work?" he asked, glancing at the time on his phone.

"Oh..." I shook my head, snapping out of my momentary trance. I'd forgotten he didn't know about my firing yet. "I don't work there anymore."

"What?" He looked genuinely surprised. "So you finally turned in your resignation, huh? I know you talked about it but I figured you'd changed your mind, considering how much time had passed."

I should have corrected him and let him know the real deal behind my termination, but I just continued to the refrigerator, pulling it open. "It was finally time. It got to the point where I couldn't drag it out anymore."

"I see. Any plans for what's next?"

"As far as my career, not really. I know I'll transition into something else soon enough." I pulled out some orange pineapple juice, pausing as I set the jug on the counter, then turning to him thoughtfully. "What do you think about us taking a trip together?"

He looked to be considering it, to my relief. "A trip, huh?"

"Why not? We've reached this truce, we're going to be here together for a little while longer, we've got nothing hindering us now. It can just be a fun getaway, wherever we want."

"For how long?"

"It could be two weeks or it could be a month. We've got the freedom and the means to do as we please; let's take advantage of it. We've never just taken a fun trip together. Other than our honeymoon, when is the last time you've traveled anywhere?"

His head reared in thought. "Years, I admit. And for no real reason, either. I just...haven't."

"Well, we can. If you want. The offer is on the table. But I really hope you consider it."

We ate breakfast together at our kitchen table for the first time since we married, falling into easy conversation. The smile hardly left my face as I looked at my husband. My heart felt so full. Why couldn't it always have been like this? Why did I feel closest to him after we made the decision to part ways? I wanted to suggest that we forget about divorcing and give it one last sincere shot...maybe even go to counseling, if he was up for it. The thought of airing all of our issues didn't excite me but if that was what it would take for Montrel and I to move forward together, I'd be willing.

Whenever I started to bring it up, though, I lost my nerve. I just kept imagining Montrel letting me down, however easily. I decided that over breakfast wasn't the time. We could spend the day together, continuing the nice rapport we currently had, and I'd slowly ramp up the romance between us, hopefully reminding him of how good we could be together. Then I'd make him a luxurious dinner, with the dessert hopefully being each other. When he was on his post-coital high, *then* I'd mention it.

After we finished eating, I offered to do the dishes and Montrel went to the living room with his laptop. My mind wandered to my new plans for the day, giddy that I had all the free time in the world now. Grinning, I swung my hips side to side as I washed the dishes, feeling like things were finally taking a turn for the better. I really felt like Montrel and I could save our marriage after all, despite our agreement the night before.

Then there was a hard banging on the front door. I glanced at the small security monitor in the corner of the counter and stiffened when I saw it was Mecca. Especially since she looked absolutely pissed.

"Hold on!" Montrel yelled, and I panicked, realizing he was going to answer the door. It was a brief moment when I wished he was still holed up in the guest room and he wouldn't get to see what I knew was going to be an ugly scene. I ran out to the living room, but he was already pulling the front door open.

"Where is that *bitch*!"

Immediately scowling, Montrel faced up to Mecca, blocking me. "Excuse me?"

"Montrel," I gently grabbed his shoulder, pulling him back. "Let me deal with this."

"Nah, I don't appreciate her just showing up, disrespecting our house like that!"

Mecca scoffed, her eyes shooting fire at me. She folded her arms across her chest and shifted her weight to one leg, radiating attitude. "Well, ask your *wife* how she disrespected *me* by fucking my damn fiancé!"

I winced, literally shaking as I stood frozen to that spot, as Montrel slowly turned and looked at me.

Chapter 13 – Montrel

"What is she talking about, Aurora?"

I couldn't believe what I'd just heard. Mecca had come pounding on my door, ready to throw hands, and I'd been all set to defend Aurora, feeling closer to her after the previous night and our breakfast together. But that was before I heard what had Mecca so pissed off.

And considering how shook Aurora was looking, I was inclined to believe she was guilty.

Rapidly licking her lips, Aurora's eyes warily shot back and forth between me and Mecca, tentative hands extended in both of our directions. "I can explain, Mecca..."

"Wait, so it's true?" I jumped in, gaping at her. I knew Aurora was no girl scout but I didn't think she'd go so far as to mess with her friend's man.

"Montrel, I ...please, let me just get this out. This is hard enough."

Mecca just stood there, nostrils flared, foot tapping, breathing fire. Her chest heaved hard and fast as she glared at Aurora, waiting on how she could possibly explain herself. I was curious, myself, and took a step back. It didn't directly involve me but I still wanted to know.

"Okay..." Aurora hedged. She took a deep breath, lifting her eyes to Mecca. "He wasn't your fiancé yet, which is what started it. I knew you were getting really anxious and impatient about Toronto proposing. So I went to talk to him to see what his intentions were, on your behalf. He admitted that he was trying to save up the money to buy you a nice ring. He'd just gotten promoted but you know he had to help with his dad's hospital bills, and-"

"Yeah yeah yeah, get on with it," Mecca snapped.

Aurora swallowed nervously. "So I told him I'd pay for your engagement ring if he promised he'd go ahead and propose. He was still kind of on the fence...not because he didn't want to marry you, but because he wanted to get the ring himself, even if he had to wait. He said it felt like he'd be less than a man, having to resort to that. So I..."

Mecca's head jutted forward. "You...?"

Sighing, Aurora dropped her hands. "I seduced him. But it wasn't anything malicious. It was totally in the effort of building his confidence back up; he knew you were getting impatient and frustrated, and he hated that it was taking him so long to get you a really nice ring on his own, and *I* hated seeing how dejected he looked. It was just about making him feel good about himself; that's all. He proposed to you two days later."

My damn jaw was on the floor. What the fuck was I hearing? And did Aurora think she was making herself sound any better? Actually seducing her best friend's man just to give him a damn pick-me-up?

Mecca just stood there, staring at Aurora, her head barely moving side to side.

"It meant absolutely nothing, to either of us," Aurora felt the need to continue, clearly not knowing how to quit while she was ahead. "It was a one-time thing. And in the end, everybody got what they wanted. Mecca..." She stupidly stepped forward. "I'm so sorry you're angry. But please understand that I was just trying to help, the both of you."

Nothing happened for a few moments before Mecca finally snapped and lunged for Aurora, clawing at her face, her hair, and anything else she could get to. Aurora screamed, trying to defend herself. I stepped in because I felt like I had to, grabbing Mecca by the waist and pulling her away, though I admit I struggled a little bit. She wasn't going to be easily deterred.

"I cannot *believe* you!" she screamed, tears now running down her face. "Your deluded-ass mind actually thinks you did me a fucking favor?? If Toronto hadn't felt so guilty, you would've taken this to the damn grave! You're supposed to be my girl! I knew you did some wild shit but I never in a million years thought you'd do no shit like this to *me*!"

"Mecca!" Aurora hiccupped, getting up from where she'd stumbled to the floor after the attack. "I'm sorry! I'm so sorry!"

"The hell you are! You're just sorry you got called out!" Mecca pushed my arms away, swiping at her angry tears as the sadness started to take over her eyes. "There is no coming back from this one, Aurora. You are so dead to me."

Those words had Aurora crumbling at the waist. "No! I can't lose you too, Mecca, please..."

"You need to get some help," Mecca spat before turning for the door. "If I wasn't sure about it before, I'm damn sure about it now. Something is off in your damn brain. And you need to get it fixed. The next woman might not let you off so easy."

With that, Mecca stormed out.

Aurora stood there sobbing, her hands crossed over her chest and clutching her shirt. In just about any other situation, I'd have taken her into my arms and tried to comfort her. But I found myself not even wanting to touch her.

"How could you do something like that?" I asked, my voice low.

She shook her head, but didn't look at me. "Please, don't."

"Don't, what? Am I not supposed to say anything about this? You expect me to just pretend like this never happened?"

"I..." She sniffed and wiped her eyes. "I get it if you feel some kind of way about it. But please don't judge me."

"Seriously?"

Her back straightened. I could see the scratches Mecca left on her face. "Yes. Seriously. I never claimed to be perfect. I made a mistake, all right? But more than anything, I'm still your wife. That should earn me some empathy and compassion from you."

Mecca had a point when she said something was off in Aurora's brain. "So you want me to be empathetic and compassionate about you seducing your best friend's man, who she'd been with for years, and you had no plans of telling her about it yourself? And what do you need any empathy for, anyway, if you think you were *just trying to help* like you said?"

"Montrel, I just lost one of my best friends. I can't do this with you right now."

"Now or later, it won't matter."

She sucked her teeth and turned away from me, hanging her head and linking her fingers behind her neck. I thought maybe she was trying to find the words to better explain herself, and I was curious as to what she would come up with.

"Ugh, *stop it*!!" she practically screamed suddenly as she whirled back around, making me jump. Her eyes looked crazed and bugged, and I felt myself go on alert. It was like a switch was flipped and she went from devastated to hysterical just like that. "You do not get to stand in judgment of me! Are you perfect, Montrel? I don't think so! And anyway, part of this is *your* fault!"

My head jerked back, my brows contorting in incredulousness. "How the fuck do you figure *that*??"

"If you weren't ignoring me at the time, *again*, I wouldn't have even had time to be worried about Mecca and Toronto's relationship! But you were too busy stomping around here like a little *bitch* so I had to occupy myself elsewhere. So before you go pointing the finger at me, realize your part in all this!"

This woman was nuts. Assorted.

I started to respond, but stopped myself. There wasn't even a need to dignify that foolishness with a response. She was just trying to absolve herself any way she could, and I wasn't taking the bait.

Leaving her standing there, I turned and went upstairs, unable to look at her anymore.

Needing to get out of the house, I went for an impromptu massage in a futile attempt to relieve some of the tension that had overtaken my body in the couple of hours I'd been up. Just when I was actually feeling positively about Aurora and me...when we had *finally* reached an understanding about us and our relationship, and I felt we could iron out the mess we'd made of things enough to part ways on a good-enough note. And true enough, Aurora was hardly a saint. But, come on. She actually seemed to think she was doing a *good* thing by seducing her friend's boyfriend. I just...my head was still swimming from that whole scene.

The massage helped a tiny bit, but unfortunately, it didn't erase the happenings from that morning. I didn't know how I was going to handle Aurora going forward. I couldn't just treat it like any of her many other indiscretions. Even if I tried to twist it to make myself focus on how she *thought* she was trying to help her friend and wasn't just intending to be a backstabbing slut, it was still going to be really hard not to look at her differently after that.

These last three months couldn't pass fast enough.

As turned off as I was by Aurora's actions, I still tried to check myself at least a little bit. I might not have done anything as egregious as she did but I was no stranger to hurting people I loved, unfortunately. All the pain I'd inflicted on Claire during our relationship certainly wasn't something I was proud of. And just like Aurora, I had tried to justify my actions and finagle my way out of looking like the bad guy, saying I was doing Claire a favor by dumping her, regardless of how insensitively I did it. And now I couldn't even sleep most nights because I was missing her so much. Remembering that humbled me considerably.

I had several missed calls from Mother when I finished with my massage, and when I saw she'd texted me, too, I was actually alarmed. Mother didn't text. She always claimed that was an uneducated, juvenile, lazy way of communicating. But she'd sent me one in all caps, asking where I was and pleading with me to call her back.

A thin thread of concern emerged as I dialed her number once I was back in my car. I wondered if something happened to her, like she'd been robbed or attacked or something. Turned out I was right about one of those, in a way.

"That bastard ran off with my money!"

The concern from moments before evaporated as I leaned my head against the headrest with a sigh. "How much did you give him?"

"Five hundred thousand dollars!"

I winced. I didn't think it was going to be *that* much. "Wow, Mother."

"'Wow'? Is that all you have to say??"

"Mother, what do you expect me to say? I tried to warn you. Told you there was something about him I didn't trust. Told you not to give him any money. You refused to listen."

"Because I trusted him!" She actually sounded like she was near tears, which was foreign. The last time I saw Mother cry had been at Father's funeral. "We'd been dating a few months and he made me feel so wonderful..."

"And that's lovely, but that's no reason to give someone half a million dollars."

"Montrel, he had a business plan. He'd been working on this since before he met me."

"Did you run any kind of background check on him? Did you get a business manager to look over the business plan? Draw up any contracts with an attorney?"

She got quiet.

"Mother, come on..."

"I do not need a lecture, Montrel. This is upsetting enough."

"Well, I'm sorry, and maybe it's insensitive to say 'I told you so', but I did."

"You could show a little compassion, you know."

That seemed to be the party line that day.

"It sounds to me like he had you so drunk off infatuation that you didn't use any common sense, Mother. You gave that man all that money without doing any kind of due diligence, and I know you know better. So again, I'm not sure what it is you expect me to say to you right now. At least he didn't bankrupt you."

"You could offer to help me find him! He's turned off his phone, he vacated his house; he just disappeared!"

"You've heard of these people called private investigators, right? Hire one of those. I don't have the bandwidth to get involved in this mess of yours right now; I have my own issues."

She actually gasped. "I am your *mother*! Whatever it is you're dealing with can be put aside!"

Of course. Instead of her showing some compassion of her own and actually asking what my issues were, she just automatically expected me to throw them aside so I could fix her fuck-up.

"Mother," I sat up straighter in my seat and started my car, "You're not going to like what I'm about to say but I'm going to say it, anyway. This, what you're dealing with? *Your* problem. You're not some senile old woman. You *let* yourself get swindled, and now you want *me* to deal with it, even though I tried to warn you. And I'm telling you that I do not have time. I've been dealing with a myriad of issues for months but you don't care about that, because you *never* bother to ask what's going on with me. All you ever want to do is talk about *your* shit, lecture, give me unsolicited advice, brag on whatever pseudo-important person you met or stupidly expensive thing you bought, and then you go about your business. You want me to have something for you that you don't have for me, and for whatever reason, you don't see anything wrong with that. But there *is* something wrong with that, Mother. And until you realize that, we don't need to communicate."

Her breath hitched. "What are you saying?"

"Like I said, you're not an idiot. I think I was pretty clear."

"Are you really distancing yourself from me? When I need you most?"

"And you still don't get it. I love you, Mother, I do. Even if I don't like you very much, I still love you, and I've shown it. And it would be nice if you loved me back. I'm done letting you stress me out. So, good luck with this James situation. I have to go."

"Montrel-"

"And let the record show that you *still* haven't asked what's going on with me."

I hung up, looking at the phone before dropping it in my lap. My eyes drifted to the rearview mirror, staring at myself for several moments before finally putting the car in reverse and leaving the parking lot.

That didn't feel great, but it needed to be done. Annie Burns may have birthed me, but she hardly acted like a mother. And I was simply no longer interested in tolerating her shit out of obligation. I was her son and I'd still see about her, but from a distance. I meant it when I said I wasn't letting her stress me out anymore.

Hell, if it wasn't for her meddling, I'd have never even met Aurora.

I was still processing that call when my phone rang again. Thinking it might be Mother calling me back, I didn't even glance at the dashboard screen displaying the caller ID. But when it immediately rang again, I sucked my teeth and took a look as I pulled up at a stop light. My eyebrows shot up when I saw it was Forrest.

It was only because I was still keyed up that I went ahead and answered.

"Yeah."

"You really know how to hold a grudge, huh?"

"Picked up some tips on that from your wife. And I've had nothing to say."

"Really, Montrel? Look...I get it. When I thought about it later, I could see how you would feel some kind of way about not being Jenna's godfather, and my explanation admittedly wasn't the smoothest. And I'm sure it didn't help that it came in the middle of all the shit you're dealing with at home. It doesn't mean you're not still important to us, though, or that we don't want you in our lives."

"One of you doesn't."

"For what it's worth, I've told Giselle she was taking this too far. It's been over two years, and from what I understand, even Claire has forgiven you by now. It would be nice if we could all just move on from that."

"Yeah, well. It's not me that's doing it."

"Where are you? Your voice sounds strange."

"I'm driving."

"I gathered that. Where are you going?"

"I don't know. Not in a particular hurry to go home, I know that."

"You should come through."

"I'm good. I've been in enough tense environments lately as it is."

"Man, Giselle isn't even here. She took Jenna to some playdate thing."

"She's gotta come back at some point."

"Montrel." Forrest's voice was strong. "We've been boys too long for this. I'm asking you to come through so we can deal with our shit. And not just that; I can tell you've got some stuff on your mind and before you say I won't wanna hear it, I'm more than willing to listen if you need to unload. I'm still here for you just like I've always been, man."

I started to rebuff his invitation again but felt myself start steering my car in the direction of his house. I missed my friend. And he was right, I did need to unload.

"I'll be there shortly."

If I didn't know better I'd think Forrest breathed a tiny sigh of relief. "I'll be here."

I got to Forrest's house in about twenty minutes. By then I'd managed to convince myself to finally be transparent about my situation. I'd always been too embarrassed to admit the full extent of it before, but that was irrelevant by this point. Pride had already kept me in my marriage at least eighteen months longer than I should have stayed so I didn't need to let it keep me from hiding the real deal from my best friend.

By the time I got to Forrest's, I was wired and ready to vent. We parked it in the den and I told him about how things *really* were in my marriage, starting from when I found Aurora jacking off the hotel employee on our honeymoon to what I found out about her just that morning. I didn't try to leave anything out, even the parts that made my face flush some with resentment or embarrassment. It felt good to finally admit all of that, and hearing the rundown, I had to wonder why the hell I still had anything to do with this woman.

Forrest looked positively floored. Several moments passed before he could even find his voice.

"I knew she was taking you through some things but I had no idea it was on *that* level," he finally marveled. "Montrel, you're married to a sex addict."

Even though I had suggested as much to Aurora myself a while back, partially in jest, I had to admit it made sense, though I was certainly no authority.

"She got really incensed when I said something about that before," I told him, mindlessly rubbing my hands together in front of me.

"A hit dog will holler, they say. I know I'm not that kind of doctor but I'd be willing to bet just about anything on it. And you've only told me the stuff you know about; there's no telling what she does when she dips out in the middle of the night or stays gone all day without a word."

He had a point. I always assumed she was probably with another man but for all I knew, that was just the tip of the iceberg. Was it the same man every time? Did she have threesomes? Orgies? Did she mess with married men? People I knew? Strangers? Hell, did she even use protection when she was with these people? The thought made me cringe, remembering the times I went inside of her raw. We'd stopped using condoms when we got married, but in hindsight, that had been foolish of me since I knew she wasn't being faithful even then. I realized there was so much about Aurora I still didn't know.

Thankfully I was tested regularly and had a clean bill of health. So that was something to be grateful for.

Heaving a heavy sigh, I flopped against the back of the couch. I didn't even have the energy to get into the issue between me and Forrest, or my still-stumped career direction or the situation with Mother. All of that would have to wait. This was plenty for now.

"I can't believe I actually chose this woman over Claire," I muttered disgustedly. "And for such an adolescent reason as sex. To even say that out loud is humiliating."

Forrest clamped a hand on my shoulder. "No need in beating yourself up. You made a dumb decision but it doesn't have to be permanent."

"Even if I divorce Aurora tomorrow, it doesn't mean I'll get Claire back. She wasn't even ready to stay in touch. I understood, and I respect it, but I still wish it was different. I've even been dreaming about her."

"You have?"

"Yeah, man. And they're so frighteningly vivid; I can almost *feel* her. I miss her more than I've ever missed anyone, but at the same time, I know I don't deserve her. I put Claire through a lot. And she's doing so well for herself now that I wouldn't want to do anything to disrupt that. I'm just grateful she doesn't hate me and has graced me with forgiveness."

"Wow, Montrel," Forrest marveled, looking as if he didn't recognize me. "You're sounding incredibly mature right now. I never thought I'd see the day."

"Thanks a lot."

He quickly held up his hands. "I didn't mean it like that."

"Whatever. It is what it is. Whatever you, Claire, Giselle, or anyone else thinks of me, I brought it on myself. And my marriage to Aurora is clearly my punishment."

"Montrel, man...yeah, you did some bad shit. But that doesn't make you a bad person. You're *not* one. You stopped trying to make excuses, owned your shit and you apologized. And I can tell you've changed. Look at what you just said a moment ago; the Montrel from two and a half years ago wasn't mature enough for that perspective. Whether you ever get Claire back in your life or not, please don't think that you deserve a lifetime of punishment."

"He's right, you know."

I whirled around to see Giselle standing in the opening of the room, looking at me with kindness I hadn't seen from her in over two years. I wondered just how much she'd heard.

She continued into the room, rounding the leather couch I was sitting on and joining me, taking my hand in hers.

"Montrel, I want to apologize to you," she announced, looking right into my eyes. "I've let myself get carried away with my anger over what happened between you and Claire. Yes, she's one of my best friends. But you are, too, and you have been since the night I met you and Forrest at that party in college. You've always held a special place in my heart for your role in me and Forrest getting together. I shouldn't have shut you out like I did, and certainly not for this long. I'm sincerely sorry for that."

I looked over at Forrest, almost as if I expected them both to bust out laughing and tell me I was being punked. But he was just looking at his wife with a small smile and pride in his eyes.

Turning my attention back to Giselle, I placed my other hand over our joined ones, a grateful smile spreading across my face. "That means a lot, Giselle. I know I deserved some vitriol."

"Some. But like Forrest said, you're not a bad person, and I know that. Treating you like the devil when you've made sincere effort to make amends doesn't make me any better than you. I'd really like it if we could get our friendship back on track."

"I'd like that, too."

She leaned over and gave me a firm hug, and I felt myself get a little emotional. I'd honestly never thought we'd get to this point. It was a relief to know that my friendship with Giselle wasn't permanently damaged like I thought.

"And there's no law that says Jenna can't have two godfathers," Forrest commented as Giselle and I separated. "Regardless of the decisions you've made in your romantic relationships, Giselle and I always knew that you'd take the best possible care of Jenna if we needed you to."

"I would. But please don't feel like you have to pacify me."

"Shut up. That's not what we're doing."

"Yeah, Montrel, Forrest and I talked about this," Giselle chimed in. "And I'll readily admit that my refusal of you being Jenna's godfather was out of spite. Forrest's brother is great but he doesn't even live around here. And Jenna *loves* her Uncle Montrel. So we really would like for you to be another godfather to her."

"I can be the *primary* godfather, right?" I pressed, only partially joking. "Like, I would get her before he would. Since I'm the one that's actually here and spends more time with her. And like you said, she *loves* her Uncle Montrel..."

Giselle giggled while Forrest just shook his head, a good-natured smile on his lips.

"Fine, you nut. If it'll make you feel better, you can be the *primary* godfather. You want us to sign it in blood, too?"

"Putting it in writing is good enough."

"Ugh. *Fine.*"

"So what to do you say, Montrel?" Giselle asked, her hands clamping my knee as Forrest muttered under his breath about how spoiled I was. Guilty. "Please say yes."

Not having the desire to keep delaying when I really wanted to accept, I just nodded graciously. "Yes."

"Yay!" Giselle threw her arms around me again, and I laughed as I hugged her back. At least that was one more thing I could be grateful for.

I ended up hanging out at their house for a few more hours, accepting their invitation to stay for lunch. It felt good having my closest friends back and I wasn't in a hurry to leave. We ate, talked, got caught up on some things (I didn't tell Giselle the depth of my Aurora issues; just that we were headed for divorce), and I spent a good amount of time with little Jenna. I didn't have a ton of experience with kids but it felt good to be silly and playful with my adorable goddaughter, who had Giselle's wild curly hair, Forrest's droopy eyes, and a mix of Giselle's light and Forrest's dark skin coloring. I loved getting that extended time with her, since the only times I'd gotten to see her before was when Giselle wasn't home or whenever Forrest would bring her over to see me. And I unashamedly melted whenever she put those little arms around my neck in a hug or laid her head on my chest. I readily admitted she had me whipped already.

"When are you two gonna start working on baby number two?" I asked Forrest as Jenna and I played with some blocks.

Forrest hunched a shoulder as he perused something on his laptop. "We're not."

I looked at him in surprise. "Really? I thought you wanted at least one more."

"We did, but with all the issues we had conceiving Jenna, nobody wants that stress again. We're fine with it being just the three of us. If God sees fit to bless us with another child, great. But we're good with what we've got."

"Wow. That's surprising but I get it. As long as you guys are happy."

"Yeah, we are. Extremely happy, actually."

By the time I finally left Forrest and Giselle's, I was actually feeling pretty happy myself. It had been an emotional day, and it felt good that some things were finally starting to turn in the right direction. I'd finally put some distance between me and Mother like I should've done years ago. My friendships with Forrest and Giselle were renewed, and I had a new goddaughter, officially. It gave me some hope that maybe, *maybe*, there'd be a way to salvage what was left of me and Aurora's relationship. As much sense as it made, I still wasn't entirely sure about Forrest's sex addict diagnosis for Aurora; maybe I just didn't want to believe such a thing about her. But perhaps I could at least get her to admit she had *some* kind of issue. That would be a first step towards us riding our marriage out as amicably as possible.

But I knew that was out the window when I got home and heard her sexing another man in my house.

This woman had a lot of damn nerve. After that whole situation earlier that morning, she actually brought some man over there. Clearly, she was trying to taunt me. Or maybe this was her way of getting back at me for what she perceived to be my part in the whole Mecca situation. Either way, I was pissed at her audacity. It was one thing to go out and do her dirt but to bring it to our house? Ultimate disrespect.

It sounded like they were in the media room. I could hear the grunts and groans and pants as I ventured down the hall, keeping my steps light so as not to tip them off that I was there. Clearly they'd been too caught up in the throes of passion to hear the front door open. Either that, or she'd reached the point where she didn't care if I heard or not. It wouldn't have surprised me if she *wanted* to get caught. She had to know I could come back at any time.

I just wanted her to see me see her. That way there'd be no way she could finesse her way out of it.

When I made it to the media room, it was dark except for the muted music video playing on the huge screen. I peeked around the doorway and could see the back of Aurora's body, glistening with sweat, straddling the lap of some long-legged man. Her hair was in a haphazard high ponytail. His hands were on her ass, guiding her as she grinded on him with an almost animalistic intensity. She was actually growling, holding onto the back of the couch they were on with both hands. The light from the screen flickered over them. I was practically transfixed as I tiptoed into the room, eyes on Aurora. Neither she nor her sex buddy even noticed as I approached; his face was buried in her cleavage and her eyes were fixated on some spot on the wall in front of her.

The guy let out a noise, then slapped Aurora's ass, giving her a gruff order.

"Bounce on this dick."

She automatically obliged as if she'd been programmed. But I felt a cold wave wash over me as I recognized that voice. But there was no way. There was just no fucking way.

No longer trying to be discreet, I stormed the rest of the way over to them. The guy lifted his head from between Aurora's breasts enough for me to make out his face. My suspicions confirmed, I felt like I was going to throw up.

Aurora was fucking her stepfather, Monroe.

Chapter 14 – Montrel

They didn't even notice me at first. It wasn't until I actually dropped onto the couch next to them that they stopped what they were doing.

"Montrel!" Aurora screamed, trying to cover her breasts. As if that would make any damn difference at that point.

"Oh shit…" Monroe muttered, looking back and forth from me to Aurora. But surprisingly, he didn't try to move or cover himself or anything. He even kept his hold on her ass.

Just like that, my shock instantly morphed into rage and I leapt off the couch, looking around for something to throw or hit them with. I both hated and loved that I didn't have a gun in the house because I surely would have used it on both of them right then.

Aurora was scrambling off Monroe's lap, looking around for something to cover herself with as she pleaded with me to give her a chance to explain.

"Explain??" I screeched, not even recognizing my own voice in that moment. I grabbed a pillow and hurled it at Monroe's head, since that was all I could get my hands on. Then I apparently remembered I had fists and lunged for him, only getting in a couple of good punches to his face before Aurora scurried over and pried herself between us, her hands braced against my chest.

"Montrel, please!" she pleaded, hiccupping. She tried to turn my face to hers but I was still glowering at Monroe, who was looking a little too unbothered for my sake. He had stood and was slowly getting his things together, in no damn hurry whatsoever. It only pissed me off more. "Montrel, baby, I know this looks bad but I can explain this!"

"Get your fucking hands off me!" I yelled, knocking her hands away. Suddenly the idea of her touching me was disgusting. "You are fucking *sick*! Both of y'all!"

"Listen to her, Montrel," Monroe coolly instructed, moving his jaw side to side and checking his face for blood before he pulled his shirt on and started buttoning it. His pants were pulled up, but the clasp remained undone. "Everything isn't as it seems."

"Shut up and get out!" Aurora turned and screamed at him, sticking her hands in her hair. It seemed the realization of what she'd done was just hitting her. "Oh my god, oh my god..."

"Don't turn this on me. This was what you wanted when you invited me over here, remember?" Monroe actually smirked as he grabbed his shoes, not bothering to put them on before he strolled out of the room. This bastard actually thought this was funny. Yeah, it was definitely a good thing I didn't have a gun.

Aurora looked at me with panicked eyes, as if what he just said could possibly make me think any less of her. The sight of her standing there, naked, knowing she'd just gotten off her stepfather's lap, *in my house*, made my stomach lurch. I ran to the nearest bathroom, a naked Aurora on my heels, slamming the door in her face and lifting the toilet lid just in time to hurl what felt like everything I'd eaten that week. I clutched the porcelain bowl as I wretched, loudly, the images of Aurora and Monroe keeping me on my knees.

What the hell kind of woman did I marry??

She was incessantly knocking at the door, asking if I was all right. I wanted to tell her to leave me the hell alone, to go lay out in traffic under a weighted blanket, but I couldn't make myself talk right then.

I don't even know how much time passed before I finally pushed myself up off the floor. My body felt heavy as I washed my hands and splashed some water on my face, looking underneath the sink for some mouthwash. I looked at the practically full bottle and briefly wondered what it would do to me if I just chugged the whole thing like Gatorade. But the thought was fleeting, thankfully. Aurora damn sure wasn't worth trying to kill myself over.

She was curled up on the floor opposite the door, knees to her chest, when I finally emerged. Her fingers tangled together in front of her face as she looked up at me, tearful and whimpering. I just shot her a steel-melting look before rolling my eyes and heading off down the hallway.

I heard her footsteps behind me, her bare feet slapping against the hardwood floor. I went to our bedroom and started pulling out suitcases. When she saw this, the tears just started flowing faster.

"Montrel, can I please explain what you just saw?"

"I'm well aware of what I just saw."

"You don't know the whole story. Please, *please* listen?"

I had just pulled open my underwear drawer but stopped and turned to her, my arms folded across my chest. Sheer morbid curiosity had me actually wanting to hear what she had to say.

She took a deep breath. "Okay, well, you know that-"

"I need you to put on some damn clothes first. I'd rather not look at you like that."

She looked surprised, but dutifully moved over to pull one of her nightshirts out of the drawer and slip it over her head, running her fingers through her wild, thick hair. Once she was covered, she continued.

"You already know Monroe and I never had a very close relationship," she began. I thought about making a snide comment but refrained. "We never developed any kind of real bond after he married my mother since he was always away so much for work, so I never *really* saw him as a father figure. I didn't even refer to or think of him as my stepfather; he was just a man my mother brought into our lives. I barely ever saw them show any affection towards each other. What you saw downstairs...that didn't start until I was well into adulthood, and *way* after my mother passed. It was totally consensual. And since I know there's no point in leaving anything out at this point...I'm the one that initially seduced him."

Shocker.

"He refused me at first," Aurora continued, crossing her arms over her stomach and looking down at her white-painted toenails. "But I took it as a challenge and just upped my efforts. Then one night, I slipped something in his drink. Nothing too bad; it was just supposed to make him extra randy and willing. And it worked. But after that night - which he remembered - he said he didn't think we needed to do it again, as much as he admitted to enjoying it."

"What'd you do the next time, club him over the head?"

I saw her ears twitch. "I let myself in using my spare key late one night and joined him in bed. Went down on him. Explained that I just wanted sex and that's it. He was hesitant but he came around. After that night, we started sleeping together kind of regularly."

"So all those times he would summon you over there, those were booty calls?"

"Not always, no. A lot of the time it really was to reprimand me for something, or just an obligatory visit. It *did* usually end with us doing some kind of sexual activity, though. I...I couldn't help myself."

"So why did you always act like you hated going? Or like you were scared of him or something?"

"*Because* I couldn't seem to help myself around him. I was never actually scared of Monroe; I was scared of what I wanted to do whenever I was around him. It wasn't like I didn't recognize how twisted it was, carrying on a sexual relationship with my stepfather, whether I thought of him as one or not. But at times...my body and my urges just take over. Just about every time I left from one of our trysts, I felt ashamed. But I never seemed to remember that when the next time rolled around."

I just stood there staring at her. I was slightly less disgusted after her explanation, but not by much.

"You need to get you some help, Aurora," I stated. "Do you not recognize that?"

"I...I don't know..."

"Well, I do. You have to realize it for yourself, though. Either way, this marriage is a wrap."

Her head snapped up. "I thought we agreed to stay together until after my birthday."

"That went out the window when I saw you fucking your stepfather. And that's bad enough, but you brought him here to do it. What, were you trying to rub it in my face? Taunt me? Did you think I wouldn't care?"

She expelled a series of quick breaths, her chest caving in. "Montrel, I'll admit that I was still angry when I invited Monroe here. It *was* out of spite and yes, I wanted you to catch us. But I realize that was wrong."

"Hell of a time to realize that, Aurora. The fact that it would even enter your mind is telling enough. You asked me before what my breaking point would be, right? Well, here we are."

"I get it; I have issues!" she exclaimed, her hands swiping her face before clutching handfuls of her hair, pacing in a small circle. "But Montrel, please understand that I don't even realize what I'm doing a lot of the time. I...I might not be the ideal wife or even the ideal friend but everything I've ever said about the love I have for you is the truth."

"It may be, Aurora. But clearly, your issues are far stronger than any feelings you might have for me. And I'm not living like this anymore. I'm leaving here tonight and will have my attorney get the divorce papers to you ASAP. I'm not spending another night under the same roof with a sex addict."

She whirled around to me, her arms flailing. "I am *not* a-"

"Will you fucking get real, Aurora?? Listen to the shit you said. You seduced your own damn stepfather; hell, you *drugged* him to get what you wanted! You said you don't even realize what you're doing, that your urges take over; that means you're powerless to it. Then you feel all this shame and remorse afterwards, but it's only a matter of time before you're giving in to it again. You have an addiction, Aurora, and it has taken over you. If I had the stomach for it, I'd challenge you to break down every encounter you've had with anyone else since we've been married, and I wouldn't be surprised if you couldn't even remember them all, or who all of them were. *You seduced your best friend's man*, Aurora, remember?? Thinking you were being some kind of damn savior. You do all this shit –and I'm sure there's *plenty* more I don't know about – with *no* regard for the consequences afterwards. Don't tell me you're not a sex addict." I snatched up a handful of my boxer briefs from the drawer and stuffed them into my open suitcase. "And the sooner you realize that, the better."

Before I could blink, she was on her knees in front of me, burying her face in my crotch as her hands fumbled with the button on my pants. The desperation on her face was as clear as day. I shook my head.

"Aurora, get up," I ordered, grabbing her hands and stepping back.

"No, Montrel, please; just let me make it up to you!" She yanked her hand from my grasp and grabbed my dick through my pants, squeezing as she looked up at me hopefully. Her other hand was tearing at her nightshirt. In that moment, I felt like I didn't even recognize her. "I can make this right! Just let me-"

"Look at yourself, dammit!" I yelled, grabbing her shoulders and shaking her slightly. "Do you see what you're doing?? Do you fucking realize that you are *always* trying to fix things with sex? That that's your answer for everything? How many times have you asked to 'make something up to me' by going for my dick? After what I *just* caught you doing not an hour ago, and the shit you just admitted to, you're here on your knees thinking a fucking blow job is going to make things right! *Look at yourself!*"

She stilled, my words sinking in for a moment before she crumbled into a ball on the floor, the realization overcoming her. Her body shook with sobs and loud wails of shame. I just stood there and looked down at her, feeling a distant sense of pity. I started to reach for her, but stopped myself. As sad as it was, I didn't trust her getting too close to me. She was going to have to pick herself up.

I went on about my packing, moving around Aurora, who continued to cry and sulk on the floor. I didn't even try to pack everything; I'd have to make arrangements to get the rest of my things another time. I just took enough to sustain me for the next few days.

When I was about to walk out of the room with my suitcases in hand, Aurora called out to me. I stopped and looked back at her.

"I'm sorry," she whimpered.

I just pursed my lips. "Yeah. You are."

I went back to my old house that I lived in prior to marrying Aurora. Something told me to hang onto it, and I was glad I did. Aurora didn't know I still had it, but I think her secret was a little direr than mine.

Being in my old space brought me a welcomed sense of relief. I never really felt at home in that house Aurora insisted we buy. I had no hand in the décor or anything, because I didn't care to. But this house was all me.

"What a fucking *day*," I muttered, flopping onto the couch and throwing an arm over my eyes. I never would have predicted things turning out like they did in a million years.

Of course I'd known Aurora liked sex. A lot. That had been evident since she emerged in her underwear after our first date and tried to seduce me. And yes, she turned me out; I might have rebuffed her on our first date but I fell under her spell on our second. She had me hooked with a capital H, spending multiple consecutive days with her, going whenever she called because I couldn't get enough. I went from not even being interested at first to not being able to get enough of her. It helped when she revealed that she was only interested in me because I had my own money and wouldn't need hers. I had honestly made up my mind to be with Claire until that night. But Aurora changed my mind, and I convinced myself that marrying her so she could get her trust fund and I could get all the amazing sex I wanted was the better move.

Man, I really had *no* idea what I was getting into.

I always thought she was just sexually free; even hypersexual. It never occurred to me that she would have an actual addiction, even though that diagnosis was still unofficial. Now that the proverbial light had been turned on, my mind raced over *so* many instances that should have tipped me off. But since I was vacillating between apathy and indulgence, I never noticed. Or maybe I just turned a blind eye. Even when I thought she was just an oversexed cheater, I still stayed, and made excuses to myself for doing so. Justified her behavior and my allowance of it. If I'm honest, I knew something was off.

Even seeing her with Monroe just now; it was clear she'd been in a zone. There was no kissing or caresses. Aurora wasn't even looking at him. From what I'd been able to see of her face, there was no emotion. Her body was just moving to get what it wanted, almost on autopilot.

Suddenly Claire's advice from the day I saw her at Jenna's birthday party rang through my head:

"Just like I came out on the other side of my shit, so can you. You just have to be willing to do what's necessary to get it going. It's not for me to say what that is but I have a feeling you know exactly what you need to do; you just haven't been able to pull the trigger yet. But you'll get to your breaking point and then nothing will be able to stop you from making that move. And there won't be any doubts or second-guessing."

She was right on the money. I'd known I needed to leave Aurora alone for a while but kept delaying actually doing it. Divorce papers had been drawn up but not served. I kept giving her the benefit of the doubt over and over, or trying to assure myself we could make the best of things. But that was over. I'd finally reached my breaking point and knew what needed to be done. No doubts, no second-guessing.

And like Claire said, I'd come out on the other side of it. And I did know exactly what I needed to do for that to happen.

The heels of my hands dug into my tired eyes, my energy officially gone. I'd call my attorney in the morning. For the time being, I just wanted to get into my bed, bury myself under the covers, and forget everything and everyone for a while.

Chapter 15 – Montrel

I jumped at the sound of loud, persistent knocks on my door. My eyes eased open to darkness, and I realized I was still underneath my comforter. I could hear rain outside.

It took me a minute to get my bearings, and remember what day it was and why I was back in my old bed. Then flashes of the previous evening began scrolling through my mind, and my minor headache bloomed into a not-minor one. The damn knocking on my door surely wasn't helping any.

Apparently they weren't deterred by the fact that I was taking my sweet time rolling out of bed and digging some slippers out of my closet.

"Who is it?" I barked as I shuffled to the door.

"It's your mother."

I froze. Sure sounded like her. But when I peeked through the peephole and yanked the door open, I can't say it looked like the Annie Burns I was used to. Her hair was out of its usual French roll or bun and hanging around her shoulders (and looked like it had been finger-combed, at best), her face was makeup-free, and she was wearing casual clothing. Well, wide-legged cotton pants and a cashmere sweater were casual for her.

"How did you know I was over here?" I asked, blocking the doorway.

"I tried you at home but no one was there. Something told me to try here. Call it a mother's hunch."

I resisted the strong urge to roll my eyes. "What do you want?"

"I'd like to speak with you, if I may."

I just looked at her.

She shifted under my glare. "And need I remind you, it *is* raining out here."

Sighing, I stepped aside. "Come in."

"Thank you."

She stepped inside, closing her umbrella before leaving it near the door. I was already back in the living room dropping onto the far end of the couch. She strolled into the room and stood for a moment, surveying (and likely critiquing) the space that was decorated in fern and umber colors, which was a far cry from her (and Aurora's) preference of damn near everything being white. I just eyed her, wondering what the hell it was she wanted. But I waited patiently. It wasn't like I had anything else to do.

When she finally finished assessing and lowered herself into the armchair, she held her Dior purse in her lap with both hands and looked at me. "This is nice, your house. I always assumed it was bigger."

"The space is sufficient. It's just me here."

"Speaking of that, why *are* you back here? Did you and Aurora have a fight?"

"You could say that."

"Was it really necessary to move out, though? Marriage requires diligence and working through difficult times. You can't just run away when things are less than ideal."

I told myself to count to ten before responding. "Why are you here, Mother? I know you didn't track me down to give me unsolicited marriage advice. Especially considering you've never come to visit me before."

Her brow bent slightly. "Of course I h-"

"You haven't. I lived in this house twelve years, and you never graced my doorstep. Not because I never invited you; I have. Several times. But you were always smooth with the excuses as to why you couldn't come by. Our visits always had to be at your house, because that was more convenient for *you*. Are you really going to try to act like you don't remember that?"

She softly cleared her throat as her eyes dropped to the floor. "All right, I acknowledge that. That's part of the reason I'm here, Montrel; I haven't been able to get the things you said when we last spoke out of my mind. It's hard to admit, but you had a point."

I blinked. Was I still asleep? "Seriously?"

"You have always tried to be there for me since your father died, and I suppose I've taken that for granted. And I've clearly forgotten that I need to return the favor. I know I don't say it nearly enough, but I *do* appreciate you, Montrel. You're my only son and I-I love you. And it wasn't until you separated yourself that I realized just how much. I..." Her fingers tightened on her purse. "I don't want to lose you from my life."

I just sat and processed her words. Heartfelt moments weren't a thing between us. Part of me couldn't help but doubt her sincerity, figuring her loneliness was driving her to say whatever she felt was necessary in order to get things back to the way they were. But the other part gave her the benefit of the doubt. Mother had a lot of faults, but she wasn't evil. She might've been snooty and selfish as hell but that didn't mean she didn't love me *at all*.

"I appreciate you saying that," I finally replied. "Though I hope you understand my caution."

"You want me to prove it." Her hand lifted briefly. "I understand. And I'm more than willing."

We'll see. "All right. Well, in any case, it's nice of you to make the effort."

A quiet moment passed, neither of us knowing what to do next. This was unfamiliar territory. I thought about offering her some breakfast, but remembered I didn't have any groceries.

"So are you willing to tell me what's going on with you and Aurora?" Mother finally spoke up. "I promise not to judge. I'm just showing concern."

"All right," I conceded with a sigh. I wasn't eager to recall the things that happened with Aurora but I did appreciate the clear effort Mother was making. "Aurora and I are getting a divorce. I left her last night."

"What happened?"

"In short, she's a sex addict."

Her purse fell from her lap and despite myself, I couldn't help chuckling. The shock on her face was hilarious.

She slowly retrieved her purse. "Are you being serious with me, Montrel?"

"I'm absolutely serious. And sadly, that wasn't the only issue. Aurora and I never should have gotten married in the first place. We didn't love each other, at least not like we should have. It was essentially a business deal."

Mother's head cocked to the side. "What do you mean?"

"Aurora only married me to get her trust fund. When you met her and started hyping me up, letting her know how well off I am, it convinced her I'd be the ideal person. She wouldn't have to worry about me trying to get her money since I have my own. That was the sole reason she got with me."

"I...I had no idea..."

"I know you didn't. She put on an act for the both of us."

"And you found this out after you married?"

"No, before. She told me the truth when I went to let her know that I couldn't see her anymore because I wanted to commit to Claire."

"I thought that you and Aurora fell in love and that was the reason you married." Mother shook her head, trying to wrap her brain around all of this new information. "If you were going to commit to Claire, how then did you come to marry Aurora?"

"Sex."

Mother's face turned beet red, and I had to resist the urge to laugh again.

"As embarrassing as that is to admit, I chose Aurora over a woman I sincerely loved because Aurora was amazing in the sack," I continued. "And the thought of having access to that every day overtook my common sense. I deluded myself into believing that helping her get her money in exchange for access to her amazing sex was a good idea."

"My goodness..."

"I'll spare you the details because I don't have the energy to get into it and also, I don't want you to have a heart attack. But Aurora has a serious problem and she needs to be focused on getting the help she needs. And I need to find what's going to make me happy and fulfilled, which I've been anything but these past two and a half years."

"I wasn't aware you were so unhappy." Mother looked away in shame. "But I suppose I couldn't have been, since I never asked. Just like you said."

I nodded, not wanting to rub it in.

"And to think that I badgered you to give Aurora another chance. If I'm honest, I didn't even know much of anything about her outside of the superficial. And I never had much of anything good to say about Claire-"

"No, you didn't," I couldn't resist. She blinked at the hard edge in my voice, and I released a long breath, rubbing the back of my neck in an effort to chill out. "But I can't blame you for losing Claire. I'm the one that made the stupid decision to choose Aurora over her, and for such an immature reason. That was on me."

"Even so, I was never very kind to her. I'm sure that didn't help any."

"It was a point of contention. And my not checking you enough for that didn't help any. As easy as it would be to point the finger at you, I messed things up between me and Claire plenty without your help. I took her for granted and didn't appreciate what I had, thinking I had all the time in the world to be ready and she'd just be there whenever I felt like I was. That was *my* foolish mistake. I'd love another chance with her but I've accepted that it probably won't happen; Claire has moved on and is doing well for herself, and I'm not trying to cause her any more headaches. Thankfully she's forgiven me, though, so..." I spread my hands briefly before clamping them together, "I'll just have to be happy with that."

Mother and I talked a while longer before she left, saying she needed to go meet with the private investigator she'd hired to track down James, who was still on the loose, apparently. She admitted that she got with him partially out of loneliness and because she wanted to 'try a different kind of man', and her willingness to invest in his business was an effort to do something with her life since she'd been feeling stagnant. Clearly something she forgot when she was scoffing at me for wanting to get my own career.

Speaking of which, Forrest called a few hours after Mother left with something that managed to take my mind off of my drama.

"Hey, do you remember Dustin Drake?"

I'd been putting away the groceries I'd had delivered and paused at the question, frowning slightly. "The name sounds familiar. We went to school with him, right?"

"Yeah. He's frat, and moved up to New York after graduation to dive into the fashion industry."

"Yeah? What, as a model or something?"

"At first, but he apparently realized he didn't have the stomach for that. What he *did* find his passion for, though, was fashion design. He's been putting in time for years working as an assistant and with a couple of theater companies, and now he's ready to break out and do his own thing."

"Good for him."

"He's down here visiting his folks and I ran into him at the barbershop. When he said that he was working on a high-end menswear line, I might have brought your name up and mentioned that you were looking to branch out, yourself. To my surprise, he absolutely remembered you and what a clothes nut you are."

"Was that his descriptor or yours?"

"You're focusing on the wrong thing, Montrel. He wants to talk to you about possibly collaborating with him on his line. Maybe even being the face of it. He follows you on social media and apparently the occasional posts you put up showing off what you have on makes him think you'd be good to work with."

The bag of avocados in my hand fell onto the counter. "Seriously? I'd think he'd want someone with actual experience. I only posted my outfits on social media for the hell of it. Surely he has a bunch of contacts that would be more adept at-"

"Dumb ass, I'm telling you that this man possibly wants to work with you. You've been looking for something to do with your life. You're into this fashion shit. This could be the opportunity you wanted. Why are you trying to brush it off?"

Hell, why *was* I trying to brush it off? I'd been beating my head against the wall trying to figure out what it was I wanted to do and now, something that seemed right up my alley was falling into my lap.

"Good point," I admitted, unable to resist a chuckle. "I guess I was just caught off guard but it *does* sound like a good opportunity."

"It could be. Of course, you two will have to talk and discuss all the particulars and see if you think you'd vibe together, so it's not a lock yet. But he's definitely eager to talk to you. I told him I'd run it by you and see what you thought, but I'm gonna tell you now, if you don't call that man back immediately I will come to that house and beat your ass until you can't move anything but your eyelids."

"There's no need to go there. I have every intention of calling him."

And I did. The more I thought about what Forrest said Dustin was looking for, the more intrigued I got. And when I called him that evening and got an even better understanding of what he was trying to do, I felt myself get excited.

"I want a new face for my line, Montrel, and nobody I've met so far has fit my vision," Dustin told me during our call. "It was getting frustrating, actually. When Forrest mentioned you, and then I saw your social media posts, it just clicked in my head. With your face and your build, not to mention your style sense, I think this could really work. And as much as I love menswear, my personal style leans more towards t-shirts and jeans. My idea of getting dressed up is throwing on a Henley."

I laughed, hoping he didn't think I was mocking him. But that was comical to me. "Wow, Dustin. I wear those around the house."

He chuckled. "I totally believe that."

"I can't help but wonder, though, why you wouldn't just do a more casual line, then."

"Done it. At least, I've assisted on those. And it was fine but it didn't really challenge me. I want to step out of my comfort zone with this. And I've always loved stylish menswear even if I don't wear much of it myself."

"Okay, I can understand that. I'm flattered that you think I'd be an asset, despite my lack of experience in the industry."

"Nobody has experience until they do. You have to start somewhere. And we're not going to Fashion Week tomorrow; this is going to be a long road. We're not starting from totally nothing thanks to my contacts and the investors I already have in place but there's still a ton of work to be done. I want this done right, and I won't cut corners. Montrel, I've waited this long to branch out on my own for a reason, and have every confidence that the Dustin Drake line will be a success. And I'd love to have you on board, if you're interested."

He didn't have to ask me twice. I was very much interested.

It was exhilarating, this whole thing, and a welcome distraction from the other things going on in my life. The divorce papers had been served to Aurora but she had yet to sign. We hadn't spoken since the night I left her crying on the bedroom floor, and I couldn't help but wonder how she was doing. Part of me wanted to check on her, but the bigger part was too stubborn to reach out.

I'd tried to block out the vision of Aurora and Monroe from my memory. It was still too embarrassing to tell anyone about, even though I knew I wasn't the one that should've been ashamed. I guess I was still blaming myself for even being in that situation, but I knew I'd have to get past that. Yes, I married Aurora for the wrong reasons, and yes, I should have focused on Claire like my heart really wanted to do. But I had no idea Aurora was a sex addict. I couldn't have predicted this outcome in a thousand years, and continuously beating myself up over my decisions wasn't going to change anything. What's done was done. I just needed to move on with my life.

A week after I left her, Aurora called. I was just getting off a conference call with Dustin and our attorneys, going over the particulars of our partnership, and the giddiness I was feeling from that was doused when I saw her name on my caller ID.

"Hello, Montrel," she softly greeted when I answered.

"Aurora." I told myself to keep my cool, though I *was* relieved to hear from her. It had occurred to me that leaving her alone in the state she'd been in that night could have led to disastrous results, with her harming herself or worse. But thankfully, that wasn't the case. "What's up?"

"I'd like to see you. Can I come over? Or can you come here?"

"For?"

"There's some things I'd like to say to you and I'd rather not do it over the phone."

"I see. Well, I hope you can understand why I'd prefer not to be alone with you. I'm willing to meet, but it needs to be in public."

A beat passed before she responded. "Fine, if that's what you want. I suppose I can't blame you for that."

So we agreed to meet at the nearby recreational baseball field where a team was holding practice. I had absolutely no interest in the sport, but figured being out in the open and near children would be enough of a deterrent in case she felt a sudden urge to try to make a move for my dick.

"Thank you for meeting me," Aurora said when we were settled on the metal bleachers flanking the field. I was surprised to see her in a baseball cap pulled low over her eyes. I'd never before seen her wear one of those. And the baggy hoodie and sweats she wore made me wonder if she was trying to be inconspicuous or if she was just in too much turmoil to worry about being cute.

"No problem. What's on your mind?"

"Montrel, I've been in a personal hell these past few days," she began, lightly scraping the nails of her right hand repeatedly along her left palm. She still wore her wedding ring. I'd taken my wedding band off the night I left our house. "After you left, I spent a good two or three days going through anger, denial, self-pity...and when I finished with all that, I had to admit that you were right with what you said. I *do* have a problem."

Glancing at her, I tried to measure my response. This wasn't a time to be petty. "I'm glad you came to that realization. Acknowledging it is the first step."

"Yeah." She sighed, biting her bottom lip. "I remember the first time I touched myself, Montrel. Like it was yesterday. I was thirteen. I'm not even sure what made me do it; I just recall exploring my body and discovering that there were ways I could make myself feel good, all by myself.

It was like a treasure trove. That first orgasm was...it was mind-blowing. And I was hooked.

"I started sneaking and touching myself constantly. And when that started not being enough, I started using objects. I didn't have the nerve to try to sneak sex toys into the house, so I was humping pillows, using electric toothbrushes, rubbing my breasts against the grooves between the tiles of the shower. Anything could be used as a possible avenue for pleasure. Then I began looking to boys for that and lost my virginity at fifteen. Sex became all I thought about; the rush of it, the various ways people could please each other. The desire became ingrained, and I needed it like I needed food and water. Even hiding it from my mother became part of the thrill. She was super conservative and wanted me to wait for marriage. If she'd had *any* idea of what I was doing, she'd have stuck me in the nearest convent."

"Wow." Hearing how all of this started for Aurora was enlightening. Most people might just think she was a tramp but it went so much deeper than that. "That makes everything make more sense."

"Even so, you didn't deserve how I treated you, Montrel. Conventional marriage or not, it wasn't fair to you because you had no idea what you were signing up for. I should have been honest with you about...me. My desires and urges for sex only multiplied over the years, and it got to where I could barely control them; when they took over, satisfying them was the only thing that mattered. It was my go-to, just like you said. But I sincerely never thought of myself as an addict. Since you left, though, I've been doing some reading up on it and I can't deny it anymore. I started seeing a therapist yesterday."

"That's great, Aurora. Really." I reached over and placed a hand on her knee, waiting for her to look at me. When she did, I gently lifted her cap enough so I could see her eyes and continued, "I'm proud of you for that. I can only imagine that coming to these realizations hasn't been easy."

"No. It's been the hardest thing I've had to do. But it's necessary. When I looked around and realized I had no one; that I'd driven my friends away thanks to my...my addiction, I had to accept some hard truths."

"Mecca still hasn't forgiven you, then, I take it?"

Aurora shook her head solemnly. "She refuses to talk to me. Blocked my calls, blocked me on social media. Wouldn't even come to the door when I went to her house. And when Bron heard what I did, he distanced himself from me, too. Even Monroe has made himself scarce. I've truly never felt more alone. And since I foolishly pissed away my job, I don't even have that to focus on. All I have left is money, which isn't as fulfilling as I thought it would be."

"I'm sorry to hear that."

She briefly glanced at me before turning her eyes back to the field. I could see the redness in them and could only imagine how much crying she'd been doing over the previous few days. "You don't have to say that, Montrel. I know I brought this on myself. It hit me after you left how much time I spent blaming you for my actions instead of taking the proper accountability. But none of this was your fault; it's all me. I'm joining a support group. Though I admit I had to talk myself into it."

"That'll be good for you, I think. Getting to hear other people's stories and how they overcame should be inspiring and give you the hope you need. And you won't feel so alone, since you'll be around people who know what you're going through and know what it takes to get through it. That support system is what you need."

"Yeah, I know you're right. Getting started is always the hardest. But I'm gonna do it." I could hear the determination in her voice. "I *need* to do it."

I rubbed her shoulder encouragingly. "And I know you will."

She flashed me a grateful smile. "Thank you for that. And...I really hope you and I can eventually get to the point where we're okay. I expect it to take some time and my focus needs to be on getting myself together first, but one day, I hope you'll be open to being in each other's lives again. I'd just hate to become a person that you try to forget you ever met."

"You have a sickness, Aurora. It doesn't make you a monster."

Her eyes roamed over my face. "So you don't hate me for how I treated you?"

"No. I thought I did but once I calmed down, I realized that you need my compassion, even if it's from afar, more than my vitriol. Especially since you recognize your problem and are taking steps to deal with it. It would be different if you were still in denial or refusing to acknowledge the truth. But you're not. So I'd rather put my energy towards wishing you well. As far as us being in each other's lives...we can worry about that down the line. Right now I just want you to focus on getting better."

She nodded, looking away. "Understood. And I suppose I can't ask for any more than that. In the meantime..." She reached into her large purse and pulled out a manila envelope, holding it out to me. "Here are the divorce papers. They're signed. I'm not going to contest anything. I just wanted to give the backstory so you'd have a better understanding of how I came to be like this, and make sure I gave you the sincere apology you deserve, to your face. I am so, truly sorry, Montrel. For everything."

I accepted the envelope with a gracious nod. "Thank you, Aurora."

Running her tongue over her bottom lip before pulling it into her mouth, she looked at me for a long moment before gently touching my cheek. Then she pulled away, sniffling before she slid off the bleachers and walked back to her car, her head facing the ground. I watched her until she got in her car and drove away, then sighed and tapped the envelope against my hand. I wasn't sure when I'd see Aurora again, or if we'd get to the point of being friends or even just occasional acquaintances. All I could hope for at that point was that she'd be okay.

Epilogue - Montrel

It was so hard to know what to pack; I'd never been to Milan.

Dustin and I were leaving the next day to scope out trends, attend some shows, and visit some textile manufacturers. We'd been hard at work over the previous months with getting all the initial company registrations and permits, narrowing down our niche and target market, deciding on color palettes and collaborating on designs and the technical pack for the manufacturer, which was like a design blueprint that contained things like dimensions, front and back views of the designs, color references, fabric composition, sizing preferences. And there was still plenty more to be done. I'd had no *idea* how much went into starting a clothing line. It was all very exciting, if at times overwhelming. But Dustin and I got along great, and he was patient and encouraging, not to mention welcoming of my input and ideas. Despite my inexperience, things were moving along quite smoothly, and I was learning a ton.

Aurora and I were officially divorced. I hadn't spoken to her again since the day at the baseball field, but she did text me to let me know that her therapy was going well, though she admitted that it was harder than expected and she'd thought about quitting. She was doing individual sessions as well as the group meetings, and while she still felt some shame for the things she'd done, she did feel encouraged being around people who could relate to what she dealt with. And once he heard she was getting help, her friend Bron reached out and offered his support, as well. I was glad for her sake that at least one of her old friendships might be salvaged.

Mother and I were in an okay place. Working with Dustin took a lot of my time, but Mother and I did meet up for dinner one night, and we had semi-regular phone conversations. I could tell she was making an effort to take more of an interest in what I had going on, and to be more encouraging, something she was never very good at unless I was doing something she wanted me to do. But when I told her about what I was working on with Dustin, she actually seemed excited for me. I could admit that I got my fashion sense from her.

She also let me know that James had been arrested after being tracked down in some tiny city in California. Turned out all the plans for his insurance business had been bogus, and Mother wasn't the first woman he'd run his game on. By that point, Mother wasn't as worried about getting her money back as she was about making him pay for what he did, especially after she learned she was one of many victims. Her embarrassment over getting swindled had evolved into angry vengeance, and she wanted to throw every possible book at him. And it turned out she *did* have a video of them coming to an oral agreement over what she was investing the money for, and him agreeing to use it for those purposes only. I had to give Mother credit for that, at least.

Forrest and Giselle were dealing with the disappointment of Giselle's recent miscarriage, which was extra painful because they hadn't even initially known she was pregnant. I hated to see them go through that and was there for them best I could be, even if I didn't always know the right thing to say. I even babysat little Jenna for them for a couple days so they could have some time alone, though the miscarriage only made them appreciate their daughter even more than they already did.

I was going down the list of things I needed to do before Dustin and I left the next day and trying to ignore the chaos my room was in. I didn't usually tolerate messes, but I blamed my nerves.

My phone rang, and I glanced towards it as I crossed a couple more things off my list before stepping over to grab it. I didn't recognize the number, so I let it go to voicemail. It immediately rang again from the same number, and again I ignored it. Then a text message came in, and I thought I was seeing things when I saw those two words on the screen:

It's Claire.

I'd never called anyone back so fast in my life.

"Hey, Montrel," Claire answered.

"Claire, hey. I must say, this is a surprise."

"I can imagine. Is this a bad time?"

"No, it's fine. Um, what's up?"

"Are you at home?"

I paused, caught off guard. "Yes..."

"If you wouldn't mind some company, I'm in your driveway. But seeing as how I just showed up without any notice, I'd totally understand if-"

Anyone that knew me knew I did *not* like to run, but I literally sprinted to my front door and yanked it open. Sure enough, there was a Volkswagen Jetta in my driveway. She'd gotten a new car since the time we were together. I looked on anxiously as the driver's side door eased open, and Claire emerged, eying me with tentativeness. She closed the car door, locked it, and strode over to me. I was gawking at her as if I couldn't believe she was really there. Part of me couldn't.

"You can hang up the phone now, Montrel," she informed me amusingly.

"Oh." My face flushed as I lowered the phone. I hadn't even realized she'd hung up when I opened the door. Feeling a little silly, I silently told myself to get it together. "I guess I'm just a little thrown right now..."

"I apologize for coming by unannounced."

"No, no, you're good. Come in."

We stood there for a few moments before Claire reminded, "You're kind of blocking the door."

"Shit!" I was acting like I'd never had a lady visit me before. I stepped aside, letting Claire enter. She couldn't help giggling at me.

"Montrel, I know this is a surprise and you're wondering what I'm doing here," she said once we were in the living room. She put her purse on the couch but didn't sit. I didn't either, since I still had no clue what to expect. "I've been debating for the past few days if I was going to come by after Aurora called me."

My head jutted forward so hard it almost tipped me over. "Excuse me?"

"Aurora contacted me and asked me to consider giving you another chance."

Okay, now I had to sit. I lowered myself onto the arm of the couch, feeling like my head was swimming. "How...what..."

"Believe me, I was just as thrown as you are right now," Claire admitted, finally sitting near the middle of the couch. She clasped her hands, resting them on her thighs. "She reached out to Forrest, who then put her in touch with Giselle, who gave her my contact information once Aurora explained her intentions. I thought she was taunting me at first. But she insisted that she didn't want any trouble and was doing what she felt like she owed you."

This was getting more and more strange. "What did she say?"

"She told me how unhappy you'd been because of her. That she had basically manipulated you to get what she wanted, seducing you when she knew you were in love with me so she could persuade you to marry her."

"So she told you about the trust fund?"

"Yeah. And she also admitted the main reason you two divorced."

My eyebrows flew up near my hairline, then I looked away, feeling tingles begin to light up my skin. I'd grown to accept what happened, but the knowledge that Claire now knew everything brought a different kind of shame.

"Part of me kind of wishes she hadn't told you about that," I muttered. "It's one thing for other people to know but...it's something else for *you* to know."

"Montrel, please don't be embarrassed." I felt her hand on my forearm. "She was as tactful as she could be but she wanted me to know what she put you through. And that despite her stepping out on you so much, you still tried to make the best of your marriage."

"I'm not sure that makes me sound any better. If anything, it paints me as delusional. Which I guess I kinda was."

"I'm not saying any of this to make you feel bad. Aurora wanted me to reach out to you because she felt you needed me. Said there were several nights where you even called out my name in your sleep."

"Oh my god." My head fell back in disbelief. "She was just the little chatterbox, wasn't she?"

"Montrel," Claire couldn't help but chuckle, "I think she was just trying to convey the depth of your feelings, that's all. She wasn't trying to embarrass you."

"Hmph."

"I was honestly floored. Not only by everything she revealed to me but by the fact that she was explaining herself to me at all. We didn't know each other. She certainly didn't owe me any apologies or explanations. But that's just how much she cares about you."

"I mean, I appreciate it, don't get me wrong. And that's very nice to hear, that Aurora advocated for me like that. But you didn't have to come back here out of pity."

"Montrel, this has nothing to do with pity. When she told me all of that, I was worried about you but also, it made me do some hard thinking. You were already on my mind a good bit after seeing you at Jenna's birthday party. And if I'm honest...I might've even peeked at your social media a couple of times recently. It was hard not to miss you, as much as I tried not to. Aurora's call just nudged me to finally do something about it. Even with everything she told me, though, she also warned me not to bother you unless I was really ready to be in your life again."

I dared to look into those green eyes. "And you're here?"

"I'm here."

We shared a look before I placed my hand over hers and slid off the arm of the couch to the cushion, landing close to Claire but still with a bit of space between us. My heart was beating fast in my chest, knowing that Claire was there because she wanted to be. I honestly never thought we'd reach this point, and had grudgingly accepted it.

"That means a lot to me, Claire." My hand rubbed hers. "I've missed you so much. And I never stopped loving you. Damn near every day for the past two years, I've wished for this; us being in the same space again. If *I'm* honest, the reason I even posted on social media wasn't just to show off; it was in the hopes that you'd see it.

"But in the time since Aurora and I split up, I've been focusing on getting my life together. I have a career now, working on a clothing line. I'm actually heading to Milan tomorrow. Relationship-wise, this is the first time I've been alone in years and it's been good for me. I'm thrilled you're here; I just want to be my best self for whatever kind of friendship or relationship we have and I'm still working on getting there."

"Aren't we all?" She smiled at me. "That's totally fine, Montrel. I'm not suggesting we jump back into anything full-force because I'm not ready for that, either. I think we both need to get to know each other again in these new stages we're in. A lot has happened over these past couple of years, for the both of us. There's no need to be in any hurry. I just had to let you know I was willing, if you were."

"I'm more than willing." I leaned a little closer, feeling myself become intoxicated by her scent, which was a mix of tangerine and baby powder. "Are you really sure about this, Claire?"

She nodded. "Believe me, I didn't finish talking to Aurora one minute and then hop in my car and head here the next. It still took some doing to come to grips with the fact that you let yourself fall under her spell despite the feelings you claimed to have for me, *and* after everything we'd been through. But that was then. You've changed, and so have I. We're not the same people as when we were together before."

"You're right about that."

"So, there's no pressure either way. I've certainly got my hands full with work and school. Congratulations on the clothing line, by the way. That seems totally up your alley."

"I appreciate it. I'm more of a collaborator and face of the brand, but seeing how everything gets done and getting to have a hand in it from the beginning is exciting."

"Well, check you out. I guess it's only a matter of time before we see this face plastered across billboards and magazines and clogging up Instagram feeds, huh?"

I laughed. "That's the plan."

Her shoulder bumped mine. "I'm proud of you."

I beamed like a kid who'd been given a gold star. I brought her hand to my lips, kissing it lightly before holding it near my cheek. "Thanks. And I'm damn sure proud of you, too. You're doing some great things, yourself."

She grinned, then it faded slightly as we sat there gazing at each other. Somehow, the space between us had disappeared and our shoulders and thighs were touching. We just sat there staring at each other for I don't know how long, me rubbing her hand on my cheek and her tracing a finger on my knee.

"So how long will you be in Milan?" she finally asked softly.

"A couple of weeks." I didn't want to say how part of me now wished I didn't have to go just yet. I was already looking forward to when I'd get back and I hadn't even left.

"Well, you have my number now. When you get back, maybe you'll give me a call?"

"No maybe about it."

Everything in me wanted to kiss her. To take her back to my messy bedroom, get on the bed, and just get lost in her until it was time for me to leave for the airport in the morning. But I wasn't going to push things. Now that I knew we were both willing to rebuild our relationship, I could be patient.

"I should go," Claire said, reluctantly easing her hand from mine and standing. "You need to get your rest for tomorrow."

"I'm not ready for you to leave."

She restrained her automatic smile by biting her lip. "You sure?"

"I'm positive." I reclaimed her hand, gently tugging her back onto the couch with me. "It's a ten-hour flight; I can sleep on the plane. Please, Claire, stay."

She nodded as our hands linked together. "I didn't really want to leave, anyway."

We ended up talking for hours, the conversation continuing as we ordered some dinner and she kept me company as I finished getting my things together for my trip. Once my suitcases were packed and set by the door, Claire and I did end up on my bed, but on opposite sides, facing each other as we talked. We were both fully clothed except for our shoes. But I still felt closer to her than I had, probably ever.

She ended up staying with me until it was time for me to leave the next morning. I gave her a long, tight hug before we parted ways, hating that I had to leave her. But at least it wasn't a good-bye. I was grateful for the possibilities of me and Claire going forward, now that we both seemed to be on the same page, finally.

Aurora might have crushed my soul, but she revived my heart by nudging Claire back to me. And I'd be damned if I was gonna blow it again.

THE END

Hey, awesome reader. I hope you enjoyed *Mrs. Soul Crusher* and the emotional story of Montrel and Aurora. I hadn't initially planned on doing a sequel when I wrote *Mr. Time Waster* but something told me there was more story to tell, and I answered the call. And I know Montrel isn't one of my most beloved characters but he's so fun to write. Hopefully he redeemed himself.

Am I done with Montrel and Claire? We'll see.

Please leave a review wherever you bought this book and/or on Goodreads, however you felt about it. Reviews mean so much to us indie authors.

The social media spiel...I'm on Instagram, Facebook, and TikTok under @AuthorJessicaTerry and on X/Twitter at @ItsJessicaTerry. If you don't mind me occasionally hopping in your inbox, sign up for my email list at www.jessicaterry.com[1]. You get free stuff when you do.

---

1.   http://www.jessicaterry.com

Also by Jessica Terry

Discussion Questions
(Mild spoilers here, so...hope you've read the book first)

1. Montrel admitted that he mainly married Aurora for sex. Given that, do you think he had reason to get upset at all about any of the things she did outside of their marriage?
2. Aurora claimed many times to love Montrel, despite her behavior. Do you think she and Montrel would have worked if not for her addiction? Or were they just not a match, regardless?
3. What did you think of Monroe?
4. If you read *Mr. Time Waster*, you know everything Montrel put Claire through. Do you think Claire should have held onto her anger towards him or did you understand her reasons for forgiving him?
5. Did you agree with Forrest about his initial decision regarding Montrel being little Jenna's godfather? Or was it understandable that Montrel got so affronted?
6. Sometimes distancing yourself from family is necessary. Did you think Montrel telling off his mother and separating himself was justified?
7. Was Bron a *real* friend to Aurora, given that he was complicit in her behavior? Would you like to see them end up together?

8. Did you feel sorry for Annie for getting swindled at all?

9. Aurora seemed to know something was off within herself, even if she initially denied being a sex addict. Do you feel Montrel finally leaving her is what made her accept reality? Would she have made any changes if he decided to stay, even if he demanded she get help?

10. Montrel wasn't exactly well-loved after *Mr. Time Waster*. We learn a lot more about him and see his growth from that story to *Mrs. Soul Crusher*. Did he redeem himself to you?

Did you love *Mrs. Soul Crusher*? Then you should read *The Beginning of Again*[1] by Jessica Terry!

[2]

Ronnie thought she had it all together until her husband surprised her with a set of moving boxes and a request for divorce. With nowhere to go, no work experience, and almost nothing of her own, Ronnie is forced to move back in with her estranged father Pat, who she hadn't spoken to in years.

Pat Duncan had problems of his own. His wife just up and left one day without a word, and he spent every day for the past twenty years waiting for her to come back. So when

---

1. https://books2read.com/u/mqrp2O

2. https://books2read.com/u/mqrp2O

his daughter comes back and disrupts the life he had settled into, it only threatens to push them even further apart.

While trying to navigate constant new changes, discoveries, and long-held secrets, this stubborn father and daughter have to learn each other all over again. Despite constantly butting heads, they have to accept that they need each other, like it or not...

Read more at https://www.jessicaterry.com/.

About the Author

Jessica Terry caught the writing bug at a young age and loves little more than holing up at home in Douglasville, GA, cranking out contemporary novels. And eating. www.jessicaterry.com

Read more at https://www.jessicaterry.com/.

www.ingramcontent.com/pod-product-compliance
Lightning Source LLC
Chambersburg PA
CBHW022024240626
47154CB00007B/2252